CROSSING PATHS FINDING HOPE

Inspired by True Stories

Rich Greer

ISBN 978-1-68517-979-3 (paperback)
ISBN 979-8-88751-722-3 (hardcover)
ISBN 978-1-68517-980-9 (digital)

All Scripture quotations are taken from The Holy Bible, New International Version, NIV. Copyright 1973, 1978, 1984, 2011 by Biblica, Inc. All rights reserved worldwide. www.Zondervan.com. The "NIV" and "New International Version" are trademarks registered in the United States Patent and Trademark Office by Biblica, Inc.

Christian Faith Publishing
832 Park Avenue
Meadville, PA 16335
www.christianfaithpublishing.com

Printed in the United States of America

DEDICATION

To Claudia, Courtney, Meredith, and Allison.
The Lord truly blessed me with a family more wonderful than I deserve!
Humility, kindness, and the love of God know no shame... They
will burst forth and shine; living on forever, despite everything!

Love You Always.

THANK YOU

To Pastor Brooks Braswell and the many from my church family who gathered around the outside of the drug store and prayed. Boom! A mission field game changer!

To Danny Gokey whose personal words of encouragement were spoken to me while a mere stranger. Wow! By the way, I love the lyrics you penned to *Hope In Front of Me*! I pray that through these written words of mine the same light of hope you expressed in your music format will burst forth and shine brightly in the written pages that follow!

To Courtney and Shale Latter who came to me in one of my darkest hours and prayed…then prayed continuously from that day on! That first prayer you shared with me began with the powerful words, "God, you've got this!" I still start my prayers each and every day with those very words of assurance!

To Mary and Thad. Well, to have a friend is a true blessing, but to have Christian friends who have always been there for you for over thirty years…undoubtedly, angels sent from heaven!

To Tony Free who, as a pharmacist like myself, came alongside me, lifted me, and oftentimes carried me during the too numerous to mention difficult times at the drug store and during the COVID-19 pandemic! I'm ready for a day off. How about you?

To Meredith Konnerth for always rushing right over to lend a hand and guide me in my computer ignorance and moments of utter frustration! You are a life saver sweetheart!

To Allision Coste who, after reading my other six books and not complaining or losing hope, still believed in me as a writer!

To Holly Newby for reading, rereading, and giving me the confidence to "pull the trigger" and awesome guidance on the title!

To the many couples, friends, and family who showed up and then showed up again and never stopped showing up and being there for me! You are the true enablers and writers of this work and much of my life story! I love you all!

PRAISE FOR CROSSING PATHS, FINDING HOPE

What if your life makes a difference? Does your life have a story to tell? What if the everyday moments that we all take for granted could bring healing to someone else's mess, or our own? The path that we walk in life is not empty and in fact each of us crosses paths with hundreds of people in any given week. All those lives have struggles and we have been given the opportunity to make those struggles better or worse for each person we meet.

This is the story of "Doc," a real pharmacist in a small town in Florida. Forty years as a pharmacist, crossing paths with others has given him an amazing story to tell! This book sheds light on only a very few of those paths that take place every day that we often know little about. Through the eyes of a single person, we see the difference each life can make; every gesture and every encouraging word makes a difference for someone else. All those paths crossing, intersecting, overflowing both bad and good on each other.

The reason to read this book? To find out just how much difference your life makes. Experience the difference firsthand that you can make by simply opening your eyes to those on your path.

Holly Newby, editor, *The North Lake Outpost*

CONTENTS

CHAPTER 1

A Hardened Heart—Seriously?

*Your prayers are answered not when we are given what we
ask but when we are challenged to be what we can be.*
—Morris Adler

"Just remember there is a message in that mess of yours, Connor
Grayson," the cardiology nurse told me while holding up her
arm and shaking her pointing finger back and forth. Then letting her hand down, she rested it deliberately atop mine as I was
starting to reach across the checkout counter for my receipt.

Touching the edge of the receipt, I quickly grabbed it and pulled
my hand away from her grasp. For some unknown reason though,
my eyes stayed locked on hers during the entire exchange; maybe
desperation on my part, wanting to transfer the hope I saw within
her somehow to my heart. But there was a voice screaming inside
obstructing the acceptance of any possibility of hope!

Involuntarily my feet began to pull me backward, away from
the cold checkout counter and the annoying nurse. In one quick
angry motion, I crushed the credit card receipt in my fist and shoved
it into the right back pocket of my jeans. Then, feeling totally out of
control, I opened my mouth and allowed the rage boiling over in me
to spew out at her.

"What's the matter with you? You're one crazy person to say
that! You make it sound like everything will be all right! Like maybe

one day, I'll just waltz back in here, throw up my hands, and tell everyone how this *mess* gave me some marvelous message? Seriously? Oh yeah, I know what's the matter with me! And I don't need you or anyone else to remind me! It's not the beginning of something good. It's the start of one big crappy ending! God, what in the world are you thinking?!"

"Maybe you should ask Him?" she snapped back at me with a half-tilted smile and sparkling eyes. "And while you're at it, Mr. Grayson, ask him to throw in some hope too! You need a lot of that all right!"

"Hope?" I shouted back, then sighed deeply before adding retaliation to my fury, "You're an idiot! Forget it, lady!"

Turning my body around and away from her, I wanted to bolt toward the door. But immediately my escape encountered interference. Suddenly, I came face-to-face and was blindsided by an older woman, carrying a handful of papers on her one side and a pocketbook in her arm on the other. Without time for avoidance, we found ourselves falling atop each other and on to the tiled lobby floor with a flurry of papers scattering all around us. We looked at each other in frustration and embarrassment as we lay there.

Glancing nervously around, it looked as if the entire waiting room had jumped from their seats and was trying to help. Several individuals quickly surrounded the woman and carefully worked together to get her back on her feet. Others got on their hands and knees, hurriedly collecting her papers. As I propped myself up with my arms, I stared in curiosity at the attention being given her. Then it dawned on me, no one had offered to help me! In fact, to the contrary, they stood by glaring, not one venturing entry into my angry domain. Who could blame them?!

Pushing myself up off the hard, gray tile, my hand rubbed against something behind me and I turned around on my knees to see what it was. There in front of me was a worn black leather-covered Bible. The few pieces of paper that hadn't already fallen onto the floor were being held precariously in place by the yellowed pages of the old Bible. Picking it up and intending to simply turn and hand it to her, one of the remaining papers fell. My eyes locked onto the typed sheet as it settled still onto the floor.

At the top of the report, just below her name, was her diagnosis. Reading the findings sent waves of electrical emotion shooting through my body. My heart, as bad and hardened as they told me it was, seemed to have received a sudden and unexpected jolt of feelings! Wait a minute! What was I feeling? And who was I kidding? She was dying and I was dying! Nothing either of us could do about that, right?

Quickly I gathered up the remaining few papers, along with the Bible, and shoved them at one of the men standing and gawking.

"The show's over," I wanted to yell at the top of my voice at everyone, but I didn't. Instead I glanced out the side of my eye and watched as he gently handed the Bible and papers to her. With an almost inaudible mumble, I whispered, "I'm sorry," as she raised her eyes to look at me.

Then, without further delay, I stood up, turned and resumed my original plan to exit the building as quickly as possible. The sliding doors separated with hardly a sound as I moved within range of the motion sensor, and I was ready to head out. With a final look back over my shoulder, my eyes turned to the old lady one last time, hoping to see for certain that she was all right. Appearing unhurt by our collision, I repeated, "I'm sorry." And truly I was sorry—for both of us!

Starting to turn my head away, I caught a glimpse of her reassurance of "I'm all right." Then she started to ask, "Are you?"

But her words dissipated in the air between us as I left the building and entered into the light of the outside world. Finally, I was free!

The lingering minutes in the lobby had seemed never-ending, but they were forever behind me now! So do I really care what they think? I tried multiple times to rationalize the question to myself. And yet I couldn't stop replaying in my mind how only yesterday I was so overly concerned with what others might think of today's finding? Questioning and wondering wildly how they would treat me and what they would say to me if it was bad news? So then why now this sudden coldness? Could it be that staring the reality of death face-to-face did this to me? But what did it matter anymore? It wasn't their problem! Why should I care?

Eagerly I made my way past the remaining two rows of cars in front of my truck. There was a strange sense of security that began to come over me the nearer I got to my old '66 Chevy hunk of junk. Not sure what it was exactly—maybe it was familiarity, maybe the closeness to my escape vehicle, or maybe the certainty of knowing I would never ever be back in that office again—but I did at last feel safe!

Though early December, the still present, intense Florida sun was beating down on me as I stood next to my truck in silence. The warmth the sunrays created throughout my body made a pleasant and welcome contrast to the previous cold surrounding I left behind in the cardiologist's office. Although angry and cold feelings still were very much alive in my heart, the intensity of the sun's warmth was a wonderful reprieve.

Tilting my head back, I looked directly up in the sky, and the glow nearly blinded me. Quickly closing my eyes, I saw bright sunspots flashing in my mind. Instinctively, I raised both hands up to cover my eyes and face. However, no sooner did the brightness disappear when the stark reality of today's news hit me! My body fell back, helplessly hitting hard against the truck.

So this is it? I wondered.

Just as my fingers were spreading apart over my eyes, a view of light came breaking through, and the sight frightened me! Looking out between the spread of my fingers, they appeared as prison bars trapping me in! Desperately I searched for more light, and with that light, I prayed that there please be hope! The view entrapped me with its hold as I slowly slid down the side of the truck, not stopping until I dropped hard onto the asphalt parking lot.

I could feel the pavement underneath me, rough and hot, yet reassuring in the fact that I did still have feelings—whatever they might be! But then, there it was again, that all-unknown question hovering over me like a vulture waiting his time and asking, "How long? How long?" But who knew for certain how long?

For now, I was still breathing! And I did just that—one deep breath, then another, again and again. Finally I felt safe enough to move my hands away from my face and I placed them beside me, flat on the pavement. Tilting my chin downward until it rested against my chest, I exhaled a sigh of relief and listened to myself deliberately take in each and every breath.

There it was! In the silence I could hear my heart beating! Intently I listened, focusing all my being onto every single heartbeat! I felt I could sense the movement of each beat, the pumping of blood through my heart chambers and its coursing out to the far most reaches of my hands and feet. To me, the sound was normal and strong! Maybe they were wrong? Maybe it wasn't that mouthful diagnosis that they labeled it? Maybe my heart wasn't slowly hardening from the apex up? Maybe it wasn't the beginning of the end like I had so dramatically said it was when lashing out at the nurse? And yes, no, I didn't know all the answers. But then maybe the doctors didn't either? Maybe there was more to my heart than they could see?! Maybe there was a reason for hope?!

Call to me and I will answer you and tell you great and unsearchable things you do not know.
—Jeremiah 33:3

CHAPTER 2

And So It Began…

*Don't judge each day by the harvest you
reap, but by the seeds you plant.*
—Robert Louis Stevenson

"Wow, aren't we here bright and early this morning?"

"And a good morning to you too, sunshine," I quickly shot back in our usual not-awake-yet morning attitude banter.

"You know what I mean! You're usually the last one to get to the drugstore every morning, especially on Monday mornings. So…just a little surprised to see you first thing like this."

"Where is the 'missed you so much Friday' and the 'so glad to see you' loving thoughts I was expecting to hear?"

"Keep wishing! But not thinking you will hear that."

"Oh, so you did miss me?"

Ashton cut her eyes over at me and gave me a firm glare. Maybe it was a kind of "miss you, welcome back" look, but I doubted it!

"Yep, thanks for caring. It's good to be back." And although it sounded sarcastic, I truly was glad to be back at work!

Without any further time wasted on morning chitchat, Ashton quickly went about her startup routines of logging onto the computers, checking the lockbox, looking at the work queue for e-scripts, and listening to the voice mails for refills and new prescriptions. She seemed to pay little notice as I slowly walked around the eighty-year-old drugstore and took in the memories of my family's store and the many reminders of the close-knit community where three generations of pharmacists had served so faithfully.

I couldn't help but smile as I picked up an old metal file box container labeled with prescription numbers dating from January through September 1942. It was World War II. My uncle had enlisted in the Navy only to return home wounded, and immediately, he got back to work and served as best he could as a pharmacist right behind the same counter where I did every day. If Uncle Roy could have hope and keep going, so could I!

As I walked over behind the counter to my work area, I turned to look at the 1939 Norman Rockwell Magic Potion painting of a druggist, which had hung there behind the pharmacists work area for as long as I could remember. Like my uncle, I had spent years of my life counting, checking, and counseling. As the story goes, he had not only hung the painting but had also placed the hand-carved sign above it. The sign read, "It's a Wonderful Life," in memory of Mr. Gower, the druggist in the movie and the loss of his son during the war.

Uncle Roy never lost his son in the war, as did Mr. Gower, but he did lose his older brother—my dad—and that was bad enough. My dad was a Navy pilot who died in a plane crash when I was six years old. Uncle Roy instantly became the male figure I looked up to, and although my mom planted and grew the seed of love for health-care in my life, it was Uncle Roy who showed me what it meant to be a pharmacist. As I watched him help patients, I knew I wanted to do the same! Uncle Roy likened me to George Bailey in the movie It's a Wonderful Life, always struggling with obstacles, expectations, and having to grow up to soon—and he was right.

Lovingly I reached up and straightened the picture, then looked around at what needed my attention. Diving right into all the notes left attached to prescriptions on the counter and the bottles with sticky notes for transfers, I knew for certain this crazy was exactly where I needed to be! It was here that I felt alive again, a man with a mission and a purpose! The words of Max Lucado in a book I recently read came to mind: "You can change your life by changing your heart." Physically it might not be possible to change my heart, but I could intentionally pour all my reserve into pressing on with my life for a purpose. I could open up all my remaining good heart fully to those around me needing hope in their messed-up life! And I could just leave it open and pour out nonstop to others until my last breath! It sounded like one heck of a good plan to me (and right now I needed a plan to keep going)!

"Doc, if you're really wondering if you were missed, you need to check out that stack over there that came this weekend...all addressed to you!"

"What's that?" I questioned as I looked up from a prescription needing a doctor call for follow-up and clarification.

"Over there." Ashton was pointing to the back counter where there was a good-sized pile of mail. "Yep, popular guy, aren't you?"

"Don't know about that," I answered while walking over to pick up the almost three-inch-high stack of mail.

What seemed exciting about the large amount of mail was that most of the envelopes were not white; rather, most were brightly colored reds, greens, silvers, and golds. All those colors meant it was Christmas card time again!

Better get that string out from behind the counter and hang it ready for a load of fabulous cards! I thought to myself. And who doesn't love getting and reading Christmas cards? Call me a little kid, if you like, but it's a tradition and highlight of the season that I will never outgrow!

Each one I opened reminded me just how blessed I was to be alive and have friends and neighbors who cared so much as to sit down and handwrite a card! Nowadays, hand-prepared and signed cards are becoming a rarity, a nonpreferred dinosaur means of communication fast being pushed out of sight and into the recesses of our memory. Perhaps the real reason I believe this transition is coming is because all three of my grown children have sent me electronic Christmas cards for years now.

Granted, I give them credit for any type communication with me—be it electronic or snail mail! And the sentimental verbiage electronically sounds just as sincere, but the entire e-mail system leaves me not near as joyful as the old timeless source of seasonal greeting. It simply is not the same!

What I have discovered though is that every year I grab hold of a bit of my holiday joy from the receiving of the brightly colored cards as well as in the reading of the notes and in the display of the them with their lovingly handwritten signatures. (Pictures and yearly update notes provide great joy and a special touch too!)

As I tore open the cards, the words varied greatly, but the message of each spoke of the same themes—faith, hope, and love. Those are the three immortal powers that God promised would last forever!

Reaching for the final card, it seemed likely to prove anticlimactic based on face value appearance alone. It was not in a fancy or bright-colored envelope, rather a run-of-the-mill white, letter-sized garden variety. As with all the others, my eyes raced to the front left-hand corner in anticipation of who it was from and what I might expect. Much to my surprise, written in place of the name and address were the two simple words—*thank you.*

My curiosity aroused even more, I hurriedly flipped over the envelope, ran my finger down the flap—tearing it jaggedly—and reached inside to discover the contents! Pulling it out divulged it to be nothing more than a simple letter of sorts, folded properly in thirds and placed neatly and correctly inside with the top fold facing down. Carefully opening back the top and bottom folds revealed a handwritten letter on college-ruled notepaper.

My eyes anxiously fixed on the clean, crisp penmanship brought to life in indigo-colored ink. I began to read…

December 2, 2019

Dear Doc Grayson,

One night back in December 2012, I was crying almost uncontrollably as I searched the Google listings for an open pharmacy that would sell me only one-half of a box of Pulmicort® nebulizer med-

ication. *My one-year-old daughter had just been diagnosed with asthma and an upper respiratory infection on top of that! With no health insurance, little money left from my last paycheck, and Christmas just weeks away, I was begging for help!*

Then I came to the last pharmacy listing under independents and others. I knew it wasn't a chain or big-box store pharmacy, but it was the only one I hadn't called—Utopia Springs Drugstore. When I called, it was almost an hour past the online posted hours of operation, yet you answered—on the second ring!

After listening to me explain my situation, you agreed to fill my daughter's prescription for what I could afford. Although I was about an hour away, somewhere on Hwy 441 between Apopka and Orlando, you promised to wait for me to get there. Believe me, I drove as fast as my secondhand mom-mobile would go!

As you had told me to do, I pulled into the single-lane drive-through when I got there. You opened the window, greeted us with a big, caring smile, and handed me a box of tissues. "Thought you might need these after the night you've had," you said with a little laugh that made me feel immediately at ease for having come to your store.

Grabbing the prescription from my purse, I handed it to you. You gently took it from me, tilted your head down to read it, and reassured me you would be back in a few minutes. In almost no time at all, you came back and opened the window again. Picking a large bag up from the counter next to the window, you stretched out your arms and handed it to me. You smiled so sweetly, then quietly and tenderly told me "Merry Christmas," and shut the drive-through window and put up the Closed sign. I was speechless as I saw you wave goodbye and turn off the lights.

The mom in me told me to open and check the prescription! To my shock the bag had two full boxes of her nebulizer medicine—exactly what had been prescribed by the emergency room doctor. You never asked me for any payment for the medicine and closed the window before I could even say thank you! Which I probably wouldn't have been able to say without crying all over the place.

I have never forgotten that night! Where I work, when a person sends us a thank-you card, it makes our day. I am really hoping this makes yours! It took a few years and hearing similar stories about you from others to realize just how genuine you are and how rare it is to find anyone, especially nowadays, with true compassion and a big heart.

I will think of you every Christmas and retell this story every year to Natalie as proof to her that loving and caring people really do exist! Even when I was just a stranger to you in need of help that Christmas night, you opened your heart and were there for us. You renewed my faith in the world by that one simple act and made it one of the most memorable Christmases ever! Natalie and I thank you dearly!

Hope you have a Merry Christmas this year and every year for as long as you live! Enclosed is a picture of my daughter, Natalie. She is eight years old now and thinks she wants to be a pharmacist! I wonder where she got that idea?

Thank you again and again from the bottom of our hearts.

Merry Christmas and Love Always,
Jenn & Natalie

Suddenly, I felt my legs begin to wobble. Extending my arm behind me, I placed my hand atop the stool next to the counter to keep my balance.

"Seven years ago," I whispered to myself aloud in disbelief, shaking my head while I propped against the stool.

Then, focusing my eyes downward, I watched as the letter slipped out of my hand and across my fingertips, drifting featherlike to the countertop. My mind was reeling, desperately searching for a memory bite with all the details of that night so many years ago. I don't know for certain how long, but time seemed to stand still. I could feel my heart beating forcefully in my chest as simultaneously my breathing escalated. Both my heart and my breathing began to reverberate loudly, pounding like drums in my ears.

Although I don't know why, I felt frozen in time and space, unable to move! My body remained perfectly still as all my energy refocused to my mind and tried to remember the descriptions Jenn had so lovingly penned about that night. Then it lit up like fireworks as all the memory of that night exploded before me in my mind.

How vividly her words in the letter accurately choreographed the entire replay of that night in my mind. Now it came alive to me again! Emotions brought forth living pictures of all that had happened that Christmas seven years earlier. The warmth of a tear trickled down my face, and slowly I could again feel life pulsating through my body. One tear was followed by another, then another as I stood there allowing my mind to relive every moment of that previously forgotten night. What a gift Jenn and Natalie had sent me—a wonderful Christmas gift!

Suddenly it all made sense to me. Seven years! It was exactly seven years ago this December that I stood, not more than two feet from where I was now, looked at my shadow against the wall and felt fear such as I had never known! It was a frightening, heart-stopping moment when I watched my entire life being torn apart by my very own shadow.

On one side, I could see light radiating the possibilities for my life continuing with faith and hope, but clearly it was struggling frantically to survive. While on the other side, there was a growing darkness, engulfing me inch by inch. I could sense that the side with the darkness might not be stopped in its quest to consume and control me! The shadow of the darkness I wished not to view was filled with my sorrow, fears, and doubts. I could feel its coldness creeping into me, wanting to take hold of me! I knew I was in the midst of a battle, one the likes of which I had never known that was being fought fiercely in my heart and mind!

On the bad side, rallying the forces, was the recent dark emotions which had arisen and nearly consumed me from the loss of my mother in October. And there riding copilot was the reconfirmed diagnosis in early December by the second cardiologist at Duke who agreed my heart was dying, which meant so was I! I was seeing inside me the dark and broken places I feared the most—the ones I tried to hide from everyone's view of me.

To cope with the bleak news, I joked about having a "hard heart" and "cold heart," but deep inside, I was scared out of my mind! Adding to that, trying to deal with my mom being gone and the awesome Christian life model she was... I threw up my hands and told my family and friends the bar she had set for me was too high. Why should I strive for it anymore? But the reality was that inside me, I wished I could be half the loving, giving, and caring person she had been!

My mom had been a public health nurse in the Blue Ridge Mountains of Virginia. And even though I went fusing and complaining as a kid, every time I accompanied her on a patient home visit, I saw in her exactly what I wanted others to see in me one day: humility, love, caring, and compassion—overflowing in a sea of hope she so tendered created with each and every patient! Guess I should have, but I never even told her the real reason I went into healthcare was because of her. Too late now, just another regret hiding in those dark places. All too well I could remember that night and the sense of them pushing in on me... The feeling was suffocating!

I was tired of fighting and at the breaking point!

"God, let this battle be over with!" I remember shouting aloud that night and pounding my fists against the wall in the drugstore.

It was that December night back seven years ago. I had chosen to stay late and settle this with myself once and for all! Whatever that meant, the line needed to be drawn in the sand, and my life needed to move forward with no looking back! My body was emotionally and physically sick from all the warfare being waged in my mind, and enough was enough! It was that very moment when the phone rang! It startled me because it was the last thing I was expecting after business hours!

Turning around, I instinctively reached for the handset and answered only a moment after the second ring. Out of repetitive habit, I said what I always say, "Utopia Springs Drugstore, how can I help you?" That's when I heard the cry of a desperate mother pleading for help. Through weeping and anguish, I was welcomed into the caring of a loving heart on the other end of the line. That heart belonged to a fighting mother not willing to give up on her child! A mother who wasn't about to stop searching until she found the breathing medication needed for her sick daughter. I knew deep down in my heart that would have been my mother too—never willing to give up on me and always putting me ahead of herself!

It was then I realized that we all have battles. But I knew anything worth having in life was worth fighting for. I knew now that life was worth fighting for!

I remember listening to Jenn open up to me in her darkest hour of problems and recognized that she had chosen to face her fears head on! She knew what her daughter's untreated illness could do to her, and she loved her too much to let anything happen to her!

Jenn had no intention of giving up and the light from her courage lit the way for me! I knew now, without a doubt, what I had to do! I had to be that light...have that hope...show that love...and be that caring person I had dreamed of being ever since I was a kid on home patient visits with my mom!

Her letter stated that I "renewed her faith in the world that night," but truth be known, it was Jenn and Natalie that brought faith and hope back to me that December night seven years earlier! It's been said, there is nothing more beautiful than a heart that is changing, and mine was doing just that! Twice now they had changed my heart and opened it to feel the reality of others. First seven years ago and again now. They turned on the light that broke through and consumed the darkness which had threatened to overshadow me!

It no longer mattered what the doctor said back seven years ago, and it no longer mattered to me what he said Friday. I had hope and my life had a purpose! Just as I had chosen the side of light and hope way back then, I choose to renew it again now! And this time, I intended to shine so bright that myself and everyone around me would need sunglasses to keep the glare down! It was time for a new pair of Ray-Bans!

So it was, that December night 2012, when it all began! A hand of hope reached for me in the dark and hardened places of my heart, snatching hold, lifting me out and on to this of journey of faith. I am certain it was that moment the phone rang when everything in me changed! It was then that I bid farewell to the demons inside me. Although times then, now, and ahead may be hard, there was no reason for my heart to be hardened to the cares and needs of those around me. By giving of my life and time to others, I would be given life—a life filled with love and joy!

Closing my eyes, I listened to my heart beating… Yes, I was still alive! Hope was beating in my heart, and so long as I was alive and my heart was still beating, there was a purpose for me in my mess of pain and fear! And with a purpose I could live out my faith and be a hope-giver to others!

People judge by outward appearances, but
The Lord looks at the heart.

—1 Samuel 16:7

CHAPTER 3

Actions of the Heart

You can't live a perfect day without doing something
for someone who will never be able to repay you.
—Coach John Wooden (UCLA)

"Throw it in the lake and watch the ripples, Papa," my grandson once told me to do with the little rock he had found on the ground next to him…and I did. As we stood on the dock watching, it wasn't long before the ripples could be seen moving across the entire lake. What he and I learned together was that there are always ripples which occur as a consequence to an action.

For me it was a bit more to it than that! I realized that ripples from our lives produce consequences that impact others—like it or not! Never before did I realize that fact more vividly than I did now, after having received the letter from Jenn and Natalie.

Too often we underestimate the power of a word of encouragement, the example of faith under fire, a hug of compassion, a smile that brightens up another's day, a quiet listening ear, and countless other acts of caring and compassion that have the potential to turn a life around. The opportunities each of us have to make positive ripples in the world around are never-ending—limitless in number!

I thought about that a lot on my first week back as it was going…well…busy! If you asked the technicians working with me, they likely would harp in with the old adage my uncle used, "Busy means job security." With that in mind, I felt blessed to be busy!

"Hope you have a Merry Christmas, Doc!"

"Thanks, and Merry Christmas to you," I replied, raising my hand and waving goodbye to one of the patients.

Then, looking down and scanning the work counter, I exhaled a sigh of relief. Be it ever how brief, for now there were no waiters or red baskets with prescriptions needing immediate attention! But just as I was getting ready to sit for a moment on the stool, Deena, one of the technicians, came walking over.

With a stern look, she said, "Don't forget, Miss Emma Anne has been waiting to see you for quite some while."

"Aww… I forgot! I'm sorry. Just haven't had a free minute."

"So go!" Deena told me, pointing the way.

Walking around to the front counter, I leaned forward and looked her way. "Emma Anne, I'm so sorry you had to wait! I took off Friday and Saturday, and I am paying for it this week!"

Moving slowly, Emma Anne pushed herself up and out of the rocking chair in the small waiting area; it required her to use both her arms to assist her legs in a concerted effort. After a few moments, she was upright, smiling, and headed my way. I was astonished how well her broad smile hid the pain and struggles she had been going through the past year.

"Doc," she looked at me and began, as her body stopped and pressed gingerly against the counter, "if I haven't told you before, you're worth the wait!"

Taking a deep breath to catch up, she began with her usual cordialities, "'I've heard you say before that it is a real blessing for the drugstore to be busy, isn't it?"

"Yes, ma'am, it sure is! What with Florida Gem, our last orange plant and biggest business closing up, half the town out of work and the entire country clawing its way out of this recession—yes, busy is an incredibly good thing! Hardly a day goes by without someone coming in and sharing how they and their family are struggling to make ends meet. So being busy means we are truly blessed!"

"And the way I look at it, Doc, it is a true blessing to have you and the drugstore in our little town helping us as we work our way out of all this." She grabbed hold of my hand and then lovingly patted it tenderly with her other hand on top of it.

Glancing down only for a second to see her hands on mine, she looked back up, and just as our eyes met, she started to cry. Deena hadn't given me any heads-up that something was wrong, so her crying caught me off guard. I wasn't sure what to do or say and decided to give her a moment.

After a couple of deep sighs, she cleared her throat and composed herself. Squeezing my hand even tighter, she began explaining herself.

"I wanted you to be the first to know, before anyone else. After all these years of pain and suffering there is finally hope! And, Doc, it's…it's a feeling I still can't put into words and one I certainly never believed I would have!"

As she paused to collect her thoughts, I wondered where she was going in her conversation. Again, it seemed best not to ask questions and simply listen. In the silence of the moment, my eyes focused on her smile and not the wrinkle and worry lines that had overtaken her face these past few years. To me, they represented a badge of courage for the battles she had so bravely fought against pain, fear, doubt, poverty, failure, and at times, depression, and hopelessness.

"I won't keep you long, Doc," she started. "I still can't believe it! Pretty soon now though… Next week they say… I will be getting a check every fifteenth of the month! Can you imagine it? They called first thing this morning, letting me officially know my disability came through! The secretary at the lawyer's office explained it all and said that in the letter they were sending, it also showed I got medical and prescription coverage! That's what she said…" Emma Anne was crying, unable to continue on.

"That's awesome news! Wow!" I shouted out and let go of her hands. Immediately, I ran around the counter and out to hug her. She squeezed me ever so tightly. Her face rested on my shoulder, and I felt tears falling down on me. "I am so, so very happy for you!" I told her.

As I eased back away a little, I could see that despair and sorrow had been completely washed away by her newfound tears of hope and joy.

"It seemed that for so long you were trying to push through your pain, survive week-to-week cleaning houses, and… But now… now you have hope! And a new beginning! Beginning, Emma Anne, that's such a wonderful place to be! Thank you, Lord!"

"Oh, I have thanked Him—again and again!" she exclaimed joyfully. "And I wanted you to be first to know! You were the first to ever stop and look me in the eyes and truly listen to me! You let me come into your busy life. No one else ever did that! You probably don't even remember when that first happened, do you?" She looked at me, cocked her head to one side, and gave a grin when she saw the look on my face.

"It's all right if you don't remember. I remember," she began to explain. "That day, when I came in the drugstore for the first time ever, you stopped what it was you were doing back there"—she motioned with her hand in the direction of the workstation—"and came up to the counter. You greeted me and then asked how you could help.

"It had been an awful day. The spinal nerve pain in my back was excruciating, and I canceled my cleaning job for the day, knowing it would kill me to try and work! I had a pain medicine prescription with one refill from another pharmacy and Susie, one of the ladies who sometimes gives me a ride, thought I should bring it to you. I only had two dollars and some change in the bottom of my purse, so what did I have to lose in giving you a try? 'Just see what he says,' she told me as we came into the store.

"It really wasn't what you said to me that day. It was more what you did! Right there, at that counter over there." She again motioned with her hand as to where I had been standing behind the front counter. "You leaned forward toward me, locked those emerald-colored eyes on mine, and stopped…just to listen to me! Don't think you actually said a whole lot at all, just allowed yourself to listen and hear the rambling of a strange old fool—me. Exactly like you are doing right now!"

Reaching out and taking hold of my hand, she continued on, "It was so very obvious to me! Though you didn't even know me, you stopped what you were doing, listened intently, and showed me you cared! I could tell in your eyes, I really could! I had someone once explain to me that a person's eyes are the doorway that opens a view into their soul and reveals their true feelings. Through your eyes, I not only saw those feelings but felt them in my heart. You didn't see me as the failure I saw myself, but as another human being just like you who happened to be on hard times."

"Emma Anne…" I tried to speak, but the words I wanted to say somehow wouldn't come out. As I released her hand and started to move my hand toward my face, she moved hers more quickly. Gently she wiped a tear from my cheek. I looked at her, and there it was again, that smile. There was no doubt about it; my heart was alive and beating with so much joy for her!

"You know," she spoke rather quietly, "I don't think a man has ever cried over me… You have been so kind to me."

"But I didn't do anything!"

"Anything?" she blurted, then grabbed my shoulder, and gave me a quick shake back and forth. "You're right, you didn't do just anything! What you did that day and have continued to do hasn't been just anything, but rather *everything* for me!"

Stepping back a foot, she got a stern look on her face and then stretched out her hand and pointed her finger right at me. "How many times, including that first day, have you given me my medications? Never once did you ask me to pay or make me feel guilty! Oh, and I guess you didn't think I noticed you pulling money out of your own wallet as I was leaving, putting it in the cash register to pay for my meds!"

"Well, I was just—"

Emma Anne cut me off in midsentence and just keep on. "You treated me with respect and caring! You got me setup at the church's crisis center for food, asked your friends to drive me to doctors' appointments in Orlando, had some local ladies give me their gently used clothes, pulled some strings and got that hotshot orthopedic specialist to see me, put $25 in my checking account every month—

28

did you really think I wouldn't notice that?—and, Lord only knows, a million other little things that made all the difference in the world to me! No, that wasn't anything? You welcomed my broken life into yours and helped me to find faith and trust again. This drugstore and you are nothing short of a godsend, I tell you!"

I was speechless, and my mind was racing. I couldn't help thinking about my mom and the impression she made on me concerning how others should be treated...

As a young boy, there were several summers, I tagged along with my mom on her job. She was a public health nurse in the foothills of the Blue Ridge Mountains of southside Virginia for over thirty-five years. At first, it seemed like cruel and unusual punishment to have to ride along in the car with her and go on home visitations to people in some of the poorest places I had ever seen or imagined. Some had no indoor running water, most used outhouses, others had dirt floors, none had air-conditioning, and their means of cooking was generally an old iron stove (which served to help provide heat in the winter). Most were farmers, some cotton mill workers, and a few coal miners. Their kids had little in the way of material things, but they always welcomed me to join in with them in whatever it was they were doing and treated me like one of their kin!

Two weeks in, I realized how much my mom loved these people and how she felt a purpose in what she was doing. From her perspective, not only was she delivering needed medical care right to their doorsteps, but she was bringing with her large heaping doses of caring—something not visible or tangible in that old black bag she toted along with her on each and every visit. While setting broken bones, delivering babies, cleaning, suturing, and dressing cuts, she was also giving them the most precious of gifts. She gave them gifts from what seemed to me a never-ending overflow of her heart— faith, hope, love, and caring.

My mom taught me not only with her actions but also with those clichés she repeated constantly: "Treat folks how you want to be treated," "What comes around, goes around," "Every day is a gift meant to be shared with others," and my all-time favorite "Son, you may be the only joy someone sees in their life. Don't hide it. Give it to them freely, and expect nothing in return." Mom clearly showed me how to treat others!

Over the years, I tested her example but have proven her right repeatedly and found that placing others ahead of myself and trying to help whenever and wherever possible always is the right thing to do! And so, so many times those simple actions toward others has shifted my own paradigm and redirected me on the way I should go. A direction I most likely would have never found focusing on myself. Even more importantly, Mom led me to discover purpose in life through serving. She had it right—life is way more enjoyable with a purpose focused on others!

I looked up at Emma Anne and reminded her, "Don't get carried away and try to make it sound like something I did. Remember to give God credit for everything that has happened in your life! He's like that, you know, having a way of showing up in the most unexpected of places, and we don't even remember to thank Him!"

"I thank Him… I thank Him every day! And I know but for His grace and mercy, I could be homeless, bedridden, or so many other terrible things! Yes, I give Him complete credit!"

"I'm so happy for you," I told her again.

With a more serious look, she asked, "Doc, think you could come outside with me for a minute?"

Glancing back over at the technicians before agreeing to go, I realized they had been eavesdropping on our conversation. Both gave me a go-ahead nod.

Emma Anne didn't wait; she had already started toward the door without me. As I followed behind, she walked out the door and across the parking lot until finally she stopped under one of the old live oak trees next to the main entrance of the parking lot. Turning around, she waited impatiently for me to catch up.

"Doc," she was excited and wasted no time, "your faith and help gave me hope to overcome all these obstacles! Now that I can see that light up ahead of me, I also see clearly that there are others, just like me, needing some of that faith and help to give them hope to get through. When I first got the news this morning, I was so happy. Then I started doubting and wondered if it would be enough.

The what-ifs started to get the better of me for a few minutes! Then I closed my eyes, and let it go…trusting and believing it would be everything I was needing and more. That's when it hit me like a brick upside my head! Right then and there I knew what I had to do!"

"What?"

"I know to some people it may not seem like much, but to me, it is more than I deserve or expected to be blessed with! I did some hard numbers calculations, double-checked, then triple-checked, and I'm certain the monthly amount will let me rent a small used trailer at one of the Ocala Forest campgrounds. Which, believe me, would be lots better than that one-room apartment I currently have in, what I call the ghetto. I also did a budget for groceries based on what I spend at Dollar General and Save-A-Lot for necessities. Plus I can still qualify to get some food from the crisis center at church. Utilities are included in the rent. My medical bills and prescriptions, a walker, and any medical supplies will be covered under my medical, and…what I'm trying to say is I can do it!"

"Well, I feel certain you can make it on what you will be receiving each month!"

"No, no, you're not getting it, Doc! I…" She started to cry before she could explain.

"It'll be all right! I mean, it is going to be all right, isn't it?"

"Yes," Emma Anne replied and quickly composed herself. "I just can't seem to turn off these darn waterfalls in my eyes today! So many wonderful things are happening all at once! Doc, it's more than all right! Right now, things are closer to perfect than they have ever been! But I still need to give back! I need to share it! I need to give some of that faith and help to others so they can see hope again in their life!"

"Emma Anne, I'm really not sure I understand."

"My intention is to use what I get to take care of my needs, which aren't that much—not my wants! We all want more than we need, right? But I decided this morning that if I focus on using this blessing only for my needs, I will have a little left over each month to help someone else! It may not be much, but every little bit helps!

Who knows, Doc, maybe I can even help someone who can't afford their medicine?

I bet there are lots of people out there with problems, bills, and whatever else who feel the world is caving in on them, and they don't know what to do. I'm sure you see them and recognize the ones who have lost hope. Might be a parent who lost a job and needs a prescription for their kids, might be a person on fixed income who had an unexpected bill and is having to choose between paying the bill or getting their heart medicine, could be one of those unwed girls who got pregnant and you're giving them their prenatal vitamins—I know about you doing that too, Doc—or maybe someone on the road to recovery from addiction who needs a ride to their new job? All I want is to be of help to someone in need! You can do that for me. I know you can!"

What she was proposing was beyond any of my wildest dreams, and it pulled hard on my heartstrings! Emma Anne realized that simply because her prayers had been answered, her story wasn't over! If anyone, it was her that could so clearly attest that life rarely goes as we plan. But when we stop and acknowledge that, despite all the confusing, worrisome, frightful, and uncontrollable moments, it is all a necessary part of our journey. A life journey making us who we are, one giving us free will to make choices. We are exactly where we are supposed to be! Right here and right now, with the chance to take hold of that faith and hope and set a purpose for our life. Most likely, the biggest opportunity we encounter will be to make a changed life! To make a change and a difference—not only in our life but in the lives of others!

How amazing this life can be! The tears easing down my face were not just for her...but also for me. This was not only Emma Anne's chance to change and make a difference; it was also my chance to make a difference in lives by using the wonderful gift she was offering each month. The choice was in front of me to potentially change someone's despair into hope, and it was up to me. Free will would allow me to declare yes or no in this situation. I could question and worry over all the what-ifs and could-bes surrounding it, or I could choose to have faith and focus intentionally and selflessly on the needs of others—giving them the much-needed gift of hope.

After wiping my face against my shirtsleeve to remove my tears, I looked up at Emma Anne and asked, "Did anyone ever tell you you are amazing? After all you've been through, you still allowed your heart to think of others! Wow! I can only imagine how exciting and liberating it must have felt with your news this morning, but then, even just as wonderful to believe that you can give others that same hope you're feeling! What greater gift could you give than putting others above yourself?"

"And that's exactly what you did for me! I just want to do the same for someone else! You know that big Helping Jar you have on the counter next to the checkout register? Why not think of this as my monthly investment into helping someone in need? Someone in search of hope, someone who might need you to reach into that jar to find the resources to help them!"

I was trying to put words together in my mind to say to her what I wanted to say. To try and express how wonderful it was what she was willing to do. But the harder I tried, the bigger the mess I was making of my words. Then I remembered reading how John Eldridge described hope, and it reminded me so much of how Emma Anne felt and what she wanted others to feel also: *Hope is the sunlight of the soul; without it, our inner being would walk about in shadows. But like a sunrise in the heart, hope sheds light over our view of everything else, casting all things in a new light.*

Before I could compose anything in my mind about this new light Emma Anne had found and express to her how I felt, she reached out and tenderly touched my arm. "It'll be all right, Doc," she reassured me, without me even giving her an answer. "You just need to have a little faith. Next month, soon as I get my first check, I will bring you money for the Helping Jar. You need to start looking out for someone to help! And I don't want to know who they are or what you do for them. Got that?! I trust you, Doc. You just do it!"

I nodded my head in agreement and smiled, trying to not let Emma Anne see my eyes starting to fill with tears.

Catching a glimpse of her ride pulling into the parking lot, she blurted out, "Gotta run!" Though she didn't look at all familiar to me, the older lady driving the rust-colored station wagon blew the horn and waved. I raised my arm and waved back.

Halfway to the car, Emma Anne turned around, rushed back over to me, threw her arms around me, and kissed me on the cheek. It felt as if my heart was exploding!

"Merry Christmas!" she exclaimed as she squeezed me tight.

Then letting go, she hurried across the grass and into the parking lot. Looking back one last time before getting in, she held her arm up and waved.

"Merry Christmas, Emma!" I shouted out joyfully to her as I waved goodbye.

And now these three remain: faith, hope and love.
                                        —1 Corinthians 13:13

CHAPTER 4

Carpe Diem! (Seize the Day!)

*I learned that the measure of life is revealed in the quality of
our relationships: with God, our families, our fellowmen.*
—Richard Paul Evans, *A Perfect Day*

We rarely get the opportunity to trace our life's pathway backward to the actual crossroad where we veered left when we should have veered hard right. No doubt we have all relived that critical juncture time and again in our minds and wished we could do it over—but we can't! Yet there are times when we are placed in or near the crossroad of another struggling between veering left or veering right. And it is precisely because of our precarious closeness to them at this all-crucial intersection that we ourselves become faced with a choice also. That choice being, whether to help them or not? Do we leave our comfort zone, open up, and share our past error of way hoping to help them in their choice, or do we steer as far clear of the split in the road, never risking vulnerability, offering direction, or lending a helping hand? I've been there, and believe me, it is a hard crossroad to be at!

There was no do-over for Emma Anne's life, but what she did get was a restart and a redirection on a new road that was beaming bright with opportunities and endless possibilities. It was a beginning! A start with a turn onto helping and caring lane. An intentional directional choice (call it a veer right or a veer left, it doesn't matter) that involved putting herself out there to help others.

I knew for certain that it would be impossible for me to forget the abounding joy I saw in Emma Anne that day or to ever block from my mind the memory of the warmth and happiness I felt in my heart as she shared with me her decision to help and offer hope to others. That day reinforced for me the fact that a simple act of sharing, whatever shape or form it might be, is something incredibly special and never to be taken for granted!

I had a friend, Noah, who waited for me in the drugstore parking lot one night just to share something that I…well, considered extremely strange at the time. Looking back, I feel certain it was one of those forks in the road for his life! When I saw him, he had the tailgate of his truck down and was sitting on it, in the dark, waiting for me to close up the store. When he saw me, he motioned me over to sit down. Never one to mince words, Noah was always direct and wasted little time getting to the point or saying what he wanted to say.

Noah explained what was troubling him. Long story short, the problem was that he was having a recurring "dream," as he put it, about the drugstore. Almost every night for nearly a month, he said, he had a dream where he felt he was a bystander watching events happening at the drugstore. What he viewed witness to was a never-ending flow of people funneling in and out on a daily basis, all needing help. The issues and dramas of their lives varied with the dreams, but each had one recurring common thread—desperation! Each had situations and circumstances in their lives that were swirling out of control. Yet all of them were coming to the drugstore seeking help.

The stories he told me were almost unbelievable! Neighbors, strangers, adults, children, and they all had genuine needs. How could it be? Despite his vividly describing details and needs, I simply could not wrap my mind around how the drugstore could be pulled into these individuals lives or, more so, how the drugstore could possibly be of help. The way he detailed out how the drugstore, the town, and the people came together to help them didn't make sense! It caught me off guard and seemed almost bizarre.

Nonetheless, Noah had enough faith in our friendship that he risked coming to tell me about the dreams. I knew he had risked doubt and ridicule from me in coming up to the store and choosing to tell me. For those reasons and more, I respected him for sharing. However, with that respect and friendship came the thought that maybe his dreams were a bit clouded these days due to his losing battle with prostate cancer. I didn't want to shoot his dreams out of the water. I nodded and told him it was a lot to process, let me think on it, and we would talk again soon. He looked a little disappointed and restated emphatically that he believed what he saw in his dreams would actually come true—sooner or later. I concluded our dream discussion with the promise that if people did come to the drugstore looking for help, I would do all in my power to help them!

"That's all I could ask for, buddy," Noah replied as he shook my hand and slapped me on the back. He then shut the tailgate and started humming a tune aloud as we walked away. Even to this day, for some unknown reason, there are times I find myself humming that tune.

Noah and I had no further nights together to discuss or debate his dreams; were they premonitions, or simply wild ideas floating around in his mind? We never decided between each other who was right or who was wrong. But looking back now, I just wish I had taken him more seriously, asked better questions, or showed more interest! Sadly, that is a time I can never recapture.

Life can be strange like that, you know. What one person holds strongly to be impossible, another believes to be entirely possible! We've been taught what to think but not how to think on our own. It seems to me that the one who believes and is willing to put it all on the line—sacrificing the risk of failure and ridicule—is the real winner, the one who usually makes a difference in this life! For me, the battle in my mind centered around fear, change, attitude, and belief. Did I want to be a victim for the rest of my life, feeling sorry for myself as my heart slowly died, or did I want to live courageously, claiming every minute, day, and week as a victory?

Up until now, I admit to playing it safe. But living is about choices, and mine have often involved ignoring, avoiding, and justifying. Those actions know my address and where to find me too well and love showing up uninvited. Too many mornings I wake up to them staring me in the face as I look in the mirror. Now though, I feel I have crossed that obligatory line in the sand and no longer can I accept those choices and actions of doing nothing! It's people like Noah who have fought the battle and looked at life, not worrying about the time they had, and believed they could do anything. Most definitely, he believed by telling me about his dreams that it would make a difference or somehow give me the courage to believe. And I do believe!

Compartmentalization for this or that, time management, contacts, and appearances... Yes, time, things, and people seem to be what we love to control the most. And God forbid if someone tries to change, rearrange, or eliminate even one of those things! We've all seen people, if not ourselves, get fixated for days and weeks with guarding these things while failing to open their eyes and see how it's hurting those around them. Amazing, isn't it, how several months later we can hardly recall what the distraction, encroachment, or threat on that thing even was?

When all our efforts at control and normalcy fail and the world around us falls apart, where do we go, what do we do, and who do we turn to? Noah showed me that an open mind, willing heart, ready hands and faith in God oftentimes can be the answer. Never do I venture to tell someone who comes in the drugstore that I know how they feel or what they're going through because we all have different life experiences, different journeys, different coping processes, and different support systems. Emma Anne and Noah both knew well and had faced the shadows of human frailty, fear, doubt, lack of faith, and absence of hope.

With unprecedented technology in the palm of our hands, we have a misconception that all the solutions for our lives can be looked up, texted in, downloaded, or grabbed hold of through the Internet. Such isn't true for most people living day-to-day in this crazy world of ours. The dreams Noah had witnessed, if nothing else, revealed how messed-up lives can get in the real world, and they presented hope, given to them through the drugstore, as the absolute for making it through those times. Imagine that, hope?

*****

We all stopped what we were doing and looked toward the entrance of the drugstore when the old brass bell over the wooden door bounced and banged louder than usual as the front door flung open. Carrying a young boy in his arms, we watched curiously as he hurried over and stood behind the customer ahead of him at the checkout counter. Almost immediately, he began pacing back and forth.

As the seconds passed, I could see uneasiness on his face. His squinted eyes, the furrowed lines on his forehead, and his tightly clasped lips clearly revealed he was vexed and unhappy with the situation. Suddenly, he let out a holler as he glared directly at me.

"Hey! You the pharmacist?"

Frustration was written across him as our eyes locked contact with each other's. Knowing it would be best for everyone, I started toward the counter with hopes to calm him down and prevent a scene.

"Yes, sir, I am. How can I help you?"

"Are you Doc?"

"I am," I answered, nodding my head and positioning myself up against the counter directly in front of where he and the boy were standing. He looked at me almost dazed and stood there now in silence.

For someone who was so impatient, he seemed ill-prepared to answer me back. Therefore, I made a pathetic stab at humor (not one of my strengths) in hopes of easing the tension of the moment. "Yes, sir, most people in town call me Doc, but you can call me Connor or LC, if you prefer. My Grandma Lovelace used to tell folks back where she grew up that they could call her whatever they liked, just not late for dinner! I guess growing up in the Depression, she thought it was a true, yet a funny thing to say." I forced a grin at my pitiful attempt at humor.

Miraculously the tightness around his face subsided and slowly the corners of his mouth tilted up slightly—not a full smile, but it was getting there. And I felt relieved. He then took a deep breath and moved in closer. Maybe he was getting up his nerve, or he didn't know how to ask whatever it was on his mind.

"All right, you've got one up on me. You know my name. So what's yours?" I asked, holding out my hand to greet him. "And how can I help you two?"

"Hayden," he answered back frankly in a stern deep-toned voice. Then, with outstretched arm, he took hold and shook my hand. With a firm grip, he moved our hands up and down so angrily that it nearly shook my entire body!

Issues. Obviously, he has issues, I thought to myself.

"And who is this big man with you?" I asked Hayden.

"Josh. His name is Josh. My wife picked it! Named him after her uncle Joshua who died in Desert Storm!"

"Well, well! Certainly, pleased to meet you, Josh." I smiled and looked at him. Lifting my hand, I placed it on his head, rubbed his hair, laughed, and attempted to break the ice a little more with both of them. Josh was such a handsome little boy, clean, well-groomed with dark curly hair that nearly perfectly matched his deep brown eyes.

"Did you know I'm almost five?" he proudly announced his age, holding up his little hand with all five fingers spread apart. Then he repeated himself, wanting to make certain I knew, "I'm five!"

"You're five! You're a big man, all right! And I bet your dad is proud of you!"

Josh quickly giggled, nodded his head in agreement, and grinned ear-to-ear. I cut my eyes over at Hayden and thought I caught a glimpse of a smile as he listened to Josh and I talk. Without warning, Josh thrust his hand toward me as if he were wanting to shake just like his dad and I had done only moments earlier. Not wanting to miss the opportunity to make Josh feel more comfortable with me, I grabbed his hand and shook it, just like I had done with his dad.

Then, looking at Hayden, I asked, "So your wife named him, huh? She—"

"Is out of the picture!" he finished my sentence with curt attitude. "Yep, for good."

"Well, all right then… What can I do for you and Josh?"

"I know you're going to think I'm crazy, but this nice old lady in the apartment down below us has been bugging me to come talk to you. She's been sort of a mother figure to Josh the past few weeks, and I felt I owed it to her to come see you. Also hoping maybe it will get her off my back, if you know what I mean? But who am I kidding. We couldn't have made it without Mrs. Gonzalez! She's been right there for us every day, helping in so many ways!"

Hayden suspended his explanation just long enough to nervously look over his shoulder and around the drugstore. He then turned back toward me and asked, "Got someplace we can talk…in private like?"

"Yeah, sure." I pointed in the direction of the half-swing door toward the consultation area (required by Florida pharmacy law) for privately discussing medications with our patients.

"How about the booth over there in the consultation area?" I asked. "And you know what, Josh? If my memory serves me right, we have a couple of coloring book and crayons you might like back there."

Josh looked at his dad with a grin, then let loose to get down, and headed toward the booth and the coloring books.

"If that's not okay, Hayden, I'll be glad to ask one of the girls if they could watch him for a few?"

"Either… Whatever… Sure, that sounds fine."

Josh had already decided for us. The door shut behind him, and he slid into the booth and began looking around for the coloring books.

"Okay, let me see here, Josh," I began, while lifting up the lid of the bench seat on the opposite side from him and looking inside.

"Wow! So cool!" Josh exclaimed in amazement at seeing the bench seat lift up to reveal the storage area underneath. "It has a secret hidden compartment!"

"What? Oh yeah, right, it has a hidden compartment!" I agreed with his assessment of the old booth. "How does Paw Patrol sound?

Think you could stay in the lines and color a picture for your dad to put on your refrigerator at home?"

"Sure!" he answered

"Josh, what do we say?"

"Yes, sir, Mr. Doc." He nodded his head firmly.

I knew I shouldn't have, but I couldn't keep from laughing at how he had referred to me—Mr. Doc! That was a first! Suppose I'll have to add that to my list of what people can call me.

Without delay, Josh began thumbing through the coloring book looking for the perfect picture to do for his dad. In no time at all, he stopped his searching and started rummaging through the tub of crayons I had placed on the tabletop next to him. The first color he chose to use in his masterpiece was a light sky-blue. Then he went straight to work.

"So, Hayden," I asked, "where do you and Josh live?"

"Right now, we live down the road—in Wiersdale. But it's looking like we probably will be moving over to Utopia Springs soon."

"Really? Wiersdale has to be a thirty-minute or more drive from here? That's a good way just to talk, don't you think?" No sooner did the last word roll off my lips and Hayden's expression shifted dramatically, and he sighed heavily.

Josh hung his head down tightly and rubbed the crayon even harder against his picture, hoping his dad wouldn't get upset. Hayden immediately saw I was looking at Josh with concern, and he shot his eyes over at him to make certain he was all right. Lifting his eyes back at me, he started explaining again.

"It's like this, Doc. My Aunt Ruth lives over here in Utopia Springs. She offered to let Josh and I live with her, rent free for as long as we need. She even proposed to watch Josh while I'm at work!" Hayden let out a sigh and dropped back hard against the booth. With outstretched arm, he patted Josh on his back. Josh glanced over his shoulder and back at his dad and smiled.

"Don't get me wrong about my Aunt Ruth... It's a great offer and all, but not exactly what I had in mind for Josh and me! You see, the thing is, Sarah left us without a lot of choices! Honestly, right now, Josh and I are bone-dry out of viable options." His words gradually trailed off and faded as he hung his head down.

"Listen, if it's prescriptions you guys need or something like that, I'm more than glad to help!"

"Thanks, but lucky us," Hayden answered, as he raised his head back up and halfway smiled, "that's one thing we have no worries for right now. Josh is like super healthy, knock on wood! No, we are good, but I really appreciate the offer!"

"Then what's up?" There seemed no better time than the present to cut through the small talk and just throw it out.

"Not that I'm proud of it or anything like that, Doc, and not like I haven't been trying…but I'm really having a hard time finding any decent steady work. Man, I have been searching nonstop! I did construction for part of the year—mostly inside carpentry finishing jobs—until the bottom fell out and construction came to a screeching halt with the recession! Since then, mostly odd-and-end stuff with a nighttime bit doing janitorial work at the Altoona Elementary School. It's taken every penny I make to keep up with groceries, rent, gas, and electric! Then Sarah…" Hayden's fist suddenly came down hard on the counter, and his voice crackled as her name came off his lips.

"So it's a job you're needing? Is that why you came?"

Hayden relaxed his fist and slid it off the counter. Slowly he repositioned himself and moved his body forward, closer to the counter edge. Locking his eyes onto mine, he said, "If you are really all that Mrs. Gonzalez says you are, and you sure seem to be, I need to come clean." Hayden stopped, raised up his hands, and rubbed his palms up and down on his face while slightly shaking his head. When he brought his head back upright, it seemed to be covered with emotions—embarrassment, frustration, failure, and a wits'-end desperation crying out from his eyes staring intently at me. Finally, his emotions began to flow out in his words.

"When things got rough, and I mean really rough, Sarah couldn't take it! She flittered around with jobs, tried waitressing, and lost three jobs in one year! And then, next thing I know, she's stressing out over everything! Nitpicking every little thing and constantly with this negative attitude! Always, always asking how we were going to make it! How we would have food on the table, afford rent, buy clothes for Josh, on and on! The woman was brutally relentless, and I'm telling you right now, the negative crap she dished out was depressing us both!"

Hayden exhaled forcefully without relenting on Sarah, "But she let it get to her! She let it consume her! Couldn't deal with the thought of having to scrimp by for a short while until things got better. She lost all hope! The worry of day-to-day living sent her to the edge! I know a lot of people think it's a long, time-consuming walk from where they are to the brink, but you wake up one day, open your eyes, and realize you're standing right there! And when you see where you are, it's downright scary!"

With a deep breath and shrug of his shoulders, Hayden continued, "You just don't get how quick it all happens. Nobody really gets it until they are there! One night, everything seems to be bopping along, and then the next night, an old girlfriend shows up. Before long, she's showing up pretty much every day, especially when I'm not there with Sarah. Then one day, I come home early. Sarah is out cold on the couch, and Josh is locked in the bedroom, banging on the door! As I'm rushing to get to the bedroom and unlock the door, I hear a crushing sound under my shoe. Lifting up my foot, I see a syringe and needle! Can you believe it? Here she's out, lying there with nothing but her bra and panties on while our son is locked in the bedroom so he doesn't see his mom shooting up!" Hayden hung his head down against his hand and propped his elbows on the countertop.

I could hear his deep heavy breathing as he sat there in silence. My heart was breaking inside for him and Josh. Reaching across the counter, I stretched out my arm and placed my hand on his shoulder. "I think I've heard enough to get the picture, son."

After several minutes of silence, I removed my hand and waited for Hayden. When he resumed, he went on to explain everything. How Sarah had left with their car and was gone for almost three weeks. The time and effort he had taken to search for her every day while trying to hold down a janitor job at night at the elementary school and work in a kitchen washing dishes three days a week to keep up with the bills. Hayden went on to describe how Mrs. Gonzalez was a godsend and she had stepped up and taken care of Josh and helped fix meals and clean some around the apartment.

His tone changed dramatically as he restarted into Sarah's story. "Two weeks ago, Josh and I were awakened by banging on the front door of our apartment. My heart was racing as I jumped out of bed and hurried to open the door. I just knew it was Sarah! Imagined she had probably lost her key. Doc, I was so ready to hold her in my arms and tell her that everything would be all right, and I would do whatever it took to make us a family again!"

"Aw, man, at least she came back," I expressed with a sigh of relief.

"Right? I wish!" he exclaimed with a tone of disappointment. "No, just the opposite! It was an Orange County deputy sheriff I saw staring sternly at me in the doorway. I remember vividly how there he was in his dark-green uniform, gold badge, and gun on his hip, waiting for me. He got straight to the point and verified who I was before giving any explanation.

"Looking down at a clipboard, he read the details of how they had discovered Sarah somewhere off Orange Blossom Trail in south Orlando. Told me they were able to positively identify her because she so clearly matched the description on her driver's license that was in the back pocket of her cutoff jeans. The sheriff's officer went on and on, throwing me information nonstop that just got blurred as the reality started to set in on me. Finally, he stopped for a moment and asked me, 'Sir, you need to understand that your wife is dead. She overdosed, and we found her body on the side of the road, less than a mile from a known crack house.'"

I watched as tears flowed from Hayden's eyes and rolled one after the other down his checks. Reaching over, he tenderly wrapped his arm around Josh and pulled him near. Lovingly, he pushed the hair back off Josh's forehead and kissed him. "I love you," he quietly whispered.

Josh tilted up his head to look at his dad. "I love you too."

As they held each other, I could feel my face warming, and my vision began to blur as tears welled up in my eyes.

"Just you and me, kid," he told Josh.

"It's all right, Daddy. I'm right here. I'm not going anywhere," Josh reassured him with the most perfect of words.

Why had he come to me, really? And who was Mrs. Gonzalez? No one came to mind. But somehow, right now at this moment, none of that very much mattered. Hayden had come needing help of some sort, and he trusted me enough, through what Mrs. Gonzalez had told him, to open up and pour out the pain being pumped non-stop from his heart. Strange, but so absolutely true, how most times we work so extremely hard at hiding our brokenness. None of us likes exposing our hurts, confusion, doubts, and fears; it leaves us looking vulnerable and weak! But sitting across from Hayden and Josh, I knew all too well it took a great deal of courage to drive all the way over here and tell me their tragic story. I can't even begin to imagine what they had been though!

The way I saw it though, Hayden and Josh were given three choices when their world came crashing down. They could have just given up, given in, or they could give it all they had. It was the hard road of giving it all they had that they had chosen. That much I felt for certain! And now, now that they had shared with me, I felt privileged to be allowed to help in this part of their journey. They had been let down enough in recent months; I wasn't about to let them down! Right now, they needed to hear it from me loud and clear.

"You're not alone," I immediately blurted out to reassurance them. Then I went on to explain, "There are good people out there who, given the chance, will help you! Real people who have the courage to step out and take a chance on you just like you were willing to come here and talk to me! I know there are individuals out there who are willing to do whatever they can to help you and Josh make it! I give you my word that I will do whatever I can to help! And we will find those individuals willing to help you!" Hearing myself tell him that I would do whatever I could to help instantly reminded me of the promise I had made to Noah!

Hayden looked over at me, and some of the weight of fear and uncertainty which had been pushing him down could be seen slowly lifting off his back, and his eyes had a new light within them.

"You may not fully see it yet, but there's hope on the horizon!" I assured him.

Hayden squeezed Josh ever closer. He looked down at his son, then up at me, and there it finally was, a smile!

"Whenever I'm struggling—which, believe it or not, happens more often than you might imagine—it helps me to stop and look around. Take a headcount of what it is that I *can* be thankful for. Children, neighbors, family, health are just a few you've already put claim to in our brief conversation today! There is probably more, but you need to identify them and own them as right-now blessings in your life."

"I think I get what you are saying. I need to let the shadows of what has happened fall behind me and allow the positives of what I do have to shine some light of hope in! Yeah!" Hayden nodded his head as his mind raced to capture and see the many beams of blessings and hope starting to break through.

"You said to me you didn't feel this move in with your aunt was what you had hoped for, so spin it around into a positive! Look at it as only a short-term stepping-stone on your journey and new beginning to where you actually do see you and Josh being. If nothing else, look at it as a time to regroup, save some money, and get your ducks in a row! When those ducks start lining up—a new steady job, things for Josh—you can take the next step. Before long, each step will come quicker, and the road will be yours for the making!"

"I get what you're saying and agree, Doc! Moving in with my Aunt Ruth will solve a lot of right-now problems for Josh and me! There will be no more rent payments each month to worry about, and someone will be there every day to help me with Josh… God, yes, things will be normal! Or I mean, as normal as they can be for us for now. Aunt Ruth really wants us to come live with her." Hayden continued on, "She encouraged me a lot yesterday when we stopped by to talk about all that had happened. She explained that falling down was just a part of life, but having the faith and hope to get back up was living! Living again is exactly what Josh and I need to start doing! We need to try and get on with things!"

"Absolutely! Your aunt sounds as if she is one smart woman, a woman who also loves you both dearly!"

"Doc, after I found out from the sheriff that Sarah killed herself with heroin, I promised myself that I would do anything necessary to keep Josh and I together! Take whatever job I could get, work however many hours it took, and move wherever we needed to in order to give us the best possible shot for making it! And we are going to make it," he exclaimed matter-of-factly.

"I believe you!"

"We will make it. You can count on that! Just last week, I saw an ad in the *Orlando Sentinel* Sunday classified for a potential job. Not sure I told you, but I sold our old Toyota Corolla to pay for Sarah's funeral, catch up on rent, and buy Josh something to wear so he would look nice for her one last time. Anyhow, I rode the Lake Seminole and Orange County transit buses for an interview for the job. Had to make four changeovers just to get there!"

"So how did it go?"

"There was this line of people, maybe eight to ten, I'm not certain, out the human resources office door. Every one of them was picking up an application to be interviewed for the one single position! I stood in line, waited my turn, got the application, filled it out, turned it back in, and told the lady at the front desk that I would wait to be interviewed. I sat and waited. Waited until almost six and still no one came out to say or tell me anything. Finally, some old dude shows up and called out my name."

"Well?"

"If he asked me one question, he must have asked me a million! I was nervous and a little tired, so when he kept bombarding me with stuff about where I lived, how I would get there, if I was reliable… Well, I got a little defensive. But I apologized immediately and told him I was sorry."

After a deep breath, Hayden continued, "I thought for sure he would be angry, and I was ready to kick myself in the butt for blowing the interview. Then he looked at me, tilted his head to the side, and said that I must really need the job to have come so far for an interview. His voice seemed one of concern, not anger. I knew right then that what I saw was a man who cared. He cared about his company and who he hired for the position—the person behind the employee. I couldn't believe it when Mr. Mroz came right out and said, 'You seem like a standup guy—exactly the type we are looking for in this position.' Mr. Mroz nodded his head as he told me! From that point on all he needed to know was that I could handle the drive and be there every day for my shift. He simply wanted to make certain I was reliable! I gave him the lowdown on Sarah and all that had happened. He understood and said it made him more certain of his decision to offer me the job!"

"So you got a job. *Yes!* What a huge blessing! Tell me all about it. Where will you be working, what will you be doing, any chance for advancement, and what's the pay?"

"Yeah, I know… It's like a miracle, right?"

"It is!"

"The job is at this big spice company, just a little southwest of Orlando and over near the attractions in Kissimmee and all that jungle of traffic. Mr. Mroz said it was a fulltime position, forty hours a week, Monday through Friday, second shift on a production line with solid opportunity to move up if I'm worth a plug nickel, or something like that, he said. Guess that means that if I show them that I am reliable, committed, and hardworking, there is a chance for advancement! He offered to start me at fifteen dollars per hour and told me to be there no later than 3:30 on the dot, next Monday afternoon. My shift is from four until midnight."

"It sounds terrific! You told him yes, right?"

"There were stipulations."

"What a minute, it is legit, isn't it?"

"Oh yeah, straight-up legit! What Mr. Mroz needs… I mean… what the stipulation is, is that…that they need to be certain they can count on me to be there every day! I have to promise him that I have transportation—something other than just the county bus lines!"

"What's the problem? Pick up the phone and call and tell him you will be there! Let him know he can count on you, Hayden!"

"But I can't do that, Doc! I don't have transportation! Remember, I sold the Toyota! I had to borrow a car from one of my neighbors just to come over and see you today! And there is no way I can tell him I'll ride the bus!" Hayden exclaimed as he turned his head side-to-side in a forceful *no* manner!

"I have to promise him I'll be there and start Monday! And, you see, it's the middle of a bimonthly pay cycle, and they have a company policy that says if you start after the fifteenth of the month, your paycheck isn't until the first of the month—the next pay period! Meaning for me, there would be no paycheck for two weeks! That's two weeks of getting to work, two weeks buying groceries and everything else without any money in the bank! Hey, don't forget Christmas is just around the corner too! How's Santa supposed to get presents for Josh? God, just listen to me. I'm starting to sound just like Sarah!"

Josh immediately looked up from coloring and over at his dad and reassured him, "Don't worry, Daddy. Santa's got Christmas taken care of! He always does!"

"I know, Josh. I know. Santa's got it covered, buddy," Hayden acknowledged as he looked away from him and rolled his eyes.

"Hold on. Hold on now! Don't let your mind throw you into a negative tailspin! All you are doing is trying to think things through out loud just like any good parent would do, Hayden! Remember, knowing what you need to accomplish is half the battle! How about we figure out one thing at a time? First thing is what to drive, right?"

"Yes, but that's a huge deal! Don't you remember I sold the Corolla? Aunt Ruth hasn't had a car for who knows how long, and my other nearest relatives are third cousins in Madison, Georgia. I haven't seen them in years, and there's no way I could ask for them for help! That's why I don't know what to do... Without wheels, this job is toast!"

I didn't respond right away because I felt it best to take a minute or two to think on the situation. With what little extra cash I had, a clunker would be about all I could buy him. That certainly was not what Hayden needed! He needed something more reliable than I could offer, and that would require help from someone else!

Jimmy had been a friend for years, and it just so happened that he and his family owned several businesses in town, including a really nice used car lot. On countless occasions, he had sent individuals to the drugstore to see me. Always calling ahead, he would ask me to fill their prescriptions and send him the bill. We did our best to make certain they got the medicine they needed while not making them feel as if it was charity. Yes, Jimmy was a good, honest guy who I felt would see this as an opportunity to help! If anyone could, he would make certain Hayden had a reliable means of transportation to his new job.

"Let me make a quick call, and then I'll be right back," I said as I held up my hand and motioned to Hayden. Getting up and walking over to my work area, I grabbed my cell phone and headed to the back of the drugstore so as not to have interruptions. Scrolling under contacts, I found his number and pushed on it to call. On the third ring, Jimmy picked up.

He required little convincing after hearing of their plight, and I offered to help with the cost as much as I could. Jimmy wanted no part of my help and said he would consider it an offense if he wasn't allowed to help Hayden and Josh on his own terms. I agreed. He asked that I give him the rest of the day to select one of their vehicles and get paperwork and tags in order. He promised the vehicle would be all ready for Hayden to come by and pick up by noon the following day!

Words couldn't come close to expressing how grateful I was and how much of a blessing this would be to them, but I tried anyway to thank him for everything he was doing. Without his generosity, it would likely be no way that Hayden could accept the job! This was the beginning of everything Hayden needed, and all the rest would fall into place. I just knew it would! I rushed back out to share the amazing news!

"Hey, I don't know what kind of ride—maybe be a car or an old truck—but I have this friend who's giving you a vehicle! Consider it done, Hayden! So now it's time to call up Mr. Mroz!"

"That's unbelievable! Don't know how that just happened, but I'll call Mr. Mroz and say yes! Absolutely!" Hayden jumped out of his seat, came around to the other side of the booth, wrapped his arms around my shoulder, and began repeating, "Thank you, thank you, thank you."

"Okay. Okay. So that takes care of the big one—the ride! But sit back down because we aren't done yet! We still have work to do on that list of things you named earlier and more to cross off!"

Hayden returned back to the other side but was so excited he could hardly sit still. It sounded as if a little laughter was starting to come out of his mouth as he nodded his head joyfully. Josh looked over at his dad, and although he didn't understand all that was happening, he could tell something had changed, and he was happy again. Without having to force it, Josh smiled from ear to ear as he lovingly watched his dad. It was as if Hayden's joy had overflowed out onto Josh. Both looked so happy for the first time since I had met them!

As much as I would have liked to stay and work out every detail, there were baskets of prescriptions starting to mount up on my desk that needed attention. After instructing Hayden to write out a list and then prioritize, I started back to my work area. Before leaving, I watched as Josh opened his coloring book to the inside front cover, where there were no pictures, and he pushed it over in front of his dad along with a crayon.

"Here you go, Dad."

While trying my best to get caught up, Hayden kept busy working on his list, and before I knew it, the better part of two hours had quickly passed. When I walked back over and took a look at the list, I was amazed at how precise and organized it was! Clearly it detailed all they needed to make it through the next thirty days.

Beside the number 1 item—transportation—he had marked a big check with the crayon Josh had given him to use! After that, there was the matter of groceries for the two of them.

For years now Ria, my wife, had been using part of her monthly income to help local food banks and shelters. Most of those years when the holiday season rolled around (Thanksgiving and Christmas), she would reach out to several local churches and ask them for the name of one family in dire need. For that month, on that family, she would use all the money she normally would have spent on food for the shelters on that family in dire need. With insider information, I knew for a fact Ria had not yet committed to any family for this Christmas! Hayden and Josh would be her family! They would be the ones she could bless with the gift of groceries! Ria was going to absolutely love every minute of getting things for Hayden and Josh!

"I already know someone willing to provide the groceries! Check that one off your list there!"

"It's just so unbelievable! This is absolutely amazing! All right then, that was quick!" Hayden looked up and smiled as he used the crayon to put another big check, this time beside item number 2 on the list!

As for up next on the list: clothes for Josh.

Right around the corner, less than three blocks from the drugstore, was the Ethel Payne Crisis Center. Never before had they let me down or turned away a family I had sent to them! Maybe it is in their charter not to turn away anyone in need, but I am so very thankful for all the times they have stepped right in to provide clothes, backpacks, shoes, and necessities to local families I sent their way. They would gladly make certain Josh had clothes for school, play, and church! I would give James, their director, a call in the morning, and he would get right on helping out! There was no question in my mind about the clothes for Josh!

"The crisis center up the street will make sure Josh has all the clothes he needs! How about you put a big check next to that one too! Yep, another one we can cross off the list!"

"Got it!" Hayden was getting happier by the moment as he put another big check on the list with the crayon.

After clothes, Hayden had listed gas money. I had been thinking for a while on that one, as I had taken a moment here and there between checking prescriptions. Kameron owned Utopia Gas Stop, where Ria and I usually filled up. Over the years, we had worked together on the high school's boosters club, and he always seemed to have a giving heart whenever kids and families in need were brought up. Although he had never asked me for any favors nor I any from him, it seemed worth a try! Earlier I had texted him and explained in general the situation. He responded back with several questions, and I shot back answers to each. I needed to look at my phone and see if he had made any decisions on their needs.

Holding my hand up again and motioning, I told Hayden to, "Wait a minute and let me check something."

I went over to where I kept my cell phone on the countertop next to my workstation and picked it up. Quickly I unlocked my phone, selected Messages, and scrolled down to his reply. It was preceded with an exceptionally long explanation and details I could hardly believe! My eyes widened as I finished reading his reply. I couldn't help myself as I blurted out, "Boom! That's what I'm talking about!"

"Everything all right?" Hayden asked apprehensively.

"More than all right!" I responded back. "That concern we both had about gas for your wheels? Well, guess what? The Lord just answered and meet that need *big time*!"

"What?" Hayden glared my way, confused by my answer.

"The local gas station owner just texted me back! If I try to condense what he said, it will lose meaning...so how about I read it to you instead.

"Let me get this straight, Doc? You are asking me to give free gas to someone I don't even know? Well, strange you should ask that. I remember my parents always told me stories about how people in little towns, like ours, cared about each other. Looked out for each other, you know? They both grew up in a small town in Iowa, and I still hear tales from them about how during the droughts and severe storms neighbors came to the aid of neighbors and helped each other get by—whatever it took! That was the way they made it through, you know? What we are having right now with this recession and all is like one of those catastrophes they faced with their neighbors! This is one of the droughts and storms of our lifetime! This crisis is our time, our turn, to pull together! I don't want to someday look back and tell my kids that I didn't care enough to try and help someone in genuine need during this difficult time! You hit it right on the head when you said it could just as easily be you or I in their shoes! I used to think my parents' stories were more fairy tale than real life. Some elaborate fabrication they made up to try and teach me a lesson of some sort. But your request for Hayden and Josh just hit me. They aren't make-believe or fairytale. They are real people in real need! Right now, today they need our help! This is real life for this guy and his son, and they have faith enough to come to us looking for help? Wow! Yes, yes! I'm honored to help! And thank you so much for asking me! At first, I was…maybe mad, but that was wrong of me! I can feel it in my heart, you know. I don't say things like that, and it sounds kind of fake, I know, but I feel something different than I ever have before. And it feels really good! Whatever it is, I can't explain it, but this voice from my parents inside me keeps telling me to help them! You can count on me, Doc! Definitely count me in! Tell him whenever he needs to fill up, just come to the station! I got this covered for him! And be sure to remind him that I don't want anything from him in return—you tell him that!"

"Unbelievable! Man, oh man! I don't know what to think?!" Hayden exclaimed ecstatically!

"I'll tell you what to think!" I looked over at him and continued, "You need to thank God! These kinds of things don't just happen miraculously on their own!"

Hayden looked over at me, still dazed at all that was falling into place for he and Josh. He smiled and nodded his head in agreement to what I said.

My mom always told me that if I would make myself available and press on as hard as I could for what was right; the Lord would surely flow through making miraculous things happen! And was she ever right! Just for the asking, there were people out there who still cared and were willing to step out to make a difference. They weren't waiting for someone else to do it, a local church or a charity, they recognized the urgency of another human being's situation and jumped right it! I will never stop believing that friends help friends, neighbors help neighbors, and family helps family to get to a better place in their lives, lifting them up and allowing them to get back on their life road!

And as for Christmas gifts for Josh, I knew just the ladies for the job!

One of the senior women's Sunday school classes has been asking me if they could help with needs for any local children! Those sweet old ladies loved to help kids more than just about anything else! I couldn't begin to count the number of times they had provided for local children in need; you name it, they had done it! Virginia came to the drugstore, which meant I had her phone number in the computer! When I got a free minute later in the day, I'd give her a call! She'd get on the phone and call everyone in her class and likely round up a truck load of gifts before week's end!

I didn't want to let Josh hear we had Christmas taken care of, so I pointed to the next item on the list, smiled, and nodded at Hayden. "Check this one off too, no problem!"

He looked at me with a huge grin and put a check beside it.

Without hesitation, Hayden suddenly blurted out, "Don't know how or when, but I promise I'll do my best to pay everyone back for all they are doing!"

How wonderful it was to see that not only was Hayden appreciative, but he was willing to give back to everyone all they had given to him! I told he not to worry about repaying anyone for anything. Consider it a gift from neighbors and friends who cared about him and Josh. They were friends who wanted to give him hope and a new beginning! I will never forget the moment when I told him to use the money that he would make at the new job to help them get a fresh start with the rest of their lives and not to give another thought to repaying anything. They were gifts, free and clear!

Hayden reached over, grabbed Josh, and started to cry. He looked at the small boy he was holding and reassured him, "Everything is going to be all right, son. Everything's going to be all right!"

What a sight! My heart overflowed with emotions as I took in fully the quiet moment as Hayden held Josh tight in his arms. Oh, the power of sincere and infectious joy! Happiness may depend on circumstances, but joy depends on God! And right now, God was so richly blessing Hayden and Josh!

Hayden finally looked at me wide-eyed and exclaimed, "I can't wait any longer! I'm heading over right now to tell Aunt Ruth the news! You have no idea what this means to me...to us!" Hayden exclaimed as he stood up, took Josh in his arms, turned, and ran out the drugstore.

Where it looked like a huge door had slammed down on the life of Hayden and Josh, the actions of caring individuals opened a gateway to a new future—one with hope! Wow, what a difference they made in the life of two complete strangers! Before now I never thought of the drugstore being used in the ways it was starting to be used! Truly it was a real-life miracle!

To me, it was like a flashing sign in the dark of night that pops out at you on the road of some long highway—CARING—bling, bling! That was what it was, all right; it was all about caring! Starting with one simple act, from one person, one time, and miraculously, it was still growing and glowing! All the things people were starting to do were changing the life of a father and son, consumed by despair and dread, into a life overflowing with hope and joy! I felt totally blown away by everything that was happening! My faith in others exploded to a realm of possibility beyond anything previously imaginable!

I was finding out that you don't have to look hard to find someone in need or someone to help! Sometimes you don't have to look at all! In fact, there are days when an unexpected cry for help comes calling—right to your doorstep—just like it did with Hayden and Josh! The question is, Will we answer?

I love mornings because with each one comes a new sunrise with a brand-new opportunity to make a difference—if only we are willing! Years ago, I discovered that there is never a longest night or darkest day that can defeat the promise and reality of a new sunrise, bringing hope for the day! Tomorrow Hayden and Josh would wake up to a new day full of hope and new beginnings!

What happened for Hayden and Josh had clearly showed me care and love! So many had shared in bringing this love: the one who spoke a kind word and offered direction (the neighbor at the apartment complex), another who went from an inch in helping to a mile (or should I say many miles on an old truck with new tires), and the one who found a change of heart—maybe it was the first time he had ever truly felt his heart (offering one of today's more expensive commodities, gasoline)!

None of those who helped Hayden and Josh woke up that morning deliberately looking for someone in need. They didn't get up and out of bed planning on helping anyone. Yet when given the opportunity, each listened to their heart, opened their eyes to the needs of others, and helped in their very own special way!

It wasn't so much about what each that helped had; it was more about how they choose to use what they had and what they did with those choices was everything to Hayden and Josh! Each showed that it is never too late to start afresh, never the wrong choice to seize the day and start caring for others and giving from the heart!

I am so very thankful for each and every day my heart is still beating! Never do I take a day for granted, and I am also thankful for every new beginning that comes with these new days! My prayer would be that the Lord allows me to be part of more of these wonderful days. Days like the one I had been so blessed to be a part of today in helping Hayden and Josh!

What is impossible for people is possible with God.
—Luke 18:27

CHAPTER 5

And Then There Were Two

*God is up to something so big, so unimaginably good
that your mind cannot contain it... What we see God
doing is never as good as what we don't see.*

—Ben Patterson

"Be aware and never forget how wonderful life is," a dear friend once gave me that advice. Yet I never heeded his words or slowed down enough to recognize the truth of his statement as much as I should have. It took his suicide for that statement to really sink in. To make me stop in my tracks and say, "Wait a minute! What did I miss here?" Gavin must have told me a dozen times in the year before he killed himself that I had a wonderful life... I didn't hear him then, but I do now!

Had I listened, I would have slowed down and taken the time to look around. Only then would I have known just how absolutely wonderful my life is! If I had only known back then, I wouldn't have complained as much as I did. I would have watched my words more carefully and not been so critical and judgmental of others. I would have quit my pouting and found contentment in what I had. I would have enjoyed a lot more sunrises and sunsets. I would have counted every day as a gift and blessing, and I would have been more honest and open with my feeling and told those around me how much I loved them—especially my wife and children! Sad to say, but I didn't do any of those things as much as I should have! Time can never be relived, but we can put past mistakes behind us and strive each day to be the person we always said we would be! Gavin taught me that there is no better time than now! Tomorrow, I've found out the hard way, may not be ours to have and hold.

Also, with the loss of my friend Gavin, I learned that I should have taken the time to stop and listen, listen with my heart and not my ears to the words of those around me. Individuals, both friends and strangers, who were crying out to find someone who cared—someone that gave a hoot about their life and their struggles. Many needing no more than a smile followed by a simple "Hope you have a good day." Others a handshake or a touch on the shoulder, reassuring them with my eyes that I am there if they need me. Still more, whom if they received a note of encouragement in the mail or via a text message would consider it a sure sign someone cared—the encouragement that people knew they existed! I cannot tell you how many times I have asked myself why I didn't notice someone next to me hurting or struggling with a problem. I internalize and tell myself it was because I wasn't listening or wasn't looking, but I pray to God it wasn't because I didn't care!

I can never forget that letter. And looking back, I recognize a lot of things have changed around the drugstore since that night with Jenn and Natalie! Where in the past it sometimes seemed a bother to spend time with a patient when we were busy, I now make the time—no matter how busy—to come around and lean against the counter and listen. Instead of "I have to," it is more of a "I get to" help someone! With that, where I used to question "Why me?" the better one is "Why not me?"

It has been truly awesome what a turnaround has transpired! Sure, the people who come to the drugstore are the same (except for a few new patients now and then), but the change is that I am different. There has been a change in me! No more looking at the wrongs but rather relooking in terms of the rights. And wow, are there a lot of rights when you take the time to stop and look! Amid the daily rush and to-dos of business I have rediscovered the joy of the moment and the happiness in helping others. String them all together moment by moment, person by person, and you make a lifetime—a meaningful lifetime of wonderful memories! Strange as it may sound, it had been there all along. I simply had chosen before not to be a part of it. Now, every day, I can hardly wait to be a part of it!

Instead of looking at Mrs. Singleton as being sick with the flu (which, of course, she was), I now saw her as this wonderful lady not only needing a prescription but as someone who could use a word of encouragement to help her through this brief period of being under the weather. So why didn't I see this before? Guess I thought telling her from behind the counter that "I hope you get to feeling better" was enough. Boy was I way, way wrong! It was not enough!

In the past, staying behind the counter put me in a safety zone, my own controlled little world. It didn't require me getting too close to anyone or risk me saying something I shouldn't, or God forbid, giving the impression that I might actually care. In other words, it was the easy way out—no caring, no involvement! In the past, I didn't take the time or make the effort to go out and see her and thank her for the phone call she made to Ria telling her how much her lady's group enjoyed the homemade cowboy cookies or the note she sent to our staff, thanking us for the kindness we showed her every time she was in the drugstore. I should have done that, a no-brainer, right… Well, I didn't. Don't we all have our own personal walls that keep us at arm's length, visible yet a safe enough distance away not to get involved? But if we go around those walls and begin to engage, listen, and care, the world changes for us and those around us!

I am not certain why, but lately my days seem to be flying by. I look at the clock, and it is ten. Then I turn around, and it is almost six! Go figure? My wife explains this phenomenon as a "change in attitude." Ria tells me it is because "Your heart and soul enjoy what you are doing." If I didn't know better, I would think she was trying to be a psychoanalyst. Good luck with that one, honey. But I think she might be right…about the enjoying what I am doing because I do enjoy what I am doing every day!

Just as another day was winding down, the phone rang, and someone informed me, "Doc, call on line 2."

"Hi, sorry you had to wait," I answered.

"Doc," an old familiar-sounding voice started. "Are you real busy?"

"Not too, too so. I've always got a minute for you, Bob. What's up?" I asked, recognizing the voice.

"It's that… I… What I mean to say is… I…" He seemed unable to straighten his tongue and get out what it was he wanted to say.

"Is something the matter? Are you all right?" I questioned with concern.

"Well, I've been thinking a lot and…"

"About what?"

"How about I tell you when I see you?" Bob answered. "But it needs to be tonight. Swing by my farm after work, and we can talk."

"Tonight?"

"Yes, tonight."

"All right," I answered. "It likely will take me thirty minutes or so to wrap things up here at the drugstore, but then I'll head on over your way. Probably seven or so?"

"Great! See you then."

What the heck was that all about? I wondered. *What was it that had Bob so shaken?*

Usually he had it all together, This was the first time I had heard him be at a loss for words.

Not that he ever would make a big deal of it, but Bob was a direct descendant of one of the original families to settle in Utopia Springs back in the late 1800s. He was born, raised, and lived here almost his entire life. Like most of the old-timers, his family roots were firmly founded in farming and agriculture. But don't let that farming thing fool you. Around here a man can wear a Stetson hat, have dirty Roper boots, drive a beat-up truck, and still be a financial success!

Bob may be what most call a good-ole-boy, but he was sharp as a tack! Nothing ever got by him! Along with a head full of brains, he had a heart bigger than the state of Florida! Although up in years— I'll be nice and say he is probably twenty years older than me—we enjoyed spending time talking with each other at the drugstore, local picnics, or outside of church on Sunday mornings. I liked being able to look him in the eye when we talked, face-to-face, so as to get a true feel for what he was thinking. And even though I was a bit anxious, I looked forward to seeing and talking with him.

I have heard it said that the road to a friend's house is never long, but I am willing to bet that whoever said that had never driven the three-mile stretch of hard, dusty washboard clay road to go see Bob! I felt like my insides had been grabbed hold of and mixed in a blender by the time I pulled up in front of his old two-story clapboard farmhouse. If memory served me correct, Bob once told me this was his parent's old homestead. He was raised here, came back here to live after college at Florida Technological University (the original name for what today is the University of Central Florida), and told me he felt comfortable enough in the old place to spend the rest of his life here. "No further discussion needed," he always added. On many occasions, he had reiterated the thought that if only more of people could get to the point in their life where they were content, what a different world it would be. Too often, we are looking for that greener pasture, the next new game, another challenge, a smarter phone, more money, or some crazy new gizmo!

Simply because he is content is not to say life has always been easy for Bob over the years. He had seen both sides of the coin—good and bad. The same could be said for most farmers, especially those in this part of Florida. Big freezes in the seventies and eighties took a tremendous toll on cash crops—particularly citrus. Then, add to it, numerous hurricanes and unstoppable sprawling growth. It was Booker T. Washington who once commented that, *"Success is to be measured not so much by the position that one has reached in life as by the obstacles which he has overcome."* If such was being used as the yard stick for measurement, Bob would be considered as a huge success because he had overcome what many viewed as near impossible obstacles! The likes of which included not only agricultural challenges but also cancer, the loss of a child, and bankruptcy.

Because life had never been easy, Bob never played it safe. Instead he lived it to the fullest and pushed forward living day-by-day, trusting in the Lord. To him, safe was a feel-good disguise word for regret, and he wanted none of that! And as if all that had happened was not enough, he now faced two new nemeses—deteriorating cardiac health and the path of old age without a son or daughter to walk it with him. Yet not even these had robbed him of his faith and joy! I looked up to Bob as someone I wanted to be like.

"What took you so dadgum long!" Bob yelled to me from the pasture next to the main house. "I could have gotten here quicker on horseback! Probably would have done just that thirty years ago too!"

We both laughed, then walked toward each other, and met halfway at the fence line. Shaking hands, we then leaned against the four-post fence and looked out over the pasture. It was a stunning sight to see as the sun started to set behind the rows of deep-green-leaved orange trees. Bob tipped his hat and wiped the sweat from his brow with his shirtsleeve.

"Beautiful night, but it has been one hot winter so far! Can't remember too many winters that were this hot and dry and only a little over a week before Christmas!"

"At your age, you would know better than me," I replied with a grin.

"Whatever. I've seen more up-and-down weather than I care to remember! Long as we are not standing here talking about some crazy hurricane eyeing in on us, we are in good shape!"

"You got no argument from me on that one! I hate the six months of talk about hurricanes, El Niño, and the likes! Glad hurricane season ended last month!"

"Me too. Now listen," Bob's tone of voice changed to one more stern. He was done with small talk and ready to get down to the reason he asked me over.

"I've been thinking a lot about you and the drugstore. Add to it, I've been thinking a lot about folks here in Utopia Springs."

"That's an awful lot of thinking, Bob! I'm hoping it wasn't all bad?" I said with a guarded laugh. "Of course, I mean, the part about me and the drugstore!"

Bob grinned and gave a chuckle, if you'd call it that. Then he started right back in again, "You know..." He pulled off his hat and hit it against his leg. With a quick look up at me, he unloaded. "Listen here! For a couple weeks, I have been doing some thinking. Thinking how you…the drugstore…are doing things, helping people here, people here in town. Do you understand what I mean! Word gets around in a small town, and I hear good things. I know you well enough to know you are doing the right thing too! What I am trying to say is…"

"For goodness' sake, Bob, just come right out and say it! I promise you are not going to hurt my feelings if it is something I did wrong! I'm only human. I make mistakes just like everybody else. Open up and hit me with both barrels!"

"All right then, Doc, but it is not about any mistakes you have made!" Bob took a deep breath, exhaled heavily, and came with it again. "You've been helping people and word gets around. Small town…not much to talk about… Word gets around about those things, you know? Folks know you…trust you…the drugstore…all that. What I want to do…maybe what you can help me…"

"Bob, so long as it doesn't involve guns or illegal drugs, it is a pretty safe bet I can probably help! Just come out and say whatever it is. I will give it my best!" With that, I slapped him on the back. We both laughed, and he put his hat back on.

"Doc, I want to give you some money," he said straight out.

"Money? For what, Bob?"

"It has been weighing heavy on my mind what you do up there at the drugstore to help people. Helping different folks with their prescriptions and all those other ways you get involved. We have been friends long enough that I know you're the real deal! A real McCoy! No two ways about it, you are the real thing! None of this all talk and no action like so many people! You follow up what you say with actions. I greatly respect that about you! I want to give you some money, and I want you to use my money to help whoever needs it—the ones who really need it the most!"

"How? Just how do you see me doing that?"

"Let's say I give you a couple hundred dollars…or maybe more…whatever amount we agree on! Every month I give you, the drugstore, whoever, and you decide how best!"

"Decide how best for what?"

"I trust you, Doc! Use the money however you think best. I don't want to know, don't need a receipt—just trying to help! I might be old—remember I said *might*—but I certainly am not blind! I see folks are in trouble, likely lots of people needing help. And I want to help them out, but don't want them to know it is from me! I want it to be anonymous! Got that, Doc. Nobody needs to know!"

Bob reached over and grabbed hold of my arm as he clarified the last condition. "I don't want to hear from anybody that I did this! You understand me? Let them think it is from you, the good fairy, Santa Claus, or the Easter Bunny—I don't care, just not from me! People will accept it from you without any problem. They will hedge on me and balk at the idea if I try to do it myself! Do this for them. I know you can!"

My mouth opened wider than barn doors as I stood there speechless over his request.

"I wouldn't leave that open for too long around here, son, you might suck in some of these flies circling round my cows." Bob laughed at me and let loose of my arm. "Now, what do you say we head up to the house and get that money so you can start to work helping people? I want to get moving with this as soon as possible. I think it will be great, Doc! People need it, and I finally feel like I can help them! It feels good just thinking about it! I have always wanted to help but never quite knew how until now! I'm telling you, it feels awful good!"

I smiled, walked beside him, and listened as he asked about Ria and our girls. His voice sounded so excited. He seemed giddier than a young boy who had just gotten his first horse.

And so it was. Without any prompting or asking, Bob had decided to stop and listen to his heart and act! Without anyone standing by with an outstretched hand begging, Bob believed with a simple child-like faith that he could make a difference, a difference in the world—the world around him just outside his door in Utopia Springs! So there were two now, Bob and Emma Anne, who had decided to help out on a regular basis those in need!

Why is it when things get to going great, we start worrying? Wondering why this is happening. Is it too good to be true? When will I wake up and realize it's a dream? Or worse, what is going to happen and make it go away? All those thoughts and many, many more crowded my mind and caused me to have doubts about what was happening. I couldn't help myself, I'm only human, and I feared it wasn't going to last!

Suddenly I felt the need to make certain I wasn't doing something wrong, illegal, or unethical. Crazy, I know, but that selfish thing of covering one's butt, making sure I wasn't exposing myself to ridicule, prosecution from authorities, or the IRS, had me scrambling to get advice from "experts." Those all-knowing professionals (in this case scenario, my accountant and my lawyer) could evaluate what was happening and reassure me I wasn't doing anything wrong. So I picked up the phone and called them.

And this, my friends, was the result of those phone calls:

> Number 1: Neither believed my story. As one said, "A little farfetched to be true, don't you think? You are wishing if you think people would give you money every month to help others!"
>
> Number 2: Neither thought, even if it was the least bit true, that I should accept money to help others, no matter what the circumstances. It opened the door for others to find out, ridicule me, or accuse me of taking the money for myself. So why put myself though such insinuation?
>
> Number 3: Neither wanted any part whatsoever with helping me set up a system to help those in need. They suggested I turn it over to a church or professional organization that had tax exempt status and had done this sort of thing before. There was no need to reinvent the wheel!
>
> Number 4: Neither believed that what little I was hoping to do would make any difference in

the big picture, so why bother? They felt
there were already enough organizations out
there that if someone really needed help,
they could reach out to one of them instead.

It was that number 4 that burned me! That was the real clincher
for me! I knew that it *would* make a big difference for some people!

I wondered what on earth had happened to us as people and as
a nation. When did we buy into selfish personal illusions and push
the idea of caring and helping those in need so far to the black abyss
of our minds? When was it we started ignoring and neglecting the
beliefs we once held so strongly to? You know, like the one about love
your neighbor as yourself! Was it when we decided we needed newer
and bigger things for ourselves, and we forgot about those hurting
and less fortunate who needed so little from us just to get by day-to-
day? Was it when we got tired of seeing panhandlers on every street
corner? Was it when we got sick of all the negative news and con-
vinced ourselves we couldn't make a difference? Maybe it was when
we decided that since everyone else was out for themselves, we should
be too? Was it when we quit being humble and felt the need to be
first, right, or justified—every time, all the time, about everything?
It seems as if, as a people, we have begun to doubt the validity of the
whole care for your fellow man thing!

And speaking of doubt, that's what I get for doubting! That's
what I get for my ever questioning what was happening at the drugstore or why it was happening! That's what I get for asking the advice
of two successful individuals who have bought lock, stock, and, barrel into the lies people now consider truth!

I was trying to compartmentalize it (like everything else in my
life) and make it fit into some nice, neat little mold I envisioned for
it. Something I could control and rationalize into being whatever it
was I wanted it to be. I think too often we try to retrofit a perfect scenario into some formed little model of our own! What I needed to do
was remove my emotional and control-freak mentality and replace it
with simple faith and trust. Two things I sure do talk about a lot and

tell others they should have, but two things I often have a hard time doing myself!

Enough was enough. It was time to take my hands off the wheel, and let go! My plans and ideas were not going to get me to where we needed to go! Margaret Atwood once summed it up by saying, *"Even with the best of maps and instruments, we can never fully chart our journey."* She was right! I needed to trust in someone bigger than myself! Reaching to my right, I grabbed a prescription pad and, in big printed letters, wrote two words—*faith* and *trust.* I then ripped the sheet off the pad and placed the paper on my to-do board mounted directly in front of me. It would serve as a daily reminder not to try to do it myself but rather to have faith! Maybe it sounds totally left field, but at least for me, it was a start! And we all must start somewhere!

As for an organized system, I told myself to just keep it simple. Accept the gifts that were given each month by Emma Anne and Bob and leave them in the Helping Jar on the front counter. When someone needed help, I would just get the money out and pay for what it was they were needing. As for prescriptions, I would personally make up any difference they needed with my own money. No one need ever know who the gift was from. Just for the record, those highly trained and highly paid professionals I consulted with are now my ex-accountant and ex-lawyer!

If there was a need for food or clothes, Ria had that figured out. In the lobby of the drugstore, she kept a canned food donation box for the Ethel Payne Crisis Center that we took over to them weekly. Additionally, Ria had committed to using part of her paycheck each week toward buying groceries and kept them in the back of the drugstore to be available for those in immediate need who couldn't wait until the center was open on Thursdays. The opportunity for giving was expanded!

One day, out of the blue, a local organization contacted the drugstore to ask if they could place a clothing and toy collection drop box next to our parking lot. It took less than a week before the receptacle was in place and ready for donations. I watched with amazement as individuals brought in bags of items and realized there was no way all the people who started dropping off items in the collection box had that many unwanted items in their closets and garages! Best I could tell from watching a few times, many of the items appeared to still be in original bags and boxes—brand-new! Never would I have imagined seeing the outpour of caring individuals from the community who came by repeatedly, week after week, to place items in the donation box.

Ria reached out to the organization and made certain that if we provided them with the name of local families in need that they would help. Every time we called with the name of a family in need, they immediately responded and helped out!

Suddenly the drugstore was able to help, either directly or indirectly, through our own resources and by referrals to local organizations and businesses. It was amazing to see how the community was pulling together and helping meet the varied needs of individuals and families! Not only was the drugstore able to help with prescriptions but also grocery items, clothing, toys, health screenings, as well as personal and financial counseling at the crisis center!

The drugstore even reached out to the local health department and women's clinic and partnered to provide medications and prenatal vitamins for single mothers-to-be! It was mind-boggling all the doors that were opening and all the resources that were becoming available to so many different people in need! Clearly God was at work! I could feel it. He was up to something big, something really big!

For we live by faith, not by sight.
—2 Corinthians 5:7

CHAPTER 6

It's All about Timing

A stopped watch is right twice daily, but watches weren't made to be stopped, they were made to tell time.
—Jeremy Kingsley

Years ago I remember how it seemed strange to me when Cara, my oldest daughter, came into our bedroom one night and asked Ria to measure the length of her hair. Tired and ready for bed, I wondered what was the usefulness of such a trivial fact? Why did it matter how long it was? Having the fullest head of hair in the family, I suspected she planned to brag about the length to her sisters. Or maybe she just wanted to tell her boyfriend? I know I certainly would like to tell him a thing or two! But what the heck, getting a little balder every day, I would be thankful just to have hair enough to measure, much less worry about the length. I was ready to blurt it out and ask why when it dawned on me. They'd probably say it was a "girl things" and not bother to elaborate further. Having three daughters, I had been given that answer many times over the years. So for the sake of sounding like a fool, I refrained from questioning her motives.

I did, however, watch with curiosity and anticipation as Cara sat on the edge of the bed and handed Ria the yard stick. I could hear Cara mumbling something about hoping it was long enough. I listened intently as she explained to her mom how she had been growing it out for more than a year and had decided it was time to cut it off (providing it was long enough—twelve inches was what she needed, I think I heard her say) and donate it to Wigs For Kids. All this in the hope some young girl without hair could have a wig made of real hair. Did I feel like a jerk for my callused thoughts!

It caught me totally off guard that Cara had gotten up the courage to put self-centeredness and vanity aside long enough to recognize there were girls out there in the world needing twelve inches of hair more than she did! And when Ria announced the length to be eighteen inches, Cara immediately jumped on the bed, grabbed her mom's hand, and the two started dancing around and bouncing up and down with excitement! There have been only a few times I remember seeing her so happy! Not only was it an awesome sight to see her so happy, but it was the first time I looked at my daughter as an adult.

Too often I think I sacrificed the hearts of my daughters for the sake of my own personal agenda or desire for perfection in the life around me (another of my many screwups). At some point, we must make a choice in the lives of our children. We must recognize who they are, who they are becoming, and provide opportunity for growth in those areas, watered regularly with generous amounts of patience and love.

It probably sounds strange to say, but this experience reminded me how life is all about timing! I am sure you are probably wondering how I came up with this brainstorm while watching Cara measure her hair, right? Well, I remember when I first went off to college at Virginia Tech and decided the time was right to let my hair grow out. Away from home, no parental peer pressure—it was time, or so I thought, to test my newfound freedom! Don't sit there acting like this scenario sounds strange to you! You've done it or something similar. You know you have!

Let's see... I think I'll dye my hair a different color, maybe cut it shorter, straighten it, curl it, put a weave in it, bleach it, shave it, grow a beard. You know you've thought about doing something crazy to your hair at some point in your life! Maybe it was that little rebel streak in the back of your mind that said, "Try this!" Usually thoughts of changing come about as a result of timing. The timing for Cara to cut her hair was right because she had matured enough to want to put others ahead of herself. She was willing to live with short hair so that some girl, probably one who had undergone chemotherapy and lost her hair, would be able to live with hair—even if it were a wig. In the world around us putting others ahead of ourselves and helping others has almost become a lost part of the heart. I was proud of what Cara had done!

Face it, we all have patterns in our life. The patterns we have developed took years to cultivate and perfect. They can be seen in the way we walk, the way we talk, the clothes we wear, the way we style our hair, the friends we go out with, the food we eat, the places we go, and oftentimes more so, in our ideas and beliefs. Change one of these patterns and people notice! Take my word. Cut twelve inches off your hair and people will certainly notice! Don't think so? Just go ahead and try changing one of those patterns of yours and see if people don't sit up and take note.

"You did something different to your hair." "Is that a new blouse?" "I didn't know you hung out with them." "When did you start eating seafood?" Patterns, patterns, they are all patterns we created for ourselves; some recent while others took years to perfect. Along with these patterns comes timing. To change or modify anyone of them, the timing must be right. Thus, patterns and timing go hand in hand.

It dawned on me as I watched Cara walk out the bedroom that I could see the patterns in my life changing, as well as the patterns and purpose of the drugstore. No longer would Utopia Springs Drugstore be just a local neighborhood pharmacy! Its purpose and focus would be on neighbor to neighbor caring and helping in a broader sense beyond just prescriptions. Based on all that had happened, the timing was right! Each day I was going to have to trust God more than the day before. Let go of the reins and let Him lead the drugstore where He would have it to go, not where I wanted it to go. Day by day the resources, inspiration, and guidance would come. Then and only then would we be able to see His presence in each and every moment.

As for me, the timing was right for a change too! No longer would I be so concerned about my hard heart or be so prideful and self-centered—my focus would change to helping others without regard for myself. I only wish I had seen the need for these changes years earlier! It took the reality check of my heart and the awareness that life is short and precious for me to open my eyes and see it wasn't all about me! But fretting over my past actions, or lack thereof, wasn't going to accomplish anything! It was time to move on and put the past behind me. Look ahead to the horizon and all the possibilities just waiting for me. One thing I did know now for sure, and that it is always the right time and the right place when it comes to caring and helping! Today, tomorrow, next week…a positive change is always a welcome change! My time to change had come!

I also realized something else about timing, something closer to the heart. It was time I told Ria! She deserved to know. Although I questioned if it might be crossing the anonymity line with Emma Anne and Bob, I knew it was the right thing to do. Ria was a part of me. After more than thirty years of marriage, I'm man enough to admit she is more than just any part. She is the better part of me! The part that makes me alive and pushes me to be a better man, the man she sees me as being. Without her, I would be lost. Sad to admit, but too many times I have thought it foolish or embarrassing to acknowledge in public that I loved her. *I do love Ria, always have, always will!* I made up my mind. That night after work, I would tell her!

When I arrived home, Ria was in the shower. Although I was anxious to tell her, it could wait until she came downstairs. Nervously I sat on the sofa in our den, of all things, pretending to read a book. I listened and waited for her to finish. As she started to make her way down the stairs, I closed the book and looked toward the foyer. When she stepped off the final stair, she turned and started toward me.

"I didn't know you were home," she said, bending forward to kiss me.

As she leaned closer, I stretched out my arm and pulled her down on the sofa next to me and kissed her again.

"Wow, what's with all this attention?"

"I need to tell you something," I immediately answered, as I slid to the edge of the sofa and turned squarely to look her in the eyes.

"Okay…now you're scaring me! You look too serious. What is it? What's the matter?"

"You're not going to believe me when I tell you what has happened…" And so I began telling her everything and didn't let her get a word in edgewise until I had finished. I just knew Ria would be ecstatic, and I couldn't wait to hear what she had to say!

When I finished, I reached to take hold of her hand, but before I could, she bolted from the room! Jumping up off the sofa and following her, I was right on her heels. I could hear her starting to cry even before she reached the kitchen. She placed her hands on the counter and hung her head down over the sink. I stopped dead in my tracks, not understanding what was the matter. Helplessly I listened for a moment to her sobbing, as she struggled to catch her breath. What had I done?! What had I said to upset her so?!

"It will be all right," I finally spoke, simply trying to reassure her. Then, moving over next to her, I placed my arms tenderly around her waist. It worried me that she didn't answer. I eased my chin down against her shoulder and just held her. It seemed like an eternity as the minutes passed.

Finally turning around to face me, she clasped her arms around me and pulled me tightly next to her. Ria dropped her face against my chest and started to cry again, this time not quite as hard as before. I tried desperately to think of something to say but decided nothing would help matters because I had no clue why she was so upset. I held her and waited until finally she began to talk. She kept her face next to my chest and never looked up as she began to explain.

"For so long I've been waiting and wondering…" Ria tried to continue, but her crying escalated, and she pulled herself into me even closer.

"For so long you've wondered what? Ria, you can tell me!"

"It's like for years I have been waiting to figure out what I was meant to do after children. What it was that I could do meaningful and useful with my life. At first, I thought maybe having been a loving and caring mother to the girls and good wife to you was all I was meant to do, but that was not it! Don't get me wrong, I… I… I don't mean you and the girls aren't important! You know family means the world to me. You know that, right?"

"Of course I know that, sweetheart."

"It just seemed to me like there was something missing, something more I was supposed to do! More I could do to make my life have an impact on the world… Well, or at least, my small piece of the world here in Utopia Springs! Something to make me feel useful! Maybe find that mysterious but real joy that comes from doing something bigger than myself! I always believed the best way for me to truly be myself was to lose myself in service to others, you know, be a help to others? Connor, I'm not kidding. For years, all I did was immerse myself in the kids! And then, I volunteered for this and that organization, helped at church and school, taught vacation Bible school, joined a women's group, went out with friends, read the latest and greatest devotionals, attended conferences—all just busyness mostly! Bet if you name it, I probably tried it! All just to find what it was that was missing in my life! What it was that I was meant to do… with my talents and gifts from God? I was beginning to think something was wrong with me, and I seriously wondered why it was I felt so unfulfilled. Why did I feel so incomplete with my life? I knew, or at least hoped, there was some grander scheme for me… But what? I kept asking and wondering."

"You're not going to believe it, but I felt the same way!" I quickly replied to her. "I knew something was missing and tried to find it everywhere too! In my career, myself, church, community service, the university, students, friends, small groups, and almost every guy motivational book known to man! I tried them all! But like you said, I knew they were just busyness, and there had to be more I could do with my life! Something worthwhile, something lasting and important. Big or small, I didn't care. I even thought about us moving up to the South Carolina low country! I thought that going back to where you were from was the answer. You know, get away and start over! But the more I thought about it, the more I believed that would have just been running away from it all!"

"Right, right," Ria harped in. "I know exactly what you are saying! I kept hoping and praying and just knew it would happen or come along and just slap me in the face! But year after year, it seemed that I was just going through the motions, trying to fill in the voids with more and more busyness. I was always looking and expecting it to come along, thinking I would figure it out on my own, but I never did. It never came along!" Ria paused for a minute and pulled away slightly. "That is, it never came along until now!" She looked in my eyes, and the tears had stopped.

"The drugstore?"

"Yes, *yes*!" Ria smiled brightly and squeezed me tight! I lifted her up onto the counter top as she started to explain herself to me. "Finally, I had that purpose in life—something bigger than me that was intended for me to do all along! Not the business or the prescriptions, but an amazing means facilitated by the business in which I could make a real impact on people. Do something of bigtime significance for others! Make a real change for betterment—I'm not sure that's a word—but I want to make things better for the people around us in our community! And I realized right away listening to you tonight that you know exactly what I am talking about and want to do the same thing too! Kind of like what we have already started, but more—much more! You and I both want to not only appreciate and be thankful for all that we have been given but we want to recognize, give, and use all that we can to help others! Life and time are too short to hold back anymore! Right?"

"Absolutely!" I agreed, nodding my head. "I feel the very same way! I used to always think it was about me, but it's not. God knows it's not about me! It's about others, making a change, making a difference one day at a time, one person at a time! As hardheaded as I am, it took me a long time to realize that! But that is precisely what we are doing at the drugstore! Looking at people and situations the way we should—with caring, hope, and love. I get it now! It's about us helping all sorts of different people with different needs every day, one person at a time! It's so clear to me now that you are being used to help people, I am being used to help people, and the drugstore is being used to help people! Absolutely amazing!"

"Right, I know, I know," Ria answered. "Guess I always thought it would be something bigger, maybe grander, that I would do to fill this longing and emptiness? But what could be bigger than this? I never knew until this past year that taking a meal to a lonely, sick older person and just sitting and listening or talking with them would feel so big to me and be so important to them! I never realized so many people never got homemade brownies until I started making them and giving them away at the drugstore! Hardly a day passes without someone thanking me, hugging me, or talking to me because of those crazy, simple brownies! And I certainly never knew by reaching out, holding a stranger's hand in the drugstore, and asking them how they were feeling could mean so much! Oftentimes it turns out that I am the only person to ask about them or care!

I am totally blown away that some of the people we help actually don't have anyone who cares! Many have no one who bothers to call and check on them, ask them if they are all right, or even wish them a happy birthday once a year. Who would have thought that the birthday cards we hand-sign and send out each month would be the only birthday wish someone got that year. It makes me want to cry when I think about all the people out there with no one who cares about them! We have so many opportunities to help people. And now… Now that others are starting to care and help… Well, we can really be used by God to make a difference!"

Ria grabbed hold of me and started to gently cry. "Connor, we can help so many people."

"Lord willing, we can and we will!"

Looking up at me, as tears streamed down her face, she placed her hand around the back of my neck and pulled me close. Placing her tender lips against mine, she kissed me and whispered, "I love you. God knows how much I love you!"

Whether you turn to the right or to the left, your ears will hear a voice behind you, saying, "This is the way: walk in it."
—Isaiah 30:21

CHAPTER 7

Weighty Words

*Try being humble! We're too prideful, too self-centered,
too me oriented, too we can figure it out ourselves... What
happened to love your neighbor as you love yourself?*
—Brooks Braswell

Several years back, I had the opportunity to visit my mom's old State Health Department in Gretna, Virginia. I have never forgotten the challenge and promise they displayed as their mission statement—*In the community, for the community.* Wow! Talk about a concise bold statement of choices! What a different world it would be if we took that challenge to heart and implemented it where we live without regard to color or socioeconomic standing of our neighbors in the community! How do you think life would change for you and your community if everyone didn't simply reside in their neighborhood, but rather choose to live vibrantly there, as fellow citizens and advocates of true caring? Being genuinely concerned about friends and neighbors, what a dynamic challenge to embrace. In truth, I doubt many of us would care to be part of such a challenge because it is simply too far out of our comfort zone!

Speaking from personal experience, I know how hard it is to move out of comfort zones. It has been and still is, at times, a challenge to let down my defenses and be who I really want to be. To allow people in close enough to see the pain and hurt that has molded and shaped me into who I am is a difficult thing to do. Sadly, far too many of us put on a front, never letting anyone in closer than an arm's length away. Not wanting them to see who we really are! I suppose we are doing nothing more than living a good show for the world to see. Oh, why not let that arm down and invite them nearer—yes, into your comfort zone!

The challenge for me was letting go of what I call my safety sail. You know what I'm talking about. That protective emotional sheet we bring out and haul up in front of us like a sail on a boat when others move in too close! It not only blocks others view but allows us to grab hold of the first wild of change we can harness (be it a change in conversation, change in location or change in attitude) and move our little sailboat the heck away from those *not open for discussion topics* as fast as the wind will carry us! That is what I call my safety sail!

After the suicide death of my best friend, Gavin, I found the courage to step out of my comfort zone and hold back hauling up my safety sail around people and topics that, frankly, terrified me. And I am talking about way out of my comfort zone! If you are reading this book, you are probably thinking that sharing my emotions and thoughts is something that comes naturally, something I have done all along. Well, you are wrong! Like most men, I never felt it was the "manly" thing to do! That's not to say that I never wanted to share my hurts and pains, but I just never felt comfortable opening up to anyone and expressing my innermost thoughts and emotions! I didn't care who you were. I just wasn't comfortable talking about a lot of personal or controversial things. And that was it; no further discussion when it came around in conversation!

Admittedly, faults are something I have way too many of, and mistakes are more numerous than the pages of this book could hold. And no, I'm not proud of myself nor do I think that by admitting I have made mistakes, it somehow miraculously wipes the slate clean. True, most of us would never intentionally harm anyone. But by not helping a fellow human being in need, aren't we doing just that—harming them? I know from my own mistakes and the missed opportunities to help others that not helping is a form of hurting, cutting deeper and wider than any bodily laceration caused by a knife!

And yes, a cut most anywhere on our body can generally be corrected by modern medicine; however, a cut to our soul can never be sutured together by even the most skilled of human surgeons! Personally, I am sick and tired of living with regrets for the what-ifs and what-could-have-beens! I am ashamed and sorry for the cuts and pains I have unrightly bestowed upon others!

After my dear friend Gavin was gone and I had a chance to catch my breath, I began thinking about where to start. When you have missed so many opportunities to be a good friend, a good neighbor, a good husband, a good father, a good son, a good uncle… you get the picture. Seriously, you don't have to dig down too deep emotionally to find those mistakes. Yet there certainly is no need to brude over them or constantly obsess over where and why we came up short in caring; that would never accomplish anything positive! Admitting and verbalizing my mistakes to those I had hurt—now that is something altogether different, a much harder issue. Writing was the medium I chose to convey my shortcoming. Call me a wimp for not doing it face-to-face, if you like, but it was a giant leap out of my comfort zone!

As I am sure you would expect, it didn't take me long after deciding to write and say I was sorry before I had composed a dozen or more letters. Maybe that seems a lot compared to your own personal number of wrongs, but for me it was just the tip of the iceberg! Once I started the process, I quickly realized that I had hurt and wronged far more people than I initially thought or would have dared to admit.

Up front, I opened each letter with the hard, cold, and obvious fact—*I was wrong*! Three words I somehow had neglected to use together in a sentence for years! I thought about not starting the letter that way, but rather by saying something more along the lines of "It was a mistake that I…" or "I didn't mean to, but…" None of those cut to the core truth of the matter that I was wrong! It was the only way to start the letters. I had to admit and state first thing that I was wrong!

Next, I came out and said that there were no excuses for what I had done! I gave no elaborate explanation, justification, or rationalization for my actions. What would be the purpose in saying I was wrong if I then tried to downplay my way out of what I had done to them? I was wrong and no reason on earth made it right for me to have hurt them—end of explanation, period! Wrong was wrong any way you looked at it!

Once I made it clear that I was the one who had screwed up, I then told them I understood if they did not wish to accept my apology or could not find it in their heart to forgive me. And no, I did not use any fancy language or mix words to make them feel guilty if they could not forgive me. Sadly, I knew there would be some who, because the hurt I had inflicted was so great, could probably never forgive me.

Let me stop right here and clarify. These were not cookie-cutter form letters or something I standardized and copied one person to the next! Each letter was written by hand (no e-mails, text messages, or computer-generated letters or cards) specific to each individual and the hurt I had caused them! The words I composed were from my heart. I chose to willingly and intentionally open up, leave it all on the table, and say what I felt. Every emotion and feeling I had so desperately wanted to say so many times over the years I finally was able to convey in written word.

Looking back now, I realize I had come to a critical fork in the road and taken the path less trodden. Opting to go down the often rough and rocky path where it no longer mattered what the person I was writing might think of me. Or what anyone else they shared the letter with might think of me for that matter! This was it! My all-out, full court press, last chance to say I was wrong with no excuses or justification for my actions! It was my time to face the music and acknowledge, as my father-in law would put it, that I had been "a jackass" with my previous actions! Whatever they might think of me now, I deserved it and probably more! But bottom line, they needed to know not only was I writing to let them know I cared about them but that I desperately hoped they could find room in their heart to forgive me! If I couldn't admit I was wrong and had made a mistake, there would be no way I could hope to help others! And I know I am not alone; we all have those people we have wronged and need to ask forgiveness from! I would leave it in God's hands, for He is the great healer and reconciler! Maybe it's time you wrote a letter to one of those people? Admit you're wrong and seek forgiveness. Then you can forgive yourself and move on with your life.

*****

I remember well how every head turned that day as she walked into the drugstore! Ria will probably shoot me for saying this, but she was beautiful! Even the loose-fitting faded blue scrubs could not hide her beauty. Standing close to six feet tall, she was slim, young, and amazingly easy on the eyes. Her hair was long, pulled back off her face with a ribbon, and wavy. When she spoke, her voice was gentle and caring yet almost commanding by her tone. Although oftentimes appearances can be deceiving, I would learn later that her appearance and voice were merely a small part of her overall beauty!

I watched from behind the prescription area as she walked across the old hardwood floors and eased up to the counter. With a smile and a calm, pleasant tone, she asked if she could speak to the pharmacist. Ashton turned and was about to ask me if I could come help her when I jumped the gun and spoke to her. Quickly, I greeted her and let her know I would be with her shortly. It's no mystery to those who use our drugstore that every patient is equally important, and I was not trying to put her off, but there were several prescriptions and patients ahead of her. She would have to wait a few minutes before I could come out and help her.

After checking the baskets containing prescriptions of patients waiting in the lobby, I then bagged and placed them atop the counter. Calling out their names, I took the time to speak with each one and asked if they had any questions regarding their medications before we rang them up at the checkout register. Once I had finished, I moved to the side counter and inquired of the young woman how I could help.

"Doc, if you've got a minute?" she questioned in a polite unhurried manner.

"Sure, what can I do for you?"

"If you don't mind, could we go somewhere more private? I promise it will just take a minute or two of your time. And I would really appreciate your help!"

"All right," I agreed and then motioned for her to come through the swinging half-door and have a seat in the consultation booth so we could talk without interruption.

"Thanks so very much," she acknowledged gratefully.

We both sat down. Then, staring across the table, I waited for her to start the conversation.

Totally unexpectedly, this previously calm demeanor woman began to rattle off information faster than a machine gun could fire out shells! With words shooting out of her mouth like bullets, the flow and topic matter jumped nonstop from here to there and everywhere! Finally, I held up my hand to stop her!

"Hold up, hold up. Slow down, young lady!" I waved my hand back and forth in front of her until I got her full attention.

"Sorry." She shrugged her shoulders as she stopped talking.

Finally, I was able to speak without her battery of words firing down on me, and I began, "Clearly something has you upset! But if you want me to help you, you need to start at the beginning and drop it down a few notches from warp speed!"

"I know, I'm sorry. I am really not myself these days! I feel like I am at my absolute wits' end! It is just that I am so upset right now, and honestly, I need somebody to talk to who will tell it to me straight—like it is! I realize you don't know me, but you know my mom, Charlotte. She has been coming in here for her prescriptions for years, and she respects you a lot! That alone says more to me than you could ever know! My mom's a tough cookie and pretty hard to deal with, but you have won her over! So maybe... What I was thinking was that you could listen to my story and give me some advice? Truthful advice, not some sugarcoated version!"

"No promises," I answered back, "but I will do my best! You know better than me where to start. So I guess when you are ready go ahead and start!"

"You want the SOAP version they put in my chart or a quick overview like we do with shift change each day, or what?" SOAP stands for subjective, objective, assessment, and plan.

"Well, I am guessing, but probably with the scrubs and medical lingo you just through out, you are in the healthcare field, right? A nurse?"

"Yes, right! Sorry, bad habit! Guess because I work around nurses and doctors so much it just comes out without even thinking! Yes, I'm an ICU nurse," she finally explained. "Usually I'm not so helter-skelter like this! Up until last month I never thought I would ever be like this..." She hesitated and then continued on, "But I am. And now I have to learn to deal with it!"

"Okay, I give up!" I told her. "What are we talking about here? Can you give me a little more info; maybe something more substantial about what is going on?"

"My bad again! How about we start over? Doc, I'm Robin. Robin Moore," she introduced herself and held out her hand to me, as if it were some formal first-time meeting.

"It is..." I was ready to say a pleasure out of habit, but that wasn't the case. I changed my mind and went with what I really thought in the moment, hoping for the best. I continued, "...interesting to meet you, to say the least!"

Thank goodness my bluntness worked! She smiled, and she managed a little giggle.

This time when she started to speak, her words were calmer. "Sometimes it's nice to just stop for a minute and laugh at yourself. I haven't done that in a while. It felt nice. Thanks for making me realize just how crazy I must sound!"

"You are certainly welcome," I said with a smile. "So, Robin, what has your world so all shook up?"

"Shook up? Yep, that pretty much sums it up!" she agreed, nodding her head. "Everything was going along great until four weeks ago. That's when it all got shook apart!"

I decided not to reply. Instead, just to sit back against the booth and listen.

"Well, let me see now…" She gazed upward, wondering how best to explain. "Like I told you already, I'm an ICU/trauma one nurse at Shand's Hospital with the University of Florida, in Gainesville. Wow, it's hard to believe—almost twenty years now! Used to joke around and say I would be an ICU nurse until they tripped me up with an IV line, tied me down to one of the gurneys, and sent me off to a nursing home! Never actually imagined that might really happen… that is, until now!"

"Why do you say that?"

"A little over a year ago, we had a real train wreck—not actual train wreck, figurative to describe an extremely complicated patient—that was life flighted to our trauma one team following an accident. The guy went head on, off his motorcycle, into the bed of a truck, and through the back window all the way into the cab and out onto the hood—sort of a human projectile meets truck. Hello! It was nasty! I don't know how he even made it to the hospital alive, but somehow he did!"

"Sounds really bad?"

"It was! There were five of us trying to stabilize him, hold him down, get IVs started, draw blood, place a tube into his chest cavity to drain out the blood… You name it, we were doing it! Pretty much the usual Friday night, full moon excitement thing going on that we see a lot of!"

"A cluster of problems for sure?"

"Not the worst I've ever seen, mind you. But it was bad! And to make matters even crappier that night, one of our more experienced nurses had called out sick at the last minute so we were a man down on the shift. The real icing on the cake though, for a disaster in the making, came when the kid in the next bed decided to code on us at the same time that we were trying to get the human bullet guy stabilized! That's when all hell broke loose! We decided to split up and tag team between the two patients! It was chaos, but really we had no choice! We called for help, but it didn't come quick enough!"

"They didn't make it?"

"Who didn't make it, the backup or the patients?"

"Both, I guess?"

"The help—finally! The patients—neither!"

"Oh, I'm sorry! That has got to be one of the downsides of trauma patients. Guess you hang on to the victories and try hard to put the nonvictories behind you." No sooner did the words come out of my mouth when Robin gave me this strange look. "But I am sure that is likely easier said than done?"

"Right, occupational hazard for sure! Take my word though, you never can completely put them behind you. Sure, they make you work that much harder the next time, but on those really dark nights, their faces come at you, one after the other in concession! That is when it gets really tough!"

"I can't even imagine! I admire you for what it is you do! Probably a no-glory job, but you make a big difference—sometimes that life-and-death difference—for a lot of people! It is the ones you save that you make all the difference in the world for, them and their families!"

"Thanks for saying so. Everyone there does the best they can, but sometimes it's still not enough!" Robin paused and then looked over toward me, but not really at me. She seemed to be off in a distant place in her mind somewhere.

"You okay?"

"Guess I won't have to deal with those faces too much longer! And I sure don't need to worry about learning from the past and working harder next time!"

"What? I don't follow you?"

"They called me into the administrative offices four weeks ago, today, and suggested—more like told me—I needed to step down!"

"All because of what happened back a year ago? Because two patients didn't make it? How can they blame you for that? No way that it is all your fault!"

"No! It's not my fault! That is not what they were saying. It—"

"If that's not what they were saying, then what was it?"

"It was because of that day, but not because they didn't make it. I remember lying almost completely on top of the one, trying my best to hold him still, get him strapped down while he was seizing and working to get an IV started all at the same time! Finally, I found a vein, inserted the needle, and just before I could get it taped down securely, it shot out and went straight from his arm into mine! Bam, just like that! In a split second! You're doing everything you possibly can to save the life of some guy you don't even know, and the next minute, you are the one who needs saving!"

"What... Robin, what are you saying?"

"I am saying that now I am the one who is the train wreck! Not some stranger on a gurney... I am the one..." Robin broke down. Placing her hands over her face, she started to cry.

Leaning forward, I reached across the counter and place my hand on her arm. I could feel she was trembling, and when she reached down and touched my hand, hers was soaked with tears. I sat and waited.

Nurses are not easily shaken, I thought to myself. *Whatever the situation was with her, I knew it was bad!*

"Doc." She finally looked up, let go of my hand, and announced to me, "I am a mess! In all my years of nursing, I never thought I would be the one with all the problems! We are trained to deal with other people's problems but never taught how to deal with our very own!"

"Being a pharmacist, I understand somewhat where you are coming from with that! Daily I give people advice or suggesting about taking this or that medication or remedy, but rarely do I heed my own words of wisdom or think I am the one needing help. I am a terrible patient, and I resort to taking medicine only as a last resort! Listening to me when I am sick, you would think I didn't have a clue how to get myself well! Hardheaded—that's what my wife Ria always tells me! And my kids say when I am sick, I am the worst patient they have ever seen!"

Robin's face slowly allowed the appearance of a little smile but nothing more. Then she started back to talk. "Boy, are you right! Health professionals are the world's worst! We think we know it all... except when it comes to us. Then we go brain-dead and lose all perspective of what we should do to get ourselves well!"

"Oh yeah, right," I agreed.

"This time though, I don't think there is much chance in the cards of getting well for me!" Robin's entire demeanor suddenly switched to being serious again. "It won't matter how much I rack my brain on this one. There are not any long-range magical solutions waiting around the bend for me!"

"What makes you say that?"

"Doc, I have AIDS and have now developed hepatitis! What's worse, my body's reacted aggressively, more so than the doctors say they have ever seen with anyone! My liver enzymes are off the wall. My immune system is shot. Now they tell me damage has already occurred, and my only hope is a liver transplant! And they can't even guarantee I will qualify with AIDS, and if I did that, I might reject it! Right now, I'm living on a cabinet full of meds—steroids, pain medications, antibiotics, and blood transfusions. Strictly borrowed time, Doc! And it stinks!"

If there had been a mirror in front of me, I feel certain I would have seen my mouth gaping wide open in disbelief! Looking at her before now, I had never imagined she was so sick! Most patients with all the liver problems she described are jaundiced (yellow tint to the skin), and their skin and hair look thin and ragged. I could only suppose that the disease had been so quick, her body outside hadn't caught up with the inside, but eventually it would! When it did, the beautiful woman in front of me would not look so beautiful any-more! The thought of what she must be dealing with made my head spin, and I felt sick to my stomach!

Robin could see I was struggling with what to say to her. As if nursing intuition, she jumped back in and saved me by continuing to explain more about her medical condition.

"They did give me priority and moved me up on the national registry! Still it could be weeks, months…who knows how long. My daughter is young enough, but not yet old enough, that she doesn't want to face the reality of what could happen, and my mom has had to help take over with a good many things. Doc, I am not a lot of help to our team, and I feel they are right to ask me to step down! My energy levels near zero, and I can't even stay focused on the usual day-to-day needs to be done around the house! In a word, worthless, and right now, that's all I am!"

"Don't say that! No, Robin, you are not worthless! Your family loves you and needs you. They don't care if you are unable to do all that you used to. They love you just the way you are! And how about your husband?" There had been no mention of him, so I hoped I hadn't asked the wrong question.

"Huh! He left us years ago and has been out of our lives, pretty much...*forever*!"

"Sorry I asked." I felt like a heel.

"Now don't give me that look and start feeling sorry for me, Doc! I am going to need your help and advice and...who knows what else. I would be willing to wager money that there will be a ton more meds they put me on! They scheduled me for weekly visits, and I plan on having them call you with all my scripts. I need you to look out for me—ask questions, double-check what they put me on, and if you see them write for anything squirrely or off the wall, I expect you to speak up! You know what I mean? I need you to be my eyes and brains for all the crap they will most likely put me on, okay? Just look at me and tell me I can count on you, all right?"

"All right, I can do that!" I promised, looking her directly in the eyes! "You can count on me, Robin!" I assured her again, this time with a smile and a nod of my head.

"Listen, my mom is taking over things with my daughter, Michelle. Fair warning, she will probably ask you a million questions about what I am on and why the doctors are writing for it. I need you to run interference! Give her some information—enough to make her satisfied—and hold back on all the side effects and adverse effects of my meds! Deal?"

"Deal," I agreed but had no idea how I could rightfully do what she was asking. Maybe just give Michelle and Mom the bare basic on indications for each drug and not volunteer more unless she asked specific questions. It would be a tightwire walk, but I felt I could agree to it, for Robin's sake.

"I am not asking you to lie to her, just leave out all the risks and downsides to the drugs. She will be worried enough without knowing all the details. You know what I am talking about? If people were to read all the side effects of any of the over-the-counters, nobody would be taking any of them!"

"Thank goodness they don't read everything is right! I would either be out of business or getting a thousand phone calls every day if they actually believed all the side effects would happen to them!"

"One more thing, Doc." Robin reached out and grabbed my hand. "Being a single mom, I have been struggling with keeping things afloat for my daughter and myself for these last few years. I have insurance and a little money left in savings, but now that I am not working…"

"I understand," I reassured her.

"I have no idea how much all this will eventually cost! The number and expenses for the medications will increase, that I know for sure! I will do the best I can, but please…please…" Robin began to cry.

"Robin," I reassured her softly, "I will be here for you! Whatever it is, I will help out! I will talk with your mom if she has any questions, you know I will. I have three girls of my own, and I will get Meghan, my middle daughter who works with me here at the drugstore, to talk with Michelle on a regular basis. As for the medications, let's just see what your insurance does and then take it a step at a time. But I will make sure you get your medicine! I will give my pastor at the church a call and get you on the prayer list. I believe that prayer makes all things possible!"

"I need all the help I can get! I knew you would understand. I knew I could count on you. Oh, I thank God you are here!"

Robin started to cry and grabbed her purse. Before I could even get up, she was up, gone, and out the door. I stood and watched as she ran to her car and then put her head down on the steering wheel and sobbed. My heart ached and told me to go out and tell her it would be all right, but deep down inside, I knew it wouldn't be. She had made a big enough step just coming in and asking for help. I only hoped that my willingness to help had given her just a little more courage to endure what was ahead. As desperately as I wanted to go out and comfort her, I also wanted her to be able to maintain as much dignity and independence as she could, for as long as she could, so I left her alone.

It would be wonderful if I could say that Robin fought the good fight and overcame all the huge obstacles to beat her disease, but she didn't. Eighteen months after I met this awesome individual, the Lord decided He needed her home with Him more than we needed her here. As for her mom and her daughter, they were there every step of the way (so were we), and we are all taking it a day at a time. The needs Robin worried about were taken care of along with many, many others. Lots of people deserve credit for that. And yes, there were fights Robin fought along the road and won, but in the end, complications of her disease beat her. She was a wonderful mom and raised a terrific daughter. She had some great relationships with friends, neighbors, church family, and left behind an awesome mother who would make certain Michelle had a wonderful life.

Of the many friends Robin made along the way, I am proud to say one of them was me! I saw in her that although difficult times lead to dark days, they did not cause defeat! God gave her a strong will, faith, and determination during all her battles, and they certainly shined brightly as an encouragement to countless HIV and AIDS patients! I will always remember the many stories she shared with me of victories and how proud she was of the role she played as a nurse in saving lives over the years. Robin truly had a lifetime of successes in the ICU that are now living, walking, and talking proof of what a difference a dedicated nurse can make in the outcome of a patient and the patient's families.

I will never forget that Thursday night she called and said she was leaving the hospital and on her way back home. Robin explained how they had given her some new medications, ones she needed to pick up that night before she went home in order to be able to sleep without too much pain. I asked her how far out she was and told her to come to the drive-through, and I would head up to the drugstore and meet her there.

I left my house around eight that night and went to the drugstore to meet her. Within an hour, she pulled into the drive-through. Her mom was at the wheel, and she was lying down in the backseat.

Her mom managed a forced smile and said a quick thank you for my coming to meet them. This was not the first time I had meet them late at night after one of her visits to the hospital; it had become almost routine, and I didn't mind in the least. I expected there would be more such calls as Robin continued to be the strong fighter while the disease progressed.

After I finished filling the prescriptions, I opened the window and handed them to Robin's mom. I looked at Robin in the backseat. She was sitting up and waiting for me.

"Bet you had a rough day? Are you hanging in there okay?"

Patting her mom on the shoulder, Robin asked her, in a soft but hoarse-sounding voice, to pull the car forward. I waited patiently as she inched the car slowly ever forward until Robin's window was next to the drive-through window opening. Robin then rolled her window down, and I moved nearer to hear what she had to say. Totally unexpectedly, she leaned out the car window and grabbed me around the neck. She pulled me toward her so quickly and forcefully that, I swear, I felt as if I left my feet.

Robin started to cry as she held me, then whispered in my ear, "I love you! Thanks so much for everything you've done for me!" And having said that, she let go and fell back onto the seat. After checking to make certain Robin was all right, her mom turned toward me and saw the tears streaming down my face. She put the car in gear and pulled away.

As I let go of the drive-through window, I fell to the floor. Pulling my legs toward me, I put my head between my legs and began to sob. Why didn't I say it? I had so, so wanted to say to her "I love you too," but I didn't. Oh, how I wish I had told her... The words just didn't come out! All I could do now was cry. That was the last time I saw Robin.

My lack of response to Robin that Thursday night and the subsequent guilt I feel over it have made me aware that there is a story about me that no one knows but Uncle Roy and myself. I have become weary from carrying it around all these years now and am overdue sharing it. I feel certain that someone besides me needs to hear this story.

My cousin Miles died in a car accident along a mountainous road in rural Southside Virginia. It was late in the afternoon, and he had taken the day off from work to rewire the electrical system in an old house of one of his friends. His front wheel left the road on a single lane, sharp curve, and when he corrected, the front drive slingshot him directly into the path of an oncoming car. The state police report stated that Miles died instantly from head trauma sustained during the collision.

Two days later, my Uncle Roy, Miles's dad, asked me if I would care to take a ride with him.

"Sure, why not," I agreed. With all the goings-on at the house concerning the funeral, any reason to get out sounded good to me. We drove only a short distance before pulling into a parking lot. Next to the lot was a ten-foot high chain-link fence protecting row after row of vehicles. Getting out of the car, neither of us spoke a word. I followed Uncle Roy's lead but kept a few steps behind him as he silently made his way along the fence line.

Several hundred feet down, he began to slow his pace considerably until finally he came to a complete halt. Grabbing the chain-link, he pulled himself slowly over next to the fence. As he pressed his face against the fence, I moved in next to him and looked out at the lot. That's when I saw it! There it was—Miles's car! Although the Honda Civic was a mangled mass of steel and had little resemblance to the way it looked when I saw it last, I knew it was his car!

I heard Uncle Roy quietly start to cry. I desperately wanted to cry along with him but somehow couldn't. Maybe I was in shock—stunned by Miles's sudden death and all the emotional moments over the past few days. I could do nothing but let my heart break open even wider inside of me and stare at his car in disbelief. Until now, the reality of Miles death had not fully hit me... Now it was suffocating me! In my mind, I could see Miles in the car with his head pressed against the metal strip next to the front window. I couldn't stand it any longer. I jerked my head and looked away.

Uncle Roy lingered a few minutes more and then turned to face back to where we had parked. My eyes remained locked on the distant tree line near White Oak Mountain, and I tried to think of the times Miles and I had spent in woods out at the farm hunting. Those were happy times… This was not! As I stood there, I felt Uncle Roy's hand slowly grab hold of my shoulder; his hand was large, rough, and strong, encompassing most all my shoulder.

"Son," he had called me that ever since my dad had died. "I never told Miles I loved him…" And he started to weep.

What I saw there next to me was a broken man. A father that, although outwardly in appearance was rough and tough, inwardly was torn asunder by his son's death. And as if the tragedy of Miles's death was not enough to weigh him down, he now faced living day-to-day with the regret of never having spoken the words *I love you* to his son, his only child! I could not begin to imagine the weight of burden he would carry! Even a hardcore ex-Marine such as my uncle could feel the pain from the excruciating burden on his back and a heart ripped open by the loss of a son!

The thirty-five years of Miles's life had come and gone so quickly! There must have been opportunity on so many occasions to have shared with Miles how he felt, but he never did. Years later, I listened while talking with Uncle Roy at the drugstore as he explained to me that he thought Miles knew. In detail, he explained how he felt he had shown Miles he loved him, although not with words, but by his actions! Uncle Roy mistakenly believed his multitude of times helping and being there when Miles needed him spoke loud enough for Miles to know his true feelings. Yet he never uttered the words *I love you*!

I read once that Abraham Lincoln remarked, "*I never met a person from whom I did not learn something; of course, most of the time it was something not to do!*" What I learned from my conversations with Uncle Roy and that last Thursday evening with Robin was that actions cannot always replace words, but actions with words always sends a clear message, especially to those we love! I also learned that I should never miss the opportunity to tell the ones I love that I love them!

I bet I can hear what some of you are thinking. It's not the "macho" thing to do. Guys don't do that! There's no need for it. Think whatever you want, but I believe there are times to do that!

I have learned to say "I love you," "Thank you," "I am sorry," and I am glad I have! What I regret is the way the lesson was learned. That I had to learn it from my uncle, at the death of his only son, and Robin! But at least, I learned it. I will always wish I had learned it before Robin's death! I live with the regret of not letting her know I loved her. If you and I do not learn from the lessons life throws us and choose to continue in our narrow, tunnel-vision, selfish ways, we are likely to repeat the same mistake over again and again! Don't wait until it is too late!

Remember, life is not some big corporation game where you put in a requisition and wait for chance to come down the pike and present you with the picture-perfect opportunity to say how you feel! No… You must make it happen! Don't sit there and wait for real-life situations to present the perfect opportunity! What kind of life is meant to be spent waiting? None! Be intentional and allow past failures at expressing how you feel to drive you onward to make you open up. Be thankful for that individual and tell that someone "I love you!" Take Uncle Roy's word for it; someday will be too late!

Forget the former things; do not dwell on the past. See, I am doing a new thing. Now it springs up; do you not perceive it? I am making a way in the wilderness and streams in the wasteland.
—Isaiah 43:18–19

CHAPTER 8

Let's Hear the Good…for a Change

*Don't waste yourself in rejection, nor bark against
the bad, but chant the beauty of the good!*
—Ralph Waldo Emerson

Washington, the city, has probably heard more speeches and more promises than anywhere else in America. But simply because the podium is never empty does not mean that the speeches are necessarily more important, the promises better, nor does it mean that they are more likely to come true. It simply means more people feel their words will be heard and listened to by a greater audience in our nation's capital than anywhere else. Bah…hogwash! You don't buy into that, do you?

Your voice can be heard anywhere! The location it is spoken is not nearly as importance as the humbleness and sincerity by which it is backed. Those of you with children know it means just as much to them to hear you utter "I love you" quietly and alone in their bedroom at night, as you tuck them in, as it does to say it in a room full of friends and family!

Words, words, words… How flippantly we let them flow off our lips! Listening to the jargon coming out of the legislative and executive branches of government these days, they both are using a common healthcare buzzword—patient-centered care—with the acronym PCC. When and why did we start using so many acronyms?

This compilation of three words has become the all-important cornerstone to healthcare reform. And no, I am not meaning to downplay healthcare or imply that this new reform will not work, but what if the amount of commitment, energy, and effort being expended by our government was equally mounted on a new initiative—neighbor-centered care (NCC)? Wouldn't life be different?

What if this movement was pushed down to the local, real people in real need, level? If a genuine belief in neighbor care (the love your neighbor as you would yourself thing, we have all heard since childhood) were to be prime on the agenda and pushed down from our governing bodies to our schools, churches, and citizens—what a change we would see in the world! I suppose it is too pie in the sky of a thought, but it would be awesome if "we could all unite for a common purpose"—thank you, Steven Anderson—with that common purpose being to see a progressive change in caring. To work collectively to foster a shift in attitude! You have never and probably will never hear a presidential candidate stand up and say, "I care about you" *and mean it* (without any underlying agenda behind his/her words)!

To explain away our repetitive actions in life as the result of being creatures of habit allows far too easy of a justification to our quirky behaviors. For example, I blame our dog's habit of getting up when the sun first peeks out every morning to my early rising each day. My wife and I both know this isn't the case—I get up early even on my days off and even whenever we are away on vacation. Who am I kidding? It's not the dog's fault! I have gotten up early for as long as I can remember. Of course, it drives Ria crazy because she likes to stay up late and sleep in. The dog simply allowed me the ability to shift blame direction and say, "It's their fault!" Our springer spaniel, Lady, allows me to justify my actions on her. That way, I don't have to hear Ria fuss at me each morning. I share this story to convey, in a roundabout way, that for change to come over an adult, it takes longer than you think! At least that is what I always believed until actions and events to the contrary shifted my paradigm and my entire thought process on the matter.

In years past, Wednesdays were set aside for doctors to be off and to play golf, as my kids would say, "back in the day." These days, however, medical offices that can afford to be closed for an entire day every week are few and far between! With marginal insurance reimbursements and increasing malpractice fees, every day and every penny is important to success. No longer are Wednesdays the slow day they were ten or twelve years ago. Just one more dinosaur to add to the ever-dwindling list of the way things were! Nowadays, the drugstore fills just as many prescriptions on Wednesday as it does on Monday, Tuesday, or any other day of the week. Thus, my energy levels are starting to wane by midweek. I like to blame it on the Wednesday phenomenon, yet it probably is just an old-age thing! By the time I close the drugstore and am in the car and on the way home, I am ready for a break!

Thankfully (that summation may sound bad as you read further, but at least I am honest), Ria had made plans to go shopping for the night with one of her friends, and my men's small group had been cancelled, leaving me alone at home, to kick back and relax this particular Wednesday night. Man was I looking forward to it! As I rounded the corner of our dirt road and started down the last stretch toward the house, it was extremely disheartening to see three pickup trucks and two cars parked out front of our house! I had spoken to Ria less than thirty minutes earlier, and she assured me she and Julie were on their way to the mall!

Slowing down to a near snail's pace, I eyed each and every vehicle I drove past. Several looked vaguely familiar, but I couldn't definitively place a face or name of an owner to any of them. Pulling closer, I realized no one was in any of the vehicles. Letting out a sigh of frustration, my curiosity and anxiousness escalated to a heightened level.

It was then I spied a small crowd gathered on the front porch. The group had made themselves right at home and were sitting in the line of rockers on the front porch, totally undisturbed by my arrival. Quickly, I parked my old Chevy truck, hopped out, and started toward them. The moment I stepped onto the porch, I realized there wasn't a stranger to me among them.

"Well, well, it's about doggone time you got here, Doc!" I heard the sarcastic greeting from Harrison, one of my old friends.

"We had already discussed it and decided that if we had to wait much longer, we'd bill you for our extremely valuable time," another harped in.

"The likes of which you wouldn't have enjoyed! That would have been one *large* bill, all right!" This remark caused the entire group to erupt in laughter.

"Hey, wait a minute," I began, trying to defend myself. "No way you can charge me for something I didn't know about! Not a one of you bothered to tell me about this meeting? You didn't call my secretary [which I don't have] and I didn't get the memo! And even if I had, I am not so sure I would have agreed to be seen with the likes of some of you! This very distinguished group is way out of my league! I'm just the little 'ole druggist,' don't you know?"

"Yeah right."

I wasn't certain who replied, but more laughter arose from the group.

"So what do I owe the honor of your presence? Don't see the sheriff anywhere, so it must not be that I've done anything illegal or that you are wanting to ride me out of town on a rail? So what is it then?"

Outwardly, I might have been joking around, but let me tell you right now, I was more than a little nervous about this crew! Not that they were hoodlums or trash, but just the opposite! They were the so-called movers and shakers, the individuals in town who made things happen! If my pastor had been there, I might have thought it to be a religious tribunal! Everyone here could review my less than perfect life and tell me to hit the road and drive me out of town! You get the picture? Nervously, I looked at each of their faces and waited for someone to come clean and tell me what exactly was going on.

The situation made me even more anxious as they began looking at each other somewhat awkwardly. I suppose that's what happens when you have too many powerful figures together all in the same place and at the same time! Too many chiefs and not enough Indians! Each one was wanting to take charge, but no one was willing to step on other's toes. What a ridiculous dilemma! I almost wanted to laugh at their apprehensiveness and fear of offending each another but decided the timing was terribly bad. Instead, I leaned up against the porch rail and watched as the power struggle continued on.

Finally, it was our state representative Jim who just happened to be present with this distinguished group, who decided to take front and center. Jim became the newly elected official spokesman.

"Well..." he began, clearing his throat and slowly rising from his rocker. He straightened himself into an upright, commanding position and began. "We've been talking among ourselves for quite some while and decided it was time we approached you with a few considerations regarding long-term planning for said individuals in our local community. To simplify the matter for you, what we are putting on the table is a visualization of how we see we could better aid the fine citizens of Utopia Springs and some of the surrounding areas. We—"

"Oh, for goodness' sake," Harrison interrupted, "get to the point, Jim! This isn't a campaign speech, you know!"

"You could, at least, ask us to come inside!" came a loud request from the rear of the group. "With it almost dusk, the bugs and humidity are setting in and—"

"You are right! Where are my manners?" I agreed. "Gentlemen, I use that term very loosely with this group, and, lady, would you like to step inside where it is cooler?"

"Thought you'd never ask" along with "About time" were just several of the remarks I heard as they made their way past me and into the den.

Surprisingly enough, there was no bloodshed over who would sit where! In little to no time, all five of my distinguished guests had made themselves comfortable on the sofas and chairs.

"I am ready whenever you are," I acknowledged, looking around the room.

Again, it was our distinguished state representative who spoke for the group. However, in what I feel certain was an unprecedented move, he didn't bother to get out of his seat and stand to address the group. He simply sat forward, edged to the front of his seat, and began.

"As I was starting to explain earlier, it has come to our attention," Jim began, "that a lot of unusual things have been happening in our fine city. Not so much unusual in a bad sort of way, but unusual as in different than any of us have seen in a long, long time way. Now, some of us older, or should I say more mature, remember the way it used to be and have seen things like this in the past but—"

"Oh for Christ's sake, Jim, didn't you hear me outside. Get to the point, man!" Harrison, who was the oldest among them, reprimanded him sharply.

"Okay, bottom line, Doc, we want to help!"

"Exactly!" Tammy, the lone female in the group, exclaimed in agreement. "We want to know what we can do to help out. What is it exactly that we can do to help you as you go about trying to help those in our community who come to you for assistance?"

"Precisely!" Jim piped in to agree.

"And what is it you all want to do?" I asked, seeking a more specific answer.

"That's what we are here for! We need to know how best we can help you and the drugstore service people in need. We have all heard stories, and after verifying them to be true—"

"Yes, we have heard some terrific things about what you are doing!" Jim interrupted to restate the point.

"What kind of stories are you talking about? I haven't told anyone anything about what we were doing! And quite frankly, I don't want everyone to know. It's none of their business!"

"Calm down, Doc. Don't get your britches all in a wad. We understand the importance of anonymity, but good news travels fast. You can't help it if people are talking. You can't hide such as this! People recognize the fact and respect you for doing good things! We just want to expand it and help as many people as we possibly can!" Harrison's words calmed me down, and the offer to help touched my heart.

"That's right, Doc! It's great that people, right here in our community, are helping others! One piece of good news, like what you have done to help folks here in town, goes a long way toward boosting people's confidence in their fellowmen! It makes this whole economic crisis seem distant and far away! When people next door decide to help their neighbors, well, it's a great thing! You know it is, and we know it is!" Tammy sounded so excited about what was happening.

"Couldn't have said it better myself," our dear politician Jim added. "Now let's get down to business and decide about what we are going to do!"

And that's exactly what they did!

I pretty much just sat back, crossed my arms, and listened, only occasionally interjecting an idea or comment here and there. It was clear they didn't need my help; there were more than enough chiefs and opinions to go around. For them, the bottom line was that they wanted to optimize the use of every possible resource at their disposal to further things along quickly and efficiently! They intended to take the concept of providing help and hope to a new level!

What a sight it was to see and hear such enthusiasm, hope, and genuine desire coming from individuals I never dreamed would do what they were purposing. It seemed so out of their norm. But I must admit, it was totally awesome!

By the time the five had finished strategizing and planning, the drugstore had more finances, more resources, and more commitments for helping the community than anyone could have ever imagined or hoped for! Everything they had agreed upon was about others—not themselves! There was no agenda or self-promotion in what they had concocted. It was an amazing and brilliant outpouring of effort and resources for the overall betterment of our community!

They laid out monetary commitments and decided to do fundraisers to heighten awareness and involve even more area residents who had, under the guise of anonymity, approached them wanting to help. They even planned to set up a resource directory for services and needs currently unable to be met by the systems already at our disposal. They even put forth the names of individuals who were willing to host what they were calling Giveback Parties to invite friends to raise money for good causes or individuals with specific short-term needs such as rent or utility payments.

It was even mentioned that the local Baptist church had started a soup kitchen ministry to provide food to individuals one day a week in conjunction with when their crisis center was open to the public! Additionally, there were commitments from local business owners who planned to volunteer their time and resources for a weekly free haircut service, a monthly free oil change day to help single moms in need, seniors, and those with financial difficulties, and there were even plans for free backpacks filled with school supplies for families with young children who couldn't afford school essentials! It seemed that the list just kept growing and growing! Doing what they knew best, this distinguished gathering used their wherewithal and connections to set into motion what never could have been accomplished by the drugstore singlehandedly.

Every idea, every commitment…everything they were attempting to do was good! No, let me restate that—it was *great*! It was *amazing*!

What they were setting forth to do for our community spoke louder than any speech by any politician in Washington! Their declaration was one of great news for a great cause—that being, people in need! As far as Washington DC goes, why it's nothing more than thirty-seven miles of delusion surrounded on all sides by reality! But this, well, when change in heart and attitude is accompanied by a commitment to help others, it can never be fully measured in dollars and cents.

A change of heart and a willingness to care and share—that's reality, not delusion! A reality that is measured in actions and consequences. What deeper joy is there to be found in life than that of giving selflessly to someone in need? Life is not about us, but rather life is about serving and helping others! And as for me ever doubting or questioning the role a simple small-town drugstore could play in the lives of those in need, well, they shut me up for good with their caring, neighborhood-based approach to helping the entire community.

The winds of economic change had destroyed and rearranged the landscape of life for so many people! It didn't matter what the news kept repeating about things getting better; people right here, right now, still were suffering! But when each of us steps out, we can make a difference! I just love what fellow pharmacist David Stanley said about small-town drugstores, *"Every customer at your counter has a story, and every person you see can benefit from your profession. There's a reason they call it community pharmacy. Don't forget it, and don't let anything take it away from you."*

Utopia Springs Drugstore was a community pharmacy. It was in the community and for the community! And with neighbor to neighbor caring it could make a difference. It could and would bring back hope to this small little piece of the world, one person at a time!

For I am The Lord your God who takes hold of your right hand and says to you, Do not fear; I will help you.
—Isaiah 41:13

CHAPTER 9

Bring It On!

A life not lived for others is not a life.
—Mother Teresa

How could I not be cranked about all that was happening?! It was as if dreams, miracles, and reality had somehow collided and morphed into this great source of amazingness! And truly it was amazing when I thought about all the resources that were now in place and entrusted to our community for use to help individuals in need, everyday people who had become disillusioned with life! I could only imagine what a difference we were going to make in the lives of those around us as we served them by meeting their needs in their moments of hopelessness and despair? I could hardly wait to start helping!

The excitement of all that had transpired and been put into place since that Wednesday night meeting a month ago was abruptly pushed back in my mind as my eyes locked onto the computer. On the work queue screen, I was jolted into reality when I saw over one hundred prescriptions waiting to be processed! There were e-scripts, refills, prior-authorizations, denials, and the list went on and on, page after page!

"Hello, real world," I said sarcastically aloud.

"I know... Monday morning! Should have known the fun couldn't last forever, but it was an awesome weekend for us. Liz had her sixth birthday!" My middle daughter, Meghan, explained with excitement radiating in her voice.

"Such a great age! Still young enough to want to be held and told 'I love you,' but not yet old enough to yell no and slam the door behind them!" I replied. "So much energy at that age too. If we could find a way to capture, bottle, and sell it, we'd be millionaires a dozen times over!"

"You're right! But I am so not looking forward to Liz growing up!"

"All I can say is that you better enjoy every minute with them while you can! Strangely enough, we can't wait for them to walk and talk and then can't wait for them to sit down and hush up for a minute or two! But I loved every day with you girls, despite the typical female drama, and would give anything to have those times back! It just all went by too quickly!"

"Liz is growing so quick! I looked at her at the party this weekend and couldn't believe she was already six. It has flown by!"

"Yep, it does!" I concluded, and then with our small talk behind us, we went to it, busying ourselves with the prescriptions in the work queue.

It has always seemed strange to me how quiet the first part of Monday mornings are in the drugstore. Everyone is either trying desperately to wake up, while slugging down coffee cup number 2 or diving headfirst into the work queue, hoping not to be drowned with inputting new prescriptions before the phone starts ringing off the hook and patients begin lining up at the counter. After forty years, I still love being a pharmacist and look forward to the opportunities that present themselves every day, especially those allowing me to help someone.

I reminded a student interning with me that if a pharmacist *only* helped one patient a day in the drugstore, that in one work year that would amount to helping over 260 patients! Multiply that by a twenty-five-year career, and you are looking at helping six thousand five hundred patients—if not more! Yep, I learned early on from Uncle Roy that helping patients, friends, neighbors, and family was what it was all about.

That peaceful calm before the storm ended too quickly as simultaneously two of the three phone lines began to ring. Ashton grabbed line 1 and I picked up line 2.

"Utopia Springs Drugstore, how can I help you?" I asked my caller.

"Move everyone to an interior room, and I mean now!" the almost frantic male voice instructed.

"What? What are you talking about, and who is this?"

"The storm... I mean *tornado* is headed right at you," he explained.

"No, no! Calm down! It's a hurricane—Irma—and the NOAA tracker showed it not hitting central Florida until sometime tomorrow afternoon!"

"Doc, not Hurricane Irma, but a spinoff tornado headed your way. Get everybody in a safe place—*now!*" he hung up, and all I heard next was dial tone.

"No time! Everybody into the storage room! Let's go, no time to explain! *Go, go!*" I yelled as loud as I could and pointed in the direction of the storeroom.

"What is it?" Ashton questioned almost hysterically as she ran past me.

"Why do we have to go in there?" Meghan questioned.

"Everybody just go and do what I say!"

As I started to shut the door to the storeroom behind me, curiosity got the better of me. Anxiously, I peered back to the window behind my workstation to get one last glimpse of the weather outside before closing us in. It was then I heard and suddenly saw the rain pelting viciously against the plate glass windows and the sound of an eerie roar with rumbling like thunder, which escalated to the point where I felt it had engulfed me, and I was overtaken with a strange fear like I had never known.

"Everybody, brace yourself and get ready!" was all I could think of to say as I slammed the door closed behind me. Quickly, I pulled a box of copier paper to block the door to help keep it from opening. I then turned to look at everyone.

I suppose none of them, except my daughter Meghan, had ever seen such fear on my face. They stared at me wide-eyed with mouths agape as the waves of wind, rain, and debris could now be heard hammering against the building and shaking the very walls of the drugstore. Meghan had lived through seven hurricanes with us at the house while growing up, and she knew storms in Florida were not to be taken lightly!

For what seemed like forever, we stood in a tightknit circle without a word spoken. We all listened and worried what might be happening outside and feared for the worst. Ashton looked over at Meghan and grabbed her hand. Meghan then grabbed mine, and I took hold of Deena's hand to complete the circle. Everyone looked at me once we all had our hands together as if expecting me to do or say something. I decided to do out loud what I was already doing silently inside.

"How about we pray," I suggested to everyone only a moment before the lights went out. And so I began…

"Heavenly Father, we come to you now with uncertainty—not knowing what has or is happening just outside these walls. But you assure us in your word that you are with us always in all circumstances. Please put a hedge of protection around Utopia Springs Drugstore and all of us gathered before you now. Wrap your loving hands around us and give us the peace of knowing you control even the most ferocious of storms. We claim this victory and thank you for all you have done, are doing, and will continue to do for us and this community. Please use us, Lord, as we leave this room to be a light in the darkness of what this storm has done and to share with others all you have done for us and continue to do for us. It is in your name we pray…"

"Amen" we all agreed. So be it, together as we concluded the prayer.

As quickly as the storm came upon us, almost as quickly it was gone, and our lives were spared. Together in the darkness, we walked out from behind the closed door of the storeroom to begin to try and piece together what had transpired and what we should do next.

There was still no electricity as we started to look around inside. We could see the building was standing in one piece, but the view outside the six-foot-high plate glass windows was another story altogether, and it wasn't pretty.

Trees had been uprooted, trash was scattered everywhere, and pieces of building, along with lots of shingles and pieces of tin roofs were all around! From the front side of the store, facing the street, we all fixed our eyes on what looked like the entire frame and roof off a house or store. As we learned later, the restaurant, only several hundred feet from the drugstore, had been almost entirely demolished. From the looks of things, everyone speculated it jumped from the restaurant and up over the drugstore before hitting the grocery store on the other side of us! We were right in the line of destruction but were spared. Thank you, Lord!

It took almost all our efforts to get the front door to move because so much debris had piled up and pushed tightly against it. The sight we saw outside was indescribable! My first assessment was to equate it to the destruction of a village in Vietnam when entered for the first time after hours of bombing—only worse. Within view were uprooted and splintered trees, a flipped RV, downed power lines, and roof debris all around. My heart was aching as my mind shifted, and I began to worry about the people of our town. What had happened? Were they all still alive?

Later we learned that the National Weather Service had confirmed that an EF-2 (Enhanced Fujita Scale—level 2) tornado had developed, as a spinoff from Hurricane Irma, with wind speeds between 110 and 135 mph and struck the city and surrounding communities—up to ten miles—at around 9:35 a.m., Eastern Standard Time. The tornado developed near Eighth Avenue, less than one-quarter mile from Utopia Springs Drugstore. It was repeated on weather outlets time and again that the last time a tornado hit Florida was April 15, 1958, over sixty-one years ago!

The initial damage reports for the city were over $24,305,000 for residential property and over $2,471,000 for commercial property. Those figures continued to escalate daily as our small community started to sift through all the devastation! Unincorporated areas around the city had damage figures above $12 million! Four other cities nearby were also torn apart by the tornado. In Utopia Springs alone, there were eleven streets that were completely impassable.

As if this unannounced destroyer wasn't bad enough, thirty-two hours later, Hurricane Irma slammed in and tore across all of central Florida—including Utopia Springs! What ensued was more damage, lots of flooding, and power outages in rural areas that lasted up to ten days! Gas—ethanol, diesel, and natural—was unavailable in a twenty-mile radius for almost a week. If you weren't one of the diligent residents who heeded warnings and always stayed prepared for hurricanes during the six months of hurricane season, you learned the hard way that bottled water and frozen foods were an almost impossible supply to acquire. Groceries were closed for almost a week!

If I had let my human frailty and frustration get the better of me, I would have likely thrown up my hands and said enough was enough and packed up for more friendly surrounding until normal necessities and basic infrastructures were back in operation. But where would my ridiculous tirade get me? And what about all the support systems we just put into place only a month? Wasn't I the one who said I couldn't wait to start helping people in need and those who had lost all hope? Wow, God, putting me to the test, huh?

With news that no lives were lost, I realized nothing was done that couldn't be picked up, cleaned up, repaired, replaced, or undone. I felt so ashamed for my ever having doubted that what had been established a month before these storms was in perfect timing and preparation for what this community would need, right here and right now. Fear, doubt, and most definitely our own agendas and plans always sabotage God's plans. I knew now, from here forward, that every day I would remind myself to stop focusing on me and all the ways I thought this or that should transpire and instead to have faith and trust fully that the Lord would take care of today and every other day just as He saw fit to take care of it!

And you know what? All those amazing support systems and contacts that were put into place just a month before the storms hit worked perfectly! The drugstore had been spared, and because we had generators, were centrally located on the main road, and didn't lose ground phone line service, we became the hub of hope for the community. Emergency response teams came in, took a look at what support systems we had in place, and coordinated small group efforts with specific tasks and started triaging and prioritizing care. Dozens of volunteers came forward to help, and in less than forty-eight hours, we had identified and met the needs of over four hundred people!

Temporary roof tarps were placed on hundreds of homes, allowing families to live dryly and safely until the insurances could assess, pay, and facilitate repairs. Coolers filled with food supplies and bottled waters were distributed to those in need. Crisis shelters were readied and stocked at two of the local public schools and provided a needed safe haven for nearly eighty families! Medical assessments were done by two local physicians and the drugstore provided medications and supplies where needed. Over two hundred of our neighbors were able to get needed medical treatment for a battery of varying injuries.

The Florida Southern Baptist Emergency Response Team prepared two hot meals a day out of the back of a converted tractor-trailer eighteen-wheeler. Untold numbers of volunteers combed the streets and, with chainsaw and able backs, cleared and reopened all the closed streets within five days. Certainly, there were more acts of service than I even know about. Miraculously the words *caring*, *neighbor*, and *hope* suddenly became a banner cry and mindset for the entire community! We all learned from the back-to-back life-threatening storms that times of helplessness, despair, and weakness are in reality opportunities for hope, caring, and love!

Life is oftentimes full of amazing moments and incredible blessing. But life also can throw at us its share of dark valleys and, yes, treacherous storms. Not a one of us will live our life unscathed! When the fear and dread of life's storms start blowing at us from all sides and we feel as if we are losing control as we watch all our plans and dreams be taken away by the storm, isn't it comforting to know there are those around us who care? Almost from out of nowhere, neighbors, friends, and former strangers opened up their hearts and poured out their love onto hundreds in need. So many in our community discovered that there is no greater happiness to be found than in showing compassion and making a difference in the life of another. Truly, a life not lived for others is not a life lived at all!

Most important of all, continue to show deep love for each other, for love covers a multitude of sins.
—1 Peter 4:8

CHAPTER 10

How Sweet It Is!

The birth of a healthy baby, a shared meal among friends,
the love of a husband and wife, and the kindness of
strangers are a few of the countless blessings of God.
—Tom Swift

For some unknown reason, I am seeing more and more tears being shed these days than ever before. What is really strange though is that I am actually starting to get used to it. I know, at first blush, that statement sounds cold and callused, but maybe it is not as bad a thing as it might sound. Because where I used to associate the appearance of tears only with sadness, now I understand that oftentimes tears are shed for joy. So I am learning to accept that even while tears may initially appear for sorrow or sadness, they can many times be turned around into tears of joy! I saw this so, so many times in the days, weeks, and months that followed after our community's double-whammy of storms! Sure, it sounds simple, but getting from that painful point of sorrow to the point of joy takes time. In the story that follows, it took months—nine months to be exact!

Remember back to when you were young (or younger), you probably often thought the world was yours for the taking. Nothing could hold you back. You were likely healthy, strong, happy, in love—or wanting to be one of those four—and had the flexibility to change directions on a dime. What in life could possibly derail you, right? But sometimes unexpectedly, life can go wrong! Change is one of those unplanned, yet inevitable, certainties in life. It can sneak up on us and, before we realize it, knock our feet right out from under us and mow us over! I feel certain that is exactly how Kendal felt when she got the news. Probably even more so, like the train itself had jumped off the tracks and hit her where it hurt the most. But let's not get ahead of things.

I had just locked up the drugstore, walked out into the parking lot, and was putting the key into the door of my old Chevy truck when I saw it. A white SUV flying around the corner, into the parking lot, and straight toward me. Holy cow! I was so alarmed by the speed at which it was approaching that I barely knew which way to move for fear, whether I moved right or left, it might hit me no matter the direction I took! I stood frozen, watching as it came to a screeching halt less than three feet in front of me!

Oh Lord, I was about to be robbed was my first thought! One of my greatest fears these days is that some gun-wielding dealer or addict will target and rob the drugstore! Having been on the receiving end of a pointed gun barrel during a pharmacy robbery on two occasions, I know for a fact it is definitely no fun to be robbed! Looking back at the times I was robbed, I was scared all right! But the real fear didn't hit me until days later after I had just left the police station and identified the robber in a lineup! That's when I suddenly understand the fact that I could have died. My life could have been taken from me in a split-second, by some idiot—all for the sake of one or two bottles of oxycodone and a couple of hundred dollars in the register. I can still tell you the model of the Smith & Wesson gun and the color of the Berber carpeting he pushed my head down into after I gave him what he wanted. How crazy is that?

With such a vision of what might possibly transpire racing through my mind, I readied myself for a gun in the face and a ludicrous request for some street-valuable narcotic—fentanyl, oxycodone! You just can't imagine the relief I felt when my eyes beheld a normal-looking middle-aged man coming toward me with nothing more than a prescription in hand—not a gun! I thanked the Lord, bent over, and placed my hands on my knees and exhaled a deep sigh of relief. I watched as he approached me in almost a jog and held the prescriptions out toward me as if they were gold.

"Doc, I need to get these filled, right away!"

"Okay, hold on! Let's see what you've got here."

I quickly took the prescriptions and read the names of the four medications he was looking to have filled. I was more than a little bit thankful to be looking at nonnarcotic prescriptions, not a grocery list for amphetamines, oxycodone, carispodal, alprazolam, and the likes!

"They're for my daughter!" he blurted out. "She needs to get started right away! Tonight! They were adamant!"

"I don't recognize her name? Can't remember having filled anything for her before, have we?"

"No, well, at least, I don't think so. She's never really needed anything—until now. They told her at the emergency room she would have to get started on them tonight, or we would have to bring her back in, and they would admit her. With all this COVID junk going on, I told her don't even think about messing with anywhere but here. I told her if anybody had it, it was you, Doc!"

"I appreciate that," I told him, trying to kick my memory into high gear and place who he was. "Remind me, what was your name again?"

"Michael."

"Michael?"

"I'm sorry, Williams. Our oldest girl, Page, went to school with your youngest daughter, Alana!"

"I knew I recognized you, sorry! Your pulling in here so fact and flying up next to me..."

"Yeah, sorry about that!"

"No worries. I'm hoping we have this one for Kendal? It's an injectable, and I normally don't carry a lot of those. But I'll have to go inside, check, and see."

"I hope you have it, Doc. She can't go the night without it. Kendal and Zach are already stressing over this whole thing. And my wife, she's with them now, is about to lose it too! You got to have 'em! Please tell me you do."

"Let's go inside and see. No need to start worrying before we even know if I have the drugs."

Anxiously he followed close behind, right on my heels. I listened and heard him call on his cell phone to inform someone that he had given me the prescriptions, and I was making sure I had them all. He promised to call back as soon as he found out more.

Once inside the drugstore, I hastily went to the keypad and disabled the alarm system. Then I went straight back to the prescription area and started looking to see if I had the medications before I asked him to fill out an information sheet on his daughter. Thankfully, we had a couple of multidose vials of the Heparin (a blood thinner); it was the medication I wasn't certain we had. Also I was glad we had the Zofran to control her nausea and vomiting.

"I've got all four of the prescription drugs!" I was happy to inform him. "I'll need to order some more of the injectable Heparin to complete the whole order, but it'll be in day after tomorrow. But no need to worry, I have plenty to get Kendal started tonight and for the next few days. I will need to get some information on her and find out if she has insurance, if you don't mind?" I asked as I handed him the clipboard with a new patient information sheet.

I seriously hoped Kendal had insurance. The four medications would easily run $200 or more! And to make matters worse, they each had eight refills, meaning she would need to be on them for a total of nine months. Without insurance that could get awfully expensive.

"Doc, she doesn't have insurance!" He shook his head as he informed me. "The hospital took what little savings they had for deposit on the ER visit. I will have to pay for the prescriptions this time, if it's not over a hundred dollars! If it's more than that, well, I get paid next Friday and can pay you the rest then. I sure hope it's not more. After this time, the kids are on their own with paying for it. I know they've got it tough, but I've had to look for work and have been doing nothing but odd-and-end jobs for the past few months. Thank goodness I even have a job right now, and if I'm lucky, it should last another week or two... After that, who knows?"

"I understand completely. Don't beat yourself up. Lately jobs have been sparse for everybody. You're not alone out there."

"You can say that again," he quickly added. As he readied to say something else, his cell phone rang. Pulling it out of his pocket, he started to answer but apologized first. "Sorry. If you'll excuse me for a minute, Doc?"

"No problem."

As I started typing the prescription information into the computer, I couldn't help but overhear his conversation. Reading between the lines, I could gather that Kendal must have lost a previous child (not so long ago) and was pregnant again. This time, it sounded as if they determined why she lost the first baby and were giving medications to prevent her body from attacking the husband's blood clotting factors and keep her body from aborting the child. If nothing else, it sounded to me as if Kendal was at extremely high risk of rejecting the baby if she didn't get the Heparin.

"Everything okay?" I asked as he ended the call and started pacing around the drugstore.

"She's got a long way to go yet, Doc. I told 'em not to worry. Not that they'll listen to me, but I tried! We'll just have to get Kendal on these medications and take it a day at a time. I'm sure you can tell by what they've ordered that Kendal's pregnant and sick. Big difference this time around, we know the risks. No more wondering why it's happening or looking for who's to blame."

"I kind of guessed some of that by the prescriptions, but it looks like Kendal and the baby will be all right, huh?"

"I hope and pray! This first trimester will be the most crucial, the doctor told us. If we can get her and the baby through that, then it should improve the odds. She and Zach lost their first child back several months ago. It just about tore them apart, and us. They had been married less than a year when she found out she was pregnant with the first. Like most young couples, they called everybody to tell them the good news. They were so excited. We all were. Then six weeks later, she loses the baby... Nobody understood or knew why. Everybody wanted to point the finger of blame, you know, but it was no body's fault really! It was a gut-wrencher, I'm telling you! I'm so sorry it happened but glad it's behind us now. Her being pregnant again kind of puts it all in the past. I'm praying it will, provided she can keep the baby until term!"

"I can only imagine how hard it must have been," I said, trying to sympathize with him for what I knew must be an exceedingly difficult situation. Ria and I were blessed with three girls and, thankfully, never experienced the pain of losing one.

"She passed the baby right out of her system one night when she got up to go to the bathroom. It was the worst night I can ever remember for my little girl. Zach called me all in a panic. Couldn't handle it and just lost it! Said they could see the dead fetus in the toilet and Kendal was crying uncontrollably. They asked the wife and I to come right over, which you know we did. We rushed over as quickly as we could. When we got there, my wife took care of Kendal, and I cleaned things up as best I could in the bathroom and bedroom. We took Kendal to the emergency room to have her checked out and make sure she was going to be okay. I mean, you know, we realized she'd lost the baby but wanted to make sure everything with her was all right. I thank God she didn't have any complications. She did have bleeding for almost a week after that, and they told her she might have some scaring down there, inside, or something like that. They didn't tell me, and I don't want to know all the details, Doc."

"It must have been awful!" I said with a caring sigh for his hurt. "But everybody must be happy that she is pregnant again. At least Kendal and Zach didn't give up. At least they tried again." I attempted to say anything I could think of to be encouraging and positive.

"Honestly, we are…scared to death! I think we're all scared right now. On pins and needles…waiting and hoping. We're just praying she can get far enough along to keep the baby, and hoping the baby is healthy. I'm telling you right now, Doc, it's scary! Scariest thing I've ever been through! The wife and I had no problems, no problems at all with our kids! I don't know why this is happening to her. It's just…" His voice trailed off, and he looked down at the floor, as if he might cry.

"I know it must be scary. And I sure can't say I know how you feel, but I am certain I would feel the same way if it were one of my girls. I have got three girls, you know. And I love them all dearly."

"I don't know all three or your girls, just your youngest—Alana. They must be all grown and married with kids of their own by now?"

"Two have been married for years. Alana just married Mr. Right last May in Charleston! Between the other two daughters, we have five grandkids so far! There is a picture of the family on the counter next to the register there." I proudly pointed to it.

"You did good, Doc! Nice-looking bunch," he said with a smile. "That dating scene was scary with daughters, wasn't it?"

"You won't hear any arguments from me on that one! When they lived at home and were dating, I had a few simple rules: Boys had to come pick them up at the front door, no blowing the horn. The guy's hair had to be shorter than the girls—easy request considering all three girls had shoulder-length hair. No body piercing on the boys—pierced ears on the girls was about all I could handle. I didn't want to see any underwear showing—who cares what color boxer shorts they have on—and their pants better not be so loose they had to hold them up when they walked. I had plenty of extra belts or safety pins I could give 'em. If they wanted to wear a cap, that was fine, so long as it was straightforward, not sideways, cockeyed, or backward... Plus a few other stipulations I custom made up as it went along. I did find it helpful to be cleaning my shotgun when they came to pick up the girls at the house. Now that really got the boys' attention!"

We both laughed and then traded a few horror stories of our daughter's dating years. It was nice to talk to another parent who cared for his children as much as I did mine. Before finishing up with our conversation, I promised him I would call and check in on Kendal and Zach and keep in touch with them during the pregnancy.

When I informed him the drugstore would be able to help with the cost of Kendal's medications, he reached across, grabbed my hand, pulled me toward him, and nearly shook my hand off. Again and again, he repeatedly thanked me and promised he would get the kids to stop in next week when things settled down a bit. I pointed to a bulletin board hanging against the wall covered in photographs.

"There is an empty spot up there just waiting for a picture of that baby when he or she comes. The community has been blessed over the past forty years will all those bouncing babies—Kendal and Zach's will be up there proudly with the rest! You just watch and see!"

His smile was one of the most contagiously happy I had seen in some time, and I smiled right along with him as both of us anticipated the day his grandbaby's picture would be added to the others on the board.

Before leaving, I wrote my cell and home number on my business card and told him to call, day or night, with any problems or questions on the medications. I heard him call home as he was getting ready to walk out the front door telling them the good news. He found the prescriptions Kendal and the baby needed.

That night, I shared with Ria about Kendal and the baby. She listened intently as I told her how they had lost a previous child and how her doctors are hoping the medications will prevent rejection and allow her to carry the baby to term. I explained how Kendal would have to give herself a shot twice every day in her belly area and how it was still touch and go and would be for months to come, but it looked positive. Ria's eyes lit up as I neared the end of the story as if she could hardly wait to tell me something.

"You'll never believe it! You just won't believe it!" Ria exclaimed as she sat on the edge of the sofa.

"What?"

"This afternoon, I got an e-mail from Amy. Not even thirty minutes before you came home, she e-mailed me again. You won't believe it! It was about taking dinner over to this young couple tomorrow night. She was determined about you and I doing it! She said the pastor specifically asked that we do it. She had something in the message about how the couple lost a child and were now expecting again. She even said there were risks she could lose this new baby if she didn't take some medicine through a syringe—just like you described for Kendal! I don't know about you…but I gives me goosebumps. I'm thinking it's the same couple. What do you think? Wouldn't that be something? We might get to go meet them tomorrow. Think what an encouragement we could be to them. It would be amazing if it were them! I'm excited. I can't wait to see if it's Kendal and Zach!"

"I'm excited too! Go check the e-mail again! Amy had to have given us their name and address in order to take them dinner."

Ria hurried into the bedroom and over to her computer to check the e-mail. Sure enough, it was Kendal and Zach! Ria jumped up from the chair and hugged me. We both danced around and shouted with joy over the news. It is so amazing when all the pieces fall into place. You know immediately that it is absolutely someone greater than you in charge, setting all the cogs in motion, making everything to move forward in the proper sequence of events. Even if we don't always understand the hows and whys, we still can have faith and believe. Ria and I sure did!

Long story short, Kendal had lots and lots of days where she was sick. The nausea medicine had to sometimes be taken two to three times a day during the first trimester, and she still had problems keeping food down and gaining weight throughout the entire pregnancy. As for the blood clotting and the risk to the baby, she gave herself Heparin (an anticoagulant—blood thinner) injections twice daily every day up until her due date. Along with that, she took special prenatal vitamins, which helped the baby to develop correctly. Time passed so quickly, and everything was looking good.

At the suggestion of one of our employees, there were numerous "themed" baby showers given. Employees, family, friends, and friends of friends were invited. Before long, Kendal and Zach had everything a young couple might need to take care of (and spoil) a new baby. The once empty bedroom that housed only a crib was now jam-packed with clothes, stroller, car seat, toys, etc. It was wonderful to see the outpouring of prayer, love, and caring that surrounded this family during a stressful, and oftentimes difficult, pregnancy.

At long last, the day came and Brian Russell—at six pounds and ten ounces—entered the world to the loving open arms of his parents, Kendal and Zach. A throng of friends and neighbors, as well as proud grandparents, welcomed his arrival home. I wouldn't be at all surprised if fifty or more people held Brian within the first week he was home from the hospital. That baby got more loving than any baby could hope for, and we all knew that he was a gift from God—no doubt about that!

Brian was just as healthy as any newborn, and the doctors said they were thrilled to let everyone know he had no complications or adverse ramifications from the medications. To quote my wife, *"He's one of the handsomest little boys I've ever seen."* You know, I'd have to agree with her (even if he didn't have a stitch of hair on his head).

*****

Back at the drugstore, things were clipping along at a steady pace when I overheard a patient ask one of the cashiers if she could add ten dollars to her debit transaction. We have tried to discourage our customers from cashback (the card transaction companies charge us a service fee for each transaction based on a percentage of the sale) and have asked the cashiers to tell them we would prefer not to give back extra cash unless it is an emergency. We nicely remind them that there are two banks, both with ATMs, less than a half mile down the road from the drugstore. Therefore, trying to be a conscientious employee, Ashton told her no.

I leaned forward and listened as the lady asked again for the ten dollars extra. I couldn't decide which direction it was going but went ahead and told Ashton it would be fine. I would approve it. The lady looked almost embarrassed that I had gotten involved, so I just assumed I must have replied in a wrong manner or tone. Feeling I should go out, try to explain, and apologize to her, I stopped what I was doing and went around to the front counter.

Before I could even apologize and say I was sorry, she interrupted. "Doc, remember I told you my son, Dustin, left last month for Afghanistan," Debra began to explain to Ashton and me.

"Yes I do. Please let Dustin know we are immensely proud of him and tell him to be careful. It's truly a shame that the news outlets don't give the respect and dignity due to our young men and women who serve so bravely to protect our country and our beliefs. I don't think any of us can truly imagine how it feels to be in a foreign country where people hate you and yet you are there to help them. I remember it was a little like that during Vietnam too."

"No, I can't imagine how it feels either, but I appreciate greatly you saying you are proud of him. Dustin always respected you, and that will mean an awful lot to him. And I am always reminding him to be careful. Doc, I need to explain why I was asking for the extra ten dollars!"

"You don't need to explain. I'm sorry"—my big mouth cut her short—"if I came across wrong. You know that I will be happy to process the extra ten dollars, if you need it. Really, it's no problem at all. I'm so sorry if we embarrassed you."

"No, no, it's my fault. I didn't explain." Debra turned and looked to make certain we both were listening. "Before Dustin left, I badgered him for an explanation as to why he was doing this. Why he was putting himself in harm's way? You know what he told me? He told me he wanted to do something to make a difference, something to help others! By choosing to serve as a Marine in Afghanistan, he felt he was helping all of us. I want to be able to do something to help too. It may not be much, but I was hoping I could leave the ten dollars here with you, in your Helping Jar. I have faith in you, and after seeing and hearing so many things you have done, I know you'll put it to good use to help someone. Doc, maybe you could use the ten dollars to help someone out, someone who really needs it more than I do. It's my way of being like my son, Dustin, feeling as if we are sharing the same passion. The same desire to make a difference. Please take the ten dollars and use it to make a difference!"

I was so caught off guard by her request that I didn't know what to say. I was speechless, in awe by her gesture of genuine caring and wish to make a difference. It was such an unexpected random act of kindness. Her sacrifice of ten dollars might not seem like much to some, but it could equate to one hundred dollars or more, in terms of budgetary sacrifice, for someone else or even a thousand dollars to yet another. But bottom line, how we use the money we have earned truly matters. Winston Churchill tied it up nicely when he explained, *We make a living by what we get. We make a life by what we give.* I totally agree!

"Doc, I've been in here and heard you pull people over to the side and hand them their medicine and tell them it was no charge.

You've done it three or four times that I can remember in the past few years. I was taken back at bit the first time. You know, just thought it was probably somebody you knew well and decided not to charge them—like a professional courtesy or something. Then the second time, I saw the lady start to cry as she walked past me with her little girl in her arms. That's when I knew. I knew you were doing something good and trying to make a difference—just like my son. I mean, Doc, what you were doing—"

"Debra," I quickly interrupted. "Let me tell you what." I reached across and grabbed her hand. "What you're doing, by giving the ten dollars, is helping a lot. A whole, whole lot! It could be the difference between a person getting or not getting an important medication, something they desperately needed. By doing what you're doing, something will be accomplished in the life of another human being that otherwise might not be possible. What Dustin is doing is just the same. We all recognize that, and it's an incredibly good thing. But what you're doing is just as big—just as important! Best of all, though, it's for the people right here at home. I promise you the ten dollars will mean a great deal to someone. Your money will make a big impact! I can't tell you how touched I am that you would even consider doing this. That you'd care enough to make this sacrifice. Thank you so much!"

Debra looked at me and gave a reluctant smile. She understood what I was saying and realized that what she was doing would make a difference. She knew she didn't have to do it, but she did it anyway. She was doing it out of love and caring, not for glory or recognition. Like son, like mother. Now isn't that a switch?

Who knows, ten dollars might have been all the extra money she had for the entire week. Yet she had chosen to give her money out of the abundance of her heart. To make a sacrifice for someone she would never see or know personally. Debra had chosen to take the emphasis off herself long enough to recognize that others around her were in greater need than she. Ever thought about doing that? Possibly for the first time in your life (or possibly not), change and refocus your attention to others. Maybe for one week, quit looking out for you and look out for someone else. Now that would make a difference!

"You tell your son to be careful now," I reminded her again as she started to leave.

"I will."

"Debra, thanks so much."

"You are certainly welcome," she acknowledged with a smile, as she looked over her shoulder and headed out the door of the drugstore.

Too often, we buy into the falsehood that generosity is mainly a character trait found only in the rich and affluent of society. Well, let me tell you from experience, that's simply not so. Being rich doesn't correlate with giving to the needs of others. In fact, just the opposite is true: middle income people give more. Researcher Arthur C. Brooks found that *"Americans at the bottom of the income distribution pyramid are the country's biggest givers per capita."* This led me to believe then that giving and caring is more a matter of the size of the heart than the size of the pocketbook.

Looking around at the world these days, I recognize that we have become a process-driven society. And that process we work so hard to drive and maintain is spelled S-E-L-F. We have crowded together so tightly this four-letter word that there is simply no room for others. I hope it doesn't happen, but someday, it could be that the rains and pains of everyday life pour down upon you or me. It's probably then, and only then, that we will wish someone would find the time or the heart to fit us in between their S-E-L-F. I once heard a lady in the waiting room at my cardiologist's office remind her husband that we all are alike in that we have 365 days a year to make a difference. She then looked at her husband and asked him when he was going to stop feeling sorry for himself and use one of those days to help someone feel a little bit better about themselves?! She then followed up and questioned him if he had room in his heart for anybody besides himself. She sure got my attention that day!

I admit it. I have made a lot of mistakes in my life. I have been self-centered and overlooked others far, far too often. If I could have any wish, I would wish to be half the person my wife and children see me as being. They see me as generally good and caring, many times putting others ahead of myself. I wish that was always the case. My time, just as yours, on this earth is limited. So why don't we make the most of it? Why can't we be the person we ought to be, the person everyone knows we can be? That's the sixty-four-million-dollar question (an expression my Grandma Lovelace used which has stuck with me).

If we knew we had only a fixed amount of time to live... Let's make it a month. Wouldn't we look at things differently? It would probably be amazing to discover how the things we think are so important suddenly would be totally meaningless. How we would choose that path of action and deeds for that final month of our life should be the blueprint of how we live our entire life. I know for me when I initially thought about the final days it caused me to have a reversal of many of my bad habits and poor actions (some inactions). More than likely, if you thought you only had thirty days to live, there would be a radical transformation from who you once were to who you now want to be for that final countdown. I still remember when they told me that my heart was dying, and I would die along with it in a month or two—it radically changed me. Ria sometimes hits me in the arm and say, "Hey, remember you are supposed to be dead, so do something before you die! And I mean now!!"

Although I haven't received word in the mail lately or been given any extended guarantee that I have more than one month to live (which I have lived far past that), I often stop and wonder what my emphasis would be today if I knew, beyond a shadow of a doubt, that I had exactly only thirty days to live? I would ask myself one big question, Will this day be used for myself, or will it be used for others? How would I populate the 1,440 minutes given to me each day? Would it be all about me, or would it be about others, like family or friends?

Think back to what was your emphasis today? What do you think it will be tomorrow? What will it be the next day? I don't have to tell you that it is up to you what you do with each gift of a day.

H. Jackson Brown threw rocks at any excuses we might have of not enough time when he penned, *"Don't say you don't have enough time. You have exactly the same number of hours per day that were given to Helen Keller, Pasteur, Michelangelo, Mother Teresa, Leonardo da Vinci, Thomas Jefferson, and Albert Einstein."* Never thought of it that way before.

What you leave as your life legacy will not be defined in one, two, or three spectacular moments but more so in the thousand to ten thousand little moments and actions you choose to do all along the way. So what are you waiting for? Push the button and deliberately choose to risk the two to three minutes it takes to put a life-changing action into motion!

*A friend loves at all times, and a brother
is born for a time of adversity.*
—Proverbs 17:17

CHAPTER 11

Choices, Choices... We All Have Choices

Evaluate every opportunity not by how much money you can earn, but by how effectively you can reflect Christ and live for Him in that situation.

—Tony Dungy

On an extremely hectic day two weeks before Christmas, Ashton, one of the pharmacy techs, came over to me with a frantic look on her face and questioned,

"Can you come up front and help this lady? I think... I mean... right away, please. She's got all her meds out on the counter in a pile and...and..."

"I will be right there," I assured her.

Quickly, I finished checking the two patient's prescriptions in the red clipped baskets on my desk and called out their names, letting them know they were ready to be picked up. I then made my way from behind the counter and headed toward the front to try and help the lady Ashton had told me about.

"Hi, there. How are you today?" I politely greeted her with a smile. My eyes couldn't help but notice all the prescription vials on the counter in front of her.

"I'm fine. Thank you for asking," she replied graciously, never even looking up.

Staring down at the counter in front of her, I suddenly understood why the cashier had been so concerned. Carefully lined up, all in a row, on the blue granite countertop were her prescription vials. Hurriedly I glanced at each, as best I could, and happened to catch her name on one of the bottles that was turned around toward me.

"So what have we got here, Mrs. Reynolds?"

"These are all my prescriptions I take each month. Of course you know that, I get 'em from you, Doc."

"Yes, ma'am, I see that. And I am so thankful you let us fill them for you."

"It's almost Christmas," she began. "Hard to believe! This year has gone by so quickly. My son called me yesterday, and he's coming down from North Carolina to see me. To be here with me for Christmas!"

"That's great. I know that must make you happy?! Having him here to spend the holidays with you and all."

"Yes, I am so thankful he will be home. He hasn't been down to see me for the past two years, and he has never been home for Christmas since he got married and had children. It will be a real treat to see him and my grandchildren this Christmas!"

"Oh wow, the whole family's going to be here for Christmas, huh? How nice that should be?!"

"It's a miracle! It'll be wonderful," she agreed, then paused. "But it makes things a little difficult for me. And that's why I am here. I need your help, Doc. Please?"

"Yes, ma'am. I will be glad to help you, Mrs. Reynolds. Tell me, though, what exactly is it you need my help with?"

"Fact is, things are kind of thin right now. I don't have a lot of money, Doc. I'm on a fixed income, and there's just no extra money coming in until the first of the month. Most months there is hardly enough to make it without some creative scrimping, if you know what I mean?"

"I grew up without a lot. And I know it is really tough on a lot of people right now. I feel certain you are doing the best you can. And it looks like you're doing a great job managing your prescriptions." I told her as I picked up one of the prescription vials for emphasis.

"Lord sure knows I try. Doc, these are all the medicines I take," she told me again, this time waving her hand over the line of vials on the counter.

"Yes, ma'am."

"I didn't find out 'til yesterday that Corbin and his family were coming. I stayed up almost all night trying to figure it out myself, but I could only come up with one solution."

"What solution did you decide on?"

Mrs. Reynolds held up one of the prescription vials as she began to explain. "I used a black marker and put on each bottle the exact number of pills I have until I get my check at the first of the month."

"Not sure I am following. Why did you do that?"

"Doc, first off, you need to look and tell me which medications I should take and which I can do without for the rest of this year. Then, I need you to double-check me and make sure I have enough pills of each of those I really need to last me between now and January second—the first falls on a Sunday this upcoming year. That's when my check comes in. Once you tell me which I can do without, then I will look at the ones you say I need and decide which I can afford to get and which I'll have to do without. I probably won't be able to get all of them that you say I need, so you may have to have a second look-see and narrow it down. It's a lot to ask of you, I know, but I need your help."

"What?" I asked, alarmed at her suggestion of prioritizing and making a to-do or to-do-without choice on her meds. "Wait a minute, Mrs. Reynolds. Let me take a look at these."

I slowly turned each of her nine prescription vials around to read exactly what the drugs where she was taking. Several I picked up and shook gently, not so much to get an idea of the amount inside but to give me time to think as I was pondering what to do. Mrs. Reynolds had done her best to mark on the label how many she had, but she expected me to calculate how many she would need to get through to the first of the month and which she could do without.

Right away, I felt torn inside. I wanted to help her, but her plan was not a good one. How could I go about this? The big problem was, every one of her medications was important! There were four heart/high blood pressure meds, three for her diabetes/blood sugar, and two critical respiratory/breathing medications. Truthfully, I felt all nine medications were necessary to keep her alive and well while her family was down visiting from North Carolina for the Christmas holiday. There was absolutely no way I could pick and choose which ones she should or should not take!

"Mrs. Reynolds," I said. I decided to question her further and give me a little more time to come up with a solution. "Why is it you only want to take part of your medications? You need to take them all. Every one is important. Some are for your heart, blood pressure, and the others are for your diabetes and breathing problems. I would just hate to say yes or no to you to stopping any of them."

"But you don't understand! I can't afford them all, Doc."

"You've been consistently getting them every month without any problems? Why now? What's so different, Mrs. Reynolds? Not wanting to sound nosey, but has something happened? Did we do something wrong and you not get all your medicine? Is that what you are trying to tell me politely?"

"No, no, it's nothing like that, Doc! It's my grandchildren. Cody and Callie are coming down for Christmas. Last time Corbin came down for the Christmas holiday, it was right before he was married and years before the grandkids were born. They have never been to see me at Christmastime. Never! I just have to get those grandbabies presents, something nice for Christmas. And I can't afford to get them presents and pay for my medications. No way can I swing both!"

"I understand completely, but you have to take care of yourself. You can't just all of a sudden stop taking your medications! I mean, you know that, right?"

"I do understand you, Doc, and I appreciate your concern for me," she said, reaching out and patting my hand. "But I can't disappoint Cody and Callie. Their dad tells me they love Christmas more than any other holiday. I can't let them down! And I want them to enjoy being here enough so that they will want to come back again. I feel like if I don't get them something nice, well, they won't have a good time and won't come back for Christmas ever again. I can't let that happen—no way! I love those two grandchildren and would do anything for them. Doc, if it means choosing between getting them Christmas presents and buying my medications, I choose them over me! Right now, they are my number one priority. But I promise you I will get back on track with everything next month. I promise! Just help me figure out what I can afford, that's all I am asking."

Mrs. Reynolds reached out and grabbed the prescription vial I was holding. Setting it back down on the counter, she started sorting through them. One by one, she carefully looked at each bottle and then started to explain.

"I know I need a few of these," Mrs. Reynolds said as she repositioned the bottles in front of me. "Let's say ten pills of this metoprolol. It is a twice a day one. And this one... I think two or three tablets of the glipizide. I can just watch what I eat more carefully and take them when my blood sugars get really high. This other one—"

"Mrs. Reynolds,"—I held up my hand and stopped her—"let's take a minute and talk about this! I know you want to give your grandchildren presents and have them enjoy Christmas, but your son and his wife should understand that you can't afford anything elaborate. Talk to them and see if they can't switch some of the tags on the presents they were going to give the children and put them as being from you. That shouldn't be too much to ask? Also, I can check with some of the ladies from church and see if they can't bring over and help you decorate a bit. My wife Ria will be glad to help provide some of the food for your Christmas dinner and—"

"Absolutely not," she emphatically let me know! "I have no intention of embarrassing my son or have him and his wife think I don't want them down or, worse, can't afford to have them down for Christmas! If they were to think that, then they might never bring Cody and Callie to see me at Christmastime again. I want them to come see me! Not just this one time, but again and whenever they can. I just can't afford all the presents right now. Please try to understand, Doc. I love my family more than anything in the world and want them to want to be with me. It's a big deal to have them come down. Every year, until now, they have gone to my daughter-in-law's parent's house in Georgetown, just outside Washington DC. They don't blink an eye at the extra expenses. It's nothing for them…but this is everything to me!"

How could I argue? I had no intentions of belittling Mrs. Reynolds and making her feel she had to take handouts in order to get by. Clearly I had embarrassed her, and I didn't mean to. She was upset and embarrassed by the whole situation. I felt by discussing it any further, I would make it worse and not better. Realizing how much this meant to her, I felt sure that if I didn't help her in some way with what she was asking, she would probably stay up the entire night fretting over it. There was no way I wanted to upset her more…but I had to do something.

"Give me a minute, Mrs. Reynolds, and I will get you going with the medications you need," I told her, picking the vials up off the counter.

Cradling her nine prescription vials in my hands, I walked back and put them on my counter. Next, I began pulling the medications from the selves. I lined each bottle up in front of me and filled it with enough medication to last her until the fifth of January. I wasn't about to let her run out of anything. This needed to be a special Christmas for her, Corbin, her daughter-in-law, and her two grandchildren. Who knows if they would ever have another together? But this one was going to be a good one. I would make certain of that! I stopped counting the medications momentarily and thought to myself, *Isn't Christmas all about giving?* God gave us the greatest gift—Jesus!

"Here you go, Mrs. Reynolds," I said, giving her a bag filled with her medications.

"So, Doc, you figured out how many I need? I can't tell you how much I appreciate everything. Now give me the bad news. How much do I owe you?" she asked opening her pocketbook and pulling

134

out a small change purse. Opening the clasp, I saw it only had a few dollar bills folded inside.

"Merry Christmas, Mrs. Reynolds, and you have a great time with that family of yours!"

"Doc, I need to know how much I owe you."

"Merry Christmas, Mrs. Reynolds." I told her again, with a big smile.

"Doc, I don't understand. What are you saying? How much are my medications?"

"Merry Christmas," I replied a third time and reached for her hand.

Mrs. Reynolds looked in my eyes and started to cry. She knew what the drugstore had done for her and for her family.

"You come around here, Doc." She directed me as tears began to stream down her checks. "I need you over on this side of the counter, right now!"

I followed her wishes and walked out through the half swinging door separating the prescription area from the patients. The very second I reached the other side, Mrs. Reynolds threw her arms around me and hugged me ever so tightly. I could feel the warm tears of joy against my neck. After a few moments, she eased away and let go. Stepping back a few steps, she looked me in the eyes.

"Merry Christmas to you, Doc. I mean it, Merry Christmas! *And Merry Christmas to all you wonderful people*! Thank you so much for everything. For the bottom of my heart, I thank you for making this Christmas the best. The best ever!"

Hurriedly she grabbed her purse and bag of medications off the counter and left the drugstore crying. I walked over to the door and watched as he made her way to her faded Ford Taurus. Carefully she opened the door and eased her old body inside. I stood to the side so she wouldn't see me watching. Mrs. Reynolds reached down and pulled out a tissue to wipe the tears from her face. Then I watched as a glow came upon her face, and she began to smile. Tears gushed from her eyes as the smile engulfed every inch of her face. I can't remember even seeing a more beautiful smile.

I stayed by the door of the drugstore and watched until her car's taillights drifted out of sight. Oh, how I wished I could be an invisible guest at her house for Christmas... What a joyous time it was going to be!

"Merry Christmas, Mrs. Reynolds!"

So whether you eat or drink or whatever you do, do it all for the glory of God. Do not cause anyone to stumble.
—1 Corinthians 10: 31–32

CHAPTER 12

One Friend to Another

Alone we can do so little; together we can do so much.
—Helen Keller

B oy, oh boy... If you didn't already know, small towns are quick to pick up on the arrival of *newcomers* (that is what they call them around here). When I hear that word, it sends chills up my spine! Reason being, over the years, I have seen that designation become a license for some non-newcomers to ignore, criticize, or even shun these folks. It's a shame too. And when that happens to these unsuspecting newcomers, it irritates the joy out of me and makes me question the motives behind it. This particular time though, I was...well...quite frankly...shocked by what it came to mean to this new couple who had settled into our little town of Utopia Springs.

There is certainly nothing out of the norm to see parents holding sick children in the drugstore. Of course, it tugs at your heartstrings to see the droopy eyes and sad expression as they press their heads against the shoulders of their moms or dads. And as much as I hate to admit it, drugstores would probably not be able to keep their doors open for awfully long were it not for sick people, young and old alike.

Looking up from checking a prescription, I almost did a double take when my eyes caught view of a young father holding his infant daughter. There, in front of the counter, stood a well-dressed man wearing a starched button-down collar dress shirt, dress slacks, and a coordinating tie to complete the look. In no way I am implying that Utopia Springs Drugstore never gets nicely attired customers; it's just a simple fact nowadays that the majority of working people do not dress in as semiformal of a manner as in years past. In other words, workplace clothing etiquette has stepped itself down a notch or two during the past decade. Casual has become the new business norm for those who still go to a physical office site. The COVID-19 pandemic of 2020/2021 created an entirely new below-casual business attire acceptability and laid the framework for stay-at-home employees.

As I looked more closely at the little girl, I noticed she had on a cute, frilly infant dress with lacy white socks and tiny black patent-leather shoes. Her hair was dark, thick, and wavy, pulled back off her face with a matching bow. Not that she wasn't adorably dressed, rather it was the sad, faraway look in her eyes that got to me. I could tell she was an extremely sick little girl.

Tightly she clung to her father and only made eye contact with me momentarily before pressing her face down into his chest.

Her dad looked tired, frustrated, and exhausted—all rolled up into one. He was struggling with the situation of waiting and trying his best to keep his composure as the technician at the counter was helping the customer ahead of him. I decided it might be a good idea to go out and see if I could help in some way.

"Hi," I began. "Need to pick up a prescription, or are you dropping one off?"

Quickly he moved over to the open counter where I was standing. Then, with loving ease, he lowered his daughter atop the counter. Although reluctant, she allowed him to sit her down but continued to cling to him with her arms wrapped tightly and holding on to the back of his shirt. He attempted to move her away just enough to reach into his shirt pocket and pull out several prescriptions. They were folded together, in half. He then looked at me and started to explain.

"I need to get these filled, please. I'm sorry, but we will need to wait." His request was short and simple, followed by, "Any idea how long it might be?"

"Let me see what you have here," I answered, reaching out and taking the prescriptions from him.

Immediately he answered me, as if for clarification or out of justification, "Kalee has never been sick before or had to have prescriptions. But she is on our insurance plan."

"All right. If you don't mind, let me get a patient information sheet for you to fill out on Kalee. And if you have your insurance prescription card with you, I will make a copy and give it right back to you."

Reaching behind the counter, I picked up a clipboard with a new patient information form attached and sat it on the counter in front of him, along with a pen. I waited patiently as he reached around to his back pants pocket for his wallet. Navigating to open it with his one free hand, he clumsily tried to find his prescription card.

"I think that might be it," I pointed and told him, seeing what looked to be a Blue Cross-Blue Shield insurance card amongst the numerous credit cards in his wallet.

"Yep, you're right, that's it," he acknowledged gratefully and then handed me the card to make a copy.

"If you would like, I can ask you the questions on the information sheet and fill it out for you. That way it will free you up and allow you to continue holding your daughter."

"That would be terrific, if you don't mind. I really appreciate it! She's just not doing well right now."

"No problem," I told him as I picked up the clipboard and began asking him for all the pertinent information. I then explained and asked him to sign the HIPAA (Health Insurance Portability and Accountability) statement. After signing the information sheet, I told him we would get the prescriptions ready as quickly as possible. He nodded his head in appreciation.

Taking the prescriptions back to the technician station, I picked up a red clip, attached it to the prescriptions, and placed them in one of the baskets for processing.

"He's waiting on these," I told Meghan.

Glancing over at my workstation and seeing it wasn't too backed up, I decided to return to the front counter. To be perfectly honest, after reading the prescriptions, I was somewhat worried about the little girl. She was sick, that much was obvious to anyone, but the dad looked as if he was swimming in a pool of hopelessness, trying to be strong, but about to fall apart. Just as I leaned against the counter and readied to start up a conversation with him, the front door opened, the overhead bell rang, and in came a woman who hurriedly made a beeline straight toward them.

Reaching their side, she held out her arms and took the little girl. Gently she pulled the child near and kissed her on the cheek. Rubbing the little girl's hair, she turned and began to talk with the dad.

Not wishing to appear nosey, I turned and headed back to look a little more closely at the prescriptions he had brought in for his daughter. The child was barely two years old and an oncology specialist in Orlando at Arnold Palmer Hospital for Children had written for some pretty powerful (and high dose) medications to control abdominal spasms, diarrhea, nausea, and vomiting. Along with those was a prescription for a topical numbing cream. The mix had my mind thinking and speculating all directions, but I wasn't sure what was the matter with Kalee.

Turning back around, I saw the woman (I now presumed to be the mom) and child had just left the drugstore. The dad was anxiously walking around in a continuous, almost circular pattern.

"I didn't get a chance to introduce myself earlier," I apologized to him, holding out my hand to shake his.

"We met once before," he told me, shaking my hand out of courtesy. "About six months ago at a Chamber-sponsored breakfast here in town."

"Okay, yes, you're right. I do remember now. So sorry for not putting that together earlier. I guess I was too busy trying to get the information on Kalee. Again, I'm sorry."

"Hey, no need to be sorry. I am sure you see a lot of people every day. You can't be expected to remember them all."

"Didn't you tell me that you and your family had moved here recently from somewhere nearby?"

"That's right. We moved over from Orlando just about nine months back. My wife was against it but caved when we were lucky enough to sell the house over there quickly and find a 1934 bungalow over here that we could afford to purchase and fix up. We got a great deal on a house here in town. But she still misses the big city. I told her to give it some time, and she would get used to it. Unfortunately now, she misses Orlando a lot more because we don't have any friends over here and with Kalee so sick and all, we'll be driving back and forth all the time. You just wouldn't believe…"

"I'm sorry Kalee is so sick. And it sure sounds like a lot of major change have hit your life all at once."

No sooner had the words left my lips when he turned around and started to walk away. Then, just as quickly as he had left, he shot back around and unloaded his problems.

"Doc, Kalee is…" His voiced tapered off as he began. Before he could even say another word, tears pushed their way out and started streaming down his face. "The doctor got the test results back from Kalee's abdominal mass." Although crying, he pushed on to tell me her story. "They found out… I mean, the doctor told us it was…" He threw both his hands up and placed them over his face. And he cried.

I stood motionless across the counter from him, not knowing what to do or what to say. I felt totally useless to his plight. Finally, I gathered up the nerve and slowly reached across the counter. It was a little out of my norm, but I placed my hand on his shoulder and gave a light squeeze, as if to say, "I'm here. I care."

Without hesitation, he looked up at me and grabbed hold of my hand, still on his shoulder. When our eyes meet, he pulled out the courage and tried again to explain.

"They told us…" he began, then paused and let out a deep heavy sigh, "that Kalee has nephroblastoma or Wilms tumor, whichever you want to call it."

Try as he might, he couldn't continue. Tears kept streaming down his face, and he let go my hand. He tried to act strong as he wiped them away with his shirt sleeve, but he was a broken man. His little girl had cancer—a word which scares even the strongest of adults!

Meghan saw how upset he was and that he was crying, so she brought over a box of tissues. Then she whispered in my ear, "His daughter's prescriptions are ready for you to check." I took the box of tissues and placed them on the counter in front of him. When he reached over and grabbed several, I asked if it would be all right for me to go back and check Kalee's prescriptions. I assured him I would be right back, and then we could talk more if he wanted. He nodded his head in agreement. Looking at his face, it appeared he was thankful to be given a moment or two to collect his thoughts and recompose himself.

When I returned from checking Kalee's prescriptions, he was still standing in the same spot, waiting on me and looking ready to talk.

"This morning they told us, for certain, that the mass in Kalee's abdomen was a nephroblastoma, which originated in her kidneys. The doctor was 100 percent certain of the diagnosis and said it's a good thing she was under the age of two and that we had brought her in immediately when we noticed the hardness in her stomach while giving her a bath. Early detection and her young age make the prognosis for survival way higher, he told us. Survival? Can you believe I'm having to think about whether or not she will live or die? She's still a baby."

"I'm so sorry she has the tumor, but at least, they feel good about the prognosis. That's a positive, right? I mean…one positive is better than no positives!"

"Absolutely, Doc, you're right. But that is about the only positive we have going for us. What I don't get is, you know, she's still just a baby. Kalee's only two years old. To me, it seems like only yesterday when she was born and now this?" He put his elbows down on the counter, hung his head down and then let out another heavy sigh.

"How is your wife? I mean, is she handling it all right?"

"I really don't know. It's still sinking in for both of us. It was only a few hours ago when we first got the news. The worst part is that they told us while we were at the hospital in the room with Kalee. She was watching us both, not knowing what was happening and then…well…when Kelley started to cry and went to hold Kalee, she lost it. Kalee started to cry and scream 'Mommy! Mommy!' She didn't understand and probably thought something had happened to Kelley. It was awful."

"So you mean to say you just found out today? This happened only a few hours ago?!"

"We just found out this morning, Doc," he answered, nodding his head. "They only told us it was a for sure thing this morning. But we knew something wasn't right. Kalee kept having diarrhea and couldn't gain any weight, and then, when we found her tummy so hard, that's when we took her in. I've got to tell you Dr. Shelton, here in town, was great! He saw her immediately and knew something was wrong. He pulled out his cell phone and called some of his contacts in Orlando right then and there. He made sure we got her seen that same day. The doctors down there couldn't believe how on top of things he was. You know how everybody in Orlando thinks there's nothing but a bunch of hicks and hillbillies out here… Well, they didn't have anything but good things to say about Dr. Shelton. I think everybody over there is wrong believing we're a bunch of uneducated hillbillies here in Utopia Springs!"

"Wow! I always thought our little town was blessed with two top-notch doctors' offices, but it's good to hear it firsthand! Sounds as if it was a God thing that he got Kalee seen so fast!"

"You better believe it, Doc! They sent Kalee over for X-rays, scans, blood works…you name it, right then and there. They told us all the result would be in within twenty-four hours, and they were. Everybody, from here to there, has been amazing—totally amazing, an absolute godsend to us! But…" He pulled back away from the counter and hung his head down and stood there in silent. After several moments, he concluded by saying, "And now the hard part starts."

"What is next, if you don't mind me asking?" I hated to sound like a busybody, but he seemed as if he wanted to talk, and genuinely,

I was concerned about Kalee. "Did they lay out some sort of treatment plan or what?"

"They did. The doctors are planning on surgery first, maybe next week, removing what they can. Then they will be using a multitherapy regimen consisting of radiation and chemotherapy along with two intravenous drugs. The combination of everything is supposed to cure her?"

"That would be wonderful!"

"It would be a *miracle* in my book! They all talked positive about her chances. I'm telling you..." Again, he hung his head down and didn't speak for a moment.

"It must be very hard," I said, trying to let him know I cared. "I have girls of my own, you know. And it would break my heart if I found out that one of them had cancer. To even think they had cancer and could die... It would scare me. Honestly, I don't know what I'd do... I just don't know?" I was babbling on and didn't mean to, but the reality of what he must be going through hit me as I was talking with him.

"Doc, let me tell you." He looked up at me, and his eyes locked onto mine. "When I heard him say Kalee had a nephroblastoma, I didn't know exactly what that meant, and all I could think was 'Why, God? Why did my little two-year-old baby girl have cancer?' It's not right." Tears welled up in his eyes and then overflowed and ran down his cheeks and landed on the countertop. "I felt as if a Mack Truck had hit me and dragged me down the road. I think it might have been less painful if a Mack Truck actually had hit me! My whole body went limp. My arms hung down beside me, feeling as if they weighed a hundred pounds. Oh my God, if I hadn't been in a chair, I think I would have fallen flat on the floor—right in front of the doctor. Then my mind went haywire and started to race in a million different directions, and I suddenly realized Kalee could die."

As the word *die* left his lips, tears again covered his face. Drop by drop, they pounded the countertop. Finally he got tired of wiping his face with his shirt and reached over and grabbed a handful of tissues to wipe his eyes.

Looking over at me, he tried desperately to catch his breath and speak again. "It's just not right. Not right at all!" The tone of his voice expressed fear and anger all rolled up into one. "Doc, how can a father think about his two-year-old daughter dying? We brought her home from the hospital, and now…now we're facing the possibility of her dying! No way that could be right. How can this be happening? Somebody blew it. There must be some sort of mistake. It couldn't be my daughter! It must be some other person's daughter who has this big-word disease I can hardly pronounce. It's not my daughter, I keep saying. But it is… It is… It's my Kalee!"

His face showed all his emotions—his fears, dread, worries, and questioning. All his worry and love for her covered him like a blanket. He didn't want to face it, but he knew he had to.

"I… I sure don't know how it feels to think that your daughter might die. And I don't have any magical answers to give you either. But know this, I do care. I care about Kalee, you, and your wife, and I promise you I'll pray for you every single day. You'll be right at the top of my list. That much you can count on. And I believe God cares and is right there with you, Kalee, and Kelley—holding you in His hands. When we are young, we can accept and believe in God so easily, but when we get older, it oftentimes becomes hard for us to open the eyes of our heart and see Him. Open up your heart, and you'll know He is there with you," I told him as I placed my hand on his chest over his heart.

He reached and put his hand over mine, without speaking. As we looked at each other, our eyes became as one. It was as if he was looking into my soul, and I was there holding out my hands to meet him when he found me. I couldn't hold back my emotions, and tears rolled down my face and joined in the pool already created by his on the counter. Neither of us spoke for this was beyond words.

Finally, I was able to assure him. "Anytime you need me, I'll be here for you. I'll give you my cell and home number, and you can call me, day or night, should you, your wife, or Kalee need medicine or something from the drugstore—anything. I mean it now… Even if you just want to vent or have somebody to listen, I'll be there! It could be my daughter, not yours. I want you to know I do care, and I'll be here if you need me. That's a promise you can count on!"

All I could do was say what was on my heart, and I had done that. I knew no words alone could ever make Kalee's nephroblastoma go away, but at least Austin knew somebody out there cared. He didn't have to say it, but he knew, and I knew, that the treatment with radiation and chemotherapy was going to be rough. They were facing a long hard road, but I meant what I said. I would be there!

"Doc..." Austin was still crying as I handed him Kalee's prescriptions. "I really appreciate you being here. I can't tell you..."

"You don't have to say anything," I reached and grabbed his hand and placed a card with my phone numbers in his palm.

"What about the medications, anything we should know? What should I tell my wife? Any problems we should expect? Any side effects that we need to know about or should be on the lookout for?"

"Tell your wife the medicines will help Kalee. Reassure her each step of the way that Kalee is in the Lord's hands. Just tell her to have Kalee take the medications the way it says on the bottles. They will start to work within an hour or so and help stop the diarrhea and vomiting she's likely to have once she starts the chemo and radiation treatments. They may make her drowsy, but that might not be a bad thing. You know, help her get a little sleep. Kalee's going to need her rest and all the strength she can muster to fight this battle. The chemo and radiation will wipe her out physically. Don't expect her to have a lot of energy. The medicines will help her rest more peacefully and allow her body to regroup. If they didn't tell you exactly where to put the cream on Kalee, give the doctor's office a call. Do remember that the cream they ordered is to be put on one hour before you go to the hospital tomorrow. It will make the insertion of the catheter less painful for her. And most of all, have faith and love on her!"

"Okay, one hour before we go to the hospital. Got it. But what is it for again?"

"It will numb the skin. I feel quite sure they will be inserting an intravenous catheter for her chemo drugs. By putting the cream on the intended insertion site, she won't feel as much pain when the doctor or nurse insert the needle."

"That'd be good. My wife and I are already starting to get freaked out over that whole IV thing. The last thing we want is to see Kalee suffering any more than she has to."

"The cream will definitely help with her pain," I reassured him. "As for the antibiotic they ordered, it's probably more preventative so she doesn't get an infection. Her immune system is going to be hit hard. She'll need all the help she can get to ward off an infection."

"Right, right… That's what the doctor said. I do remember that."

"Listen," I said, placing my hand over the bag so he wouldn't be trying to read everything about all the drugs while I was talking to him. "I know it's an awful lot to remember. Don't try to keep it all in your head. You need to write things down on paper…questions, concerns, whatever it is that's gnawing away at you. Make a list and ask your doctor or call and ask me if it's a drug or side effect question. Keep reminding yourself of how positive they felt about her prognosis. Keep repeating that to each other—that Kalee's going to make it and God is there with you. When Kalee gets sick, keep saying to each other that this is a good thing. It's the medicine working to rid her body of the tumor. Each day she pushes on and each course of therapy she completes is one step closer to her being well. Being healed. Win the now, then focus on winning tomorrow. Pretty soon the victories will start adding up. Remember to keep prayer at the top of your priority list."

"You're so, so right, Doc! We need to pray, stay upbeat and hopeful. Absolutely! With hope, faith, and God, we can get through this. I appreciate everything, Doc. And I do want to take you up on that offer you made earlier."

"What offer is that?"

"To pray for us every day. I really believe that can make a difference."

"You know," I started, "too many people underestimate the power of prayer—Christians and non-Christians alike."

"They sure do."

"If you don't mind, I'll have them put Kalee on the prayer list at church too."

"Mind?! Heck, no, I don't mind! I'd appreciate it. That would be great. And thanks again for everything, Doc."

"No problem. You keep me posted on how well she's doing and let me know the minute they tell you that tumor has gone, and she's cured."

A big smile came on his face as I concluded with the word *cured*.

"I'll keep you up-to-date, Doc. You can be sure I'll let you know how things go. Thanks again. Thanks so much for everything." He told me as he grabbed the bag of meds for Kalee and left the drugstore.

Though I genuinely believe that listening is one of the truly great gifts we can give another, I often find myself thinking ahead as someone is talking and even readying myself with an answer long before I know what the concern or need fully is. If I can allow those hurting or in need to talk and share their pain, concerns, heartache, it generally means a great deal more to them than any mere words I could express. For I have found that although trouble and chaos may be pouring out of the hurting individual standing only a few feet in front of me, peace is there inside of them waiting to be called out. Thus, it is often up to us to listen and then lovingly extend a bit of that peace to them in the form of caring, concern, prayer, faith, hope, and a willingness to help.

After Austin had gone, I went back to my counter, bowed my head and said a prayer for Kalee. Then I tried to catch up on several baskets with prescriptions needing to be checked for patients waiting and other patients that would be in shortly. As I focused my energy back on the prescriptions, I lost track of the front and patients coming in, and before I realized it, Deena—one of the technicians—was standing next to me.

"I didn't know if you heard me or not, but there's a lady out front who's been waiting to talk to you for a few minutes."

"I'm so sorry," I answered. "I didn't hear you. Let her know that I'll be right with her."

As fast as I could, I made my way around to the front counter, but all three of the prescription drop-off and pick-up points were occupied by women. I wasn't sure which one it was that needed my help. Deena saw my confusion and pointed me in the direction of the far counter.

The lady had her back to the counter and was on her cell phone as I made my way to her. Standing directly behind her, I was unable to see her face. Based on what Deena had said, I expected that she had been waiting for some time, so I tried to be patient. After several minutes, I cleared my throat to let her know I had arrived. Immediately, she turned around.

"Oh, I'm so sorry," she apologized and told the person on the other end of the phone she'd call them back in a few.

"That's all right," I said, embarrassed to not have recognized Kalee's mom—Kelley.

"Doc, you mind stepping outside for a minute?"

"Not at all."

I turned to Deena and told her I would be right back.

Kelley walked hurriedly ahead of me and out the door of the drugstore. Without stopping to even look and see if I was behind her, she made her way over across the parking lot to a late-model white Chevy Traverse parked in the shade. As we approached the vehicle, Austin opened his door and stepped out of the car. Then Kelley opened the back door and carefully picked up Kalee. She turned back around and brought Kalee over next to me.

"She's been through a lot today and she's not feeling well, but I want you to hold her. We talked about it, and we both feel it's important that you hold her, and she knows who you are."

Being a small-town druggist, I certainly have held my share of babies over the years. In fact, on the wall behind my workstation is a collection of photographs of babies and children we have had the opportunity to help at the drugstore. Whenever I am feeling down in the dumps, it only takes a minute to get me out of my slump. I simply turn around and look. I allow my eyes to meander over the gorgeous smiles and faces of children we have been blessed to be able to provide medicine to and helped get well. It is our Praise Wall, one of the greatest pick-me-ups in the world!

But at the very moment when she placed Kaylee in my arms, it was somehow different. I didn't hesitate one second in pulling her near and cuddling her tight against my chest. Even though I knew she was terribly sick (and scared of this stranger holding her), she looked beautiful to me. I rubbed my hand across her hair and pushed it back off her pale face.

It wouldn't be long, I thought to myself. And she would lose all those lovely locks. It made me feel sad to think of that. I looked into those big brown eyes staring back up at me and questioned, as her parents probably did, how someone so small and helpless could be so sick. With that thought, I pulled her even closer, and then, after a moment or two of simply holding her near me, I reluctantly gave her back to her mom.

"Thank you," I said, trying to hold back a tear. "Thank you for letting me hold Kalee. She is absolutely beautiful. What a blessing she is to us all."

"We sure do think so," Kelley answered back, with a big smile on her face.

"Remember, I'll be here if you need anything. Just call me. I'll be praying for Kalee every day. She'll get through this. We will all help her get through this. You watch and see. Just trust God and keep praying."

"We need a lot of that right now."

Looking back at Austin, I reminded him, "Keep me posted on the treatment. I want to know how everything's going. And call me anytime you need something."

"I will," he agreed as he got back in the car.

After getting Kalee back secured in her car seat, Kelley placed her hand gently on my arm. Turning to face her, she reached her arms around me and gave me a hug.

"I'm so thankful you're here..." Her words tapered off, and she began to cry. Releasing me from her arms, she quickly opened the car door and got in.

I knew if I didn't turn and walk away, I'd be crying too. As I made my way back to the drugstore, I heard their car start up and pull away. I looked back around for one last look. Kalee was in a car seat in the back, and the mom had scooted over next to the dad up front.

I have learned over the years that illness can either pull people together or push them away. I was terribly sorry for Kalee's cancer, but I was glad it had pulled her family together and not pushed them away from each other. As the weeks and months would pass by, they were going to need each other. And I hoped, if only in some little way, that I would be able to be there and help if, or when, they needed anything.

Placing my hand on my chest and closing my eyes, I could still imagine Kalee next to me. Her small body pressed tight next to mine. The sound of her heartbeat was now part of my heartbeat. I could still hear and feel it inside me. We shared a common cause now—beating the nephroblastoma. I'll always remember those few moments I held Kalee in my arms. It made me realize my heart was still alive and well and needed to beat stronger to be there for her in this battle with cancer. Every time I stopped and said a pray for her, I'd hold tight to that memory of her next to my heart. I am so grateful Kelley had the discernment to allow me to hold Kalee.

President Johnson's wife, Lady Bird Johnson, once said to someone that the secret was to *"Become so wrapped up in something that you forget to be afraid."* I think that's how it usually is with cancer treatment. You must wrap yourself up in the hope for a cure and have faith enough to forget what the odds and the obstacles are. I decided I would follow her advice and put fear out of my mind. I resolved to become totally wrapped up in faith and prayer for Kalee. The Lord could win this battle.

It wasn't long before the entire town had heard about Kalee and her family. Her battle became their battle. Kalee's name appeared prominently on the prayer lists at the four major churches in town—Baptist, Methodist, Presbyterian, and Seventh-Day Adventist. She was the recipient of monies received at several fundraisers (Bar-B-Que and Chicken Dinner). Local community and women's groups brought meals to the family on a regular basis. Everyday citizens made the drive to the children's hospital in Orlando to show their support for Kalee and her parents. Even their yard maintenance was taken over by one of the local yard care business, and the list of caring and support for these so-called newcomers seemed almost endless.

And prayer...prayer for Kalee was something openly talked about by all of us in town! We knew it was critical for her recovery. Prayer seemed to unite us for a common goal. It pulled everyone together with one singular hope—the healing of Kalee.

If you are anything like me, you are sitting on the edge of your seat wanting to know what happened to Kalee. Thank God this is a story with a happy ending. This time, the long hard journey of treatment was successful and led to remission of the disease.

Although the treatment regimen was hard—extremely hard at times—it worked. For almost an entire year, Kalee's nephroblastoma lingered as she underwent aggressive chemotherapy injections and bombarding radiation treatments. Finally, one day the lab results came back with glorious news—no trace of the disease! Thank you, Lord, and thank you to everyone who showed such an abundant outpouring of caring and love upon these newcomers!

Austin came in the drugstore on the day they got the news of the nephroblastoma disappearance.

"No sign of the cancer!" Austin shouted as he walked toward me.

He was so excited and so grateful for everything that everyone had done. And I was so thrilled by the good news that I can't even remember all the other things we talked about that day...except one.

"Doc," he began, "you remember I told you my wife hated moving to Utopia Springs? She thought I had brought her to the end of the earth."

"Oh yeah, I remember. That was a while back though."

"Not really that long. But you will never guess what she told me when we got the good news on Kalee."

"What's that?"

"She admitted she was wrong. Told me she shouldn't have said she hated Utopia Springs. Went on to say this was the best place in the world to live! I never dreamed she'd ever say that. But people really care around here, she said. Even made me promise that we'd never move. Unless we need a bigger house. We would stay in Utopia Springs no matter what though. Maybe one day, we may have to move into something with a little more room for a bigger family but still here in town. She said we'd found a permanent home here in Utopia Springs, and nobody was going to take that away!"

"And...uh...what's this talk of a bigger house? Something we need to know about?"

"Oh, maybe," he answered with a sheepish smile. "We'll see, Doc, we'll see." With that final comment, he turned and headed out the door of the drugstore.

"Tell Kalee we love her!"

With a wave of his hand, he motioned goodbye and answered, "Will do."

Now that the chemo treatments are over and the nephroblastoma is gone, Kalee's hair has finally started to grow back. Behind me, on our Praise Wall, I have a beautiful picture of Kalee. She's growing taller by the day and talking up a storm! Can't hardly shut her up some days.

Every time I see Kalee, she serves as a wonderful reminder to me, and the entire town for that matter, of how faith, love, and caring are unstoppable, especially when people see a need and act on it! And those actions, well, they can make all the difference in the lives of those around us. I am so thankful and proud for how our small town cared for and gathered round with one heart and one mind to help and hold Kalee and her family in their arms during their time of pain and suffering. Yes, God is great—all the time!

My command is this: Love each other as I have loved you.
—John 15:12

CHAPTER 13

Great Is Thy Faithfulness

Fear is the virus. Faith is the vaccine.

—John Frost

A year and a half in and now this? As if over a year of the COVID-19 pandemic hadn't slowly eaten away at life as I knew it before, now this had to happen! The second wave (labeled the Delta variant) of this merciless, invisible demon of a virus had grabbed hold of my dearest life treasure—Ria! And it wasn't simply Ria in our little town who had been hit with a hard punch of terrifying reality.

The most ferocious attack by the beast COVID-19 occurred in late August 2021. In the span of only two weeks, he had taken the lives of sixteen from us! Although Utopia Springs population is barely over three thousand, there were only a handful of families that hadn't felt a blow from the coronavirus. As of the first week in September 2021, there had been over 1,046 residents who had tested positive and sixty-nine had died from the virus. Being the only drugstore in town, most in our community diagnosed with the virus had been to see us for prescriptions, and we considered each not only neighbors, but also friends.

In those two devastating weeks of August, included in the sixteen were a husband and wife (three days apart), two adults over sixty, five adults in their fifties, four adults in their thirties (one thirty-nine-year-old husband and a father of a twelve-year-old son and a nine-year-old daughter), a twenty-six-year-old young male employed at Chick-Fil-A, a twenty-three-year-old single mom of two beautiful girls and, tragically, a nine-year-old little girl. This killer was unrelenting, cruel, and totally nondiscriminatory!

The vast and perplexing array of emotions, the ups and downs, the financial difficulties, the uncertainty, and so, so much more just can't be compacted into any one word or sentence to describe how I feel at this moment. This thing which I am unable to describe has not only infected Ria but has so overtaken (not infected) me as to nearly totally drain me of all my mental, physical, and spiritual fortitude. So as I stand here gazing out the window in Ria's hospital room, I am desperately trying to push my mind and emotions back into the realm of the positives and out of the negatives. I need to take hold of that faith, which I know is somewhere in me, and propel hope to the forefront. If only I could think with my beat-up heart instead of this humanistic logic in my brain. I am struggling so right now!

I see only darkness outside this window and feel for certain it could merge with and be nearly identical to the darkness I have felt within me so many times during the two weeks since Ria was diagnosed as positive and admitted with life-threatening respiratory complications to the hospital. How seemingly dark and impenetrable have been the never-ending days of fear and dread. I am well aware that I cannot fight this battle, nor can I win this battle, on my own.

"Lord," I began to pray out loud, "I know there is still hope on the horizon. Please help this doubting mind of mine to have faith and believe that you are in charge of this monster. Take Ria in your precious hands, hold her near to you, and have your will and way in her life. Give me hope! I love her so, Lord…"

I was still facing the window as I finished my plea to God. As I opened my eyes, a spark of light caught my attention. Trying to focus on where it was coming from, it disappeared, and I couldn't seem to find it anywhere. Just probably a reflection off something, a passing plane in the distance, or simply my imagination. Whatever, I couldn't find it.

Once I quit searching for the source of the light, I shook my head and wondered why I somehow felt different. Was it because I had finally admitted and unloaded all this burden to the Lord? Was it the result of my letting go of the wheel and trusting God to lead us on through this virus? Or maybe it was just a little adrenaline that was left inside of me, and it came out with curiosity and excitement over that darned light? I didn't know what it was?

But one thing I did know for certain, there was a newfound feeling in me that had not been there in weeks. Whatever it was and wherever it came from didn't really matter right now; the jump-start was a much needed and blessed arrival. Then suddenly without warning, I shivered momentarily, the way I do when I am hit with an unexpected blast of cold air on a winter day. What the heck was that?

Enough with these distractions, I told myself.

I reached within and tried to pull myself back together and focus on the reality and concerns of right now.

There was no need to fear, I thought to myself. *God has got this. He holds today, tomorrow, and forever in His hands.*

Right then, I stopped myself. I took a deep breath, exhaled slowly, and spoke a quiet agonized whisper, "Please give me faith and hope, Lord."

My focus shifted, and I saw not the darkness outside but the reflection of my own face, staring back at me in the glass. Of course, most of it was covered by this darned facemask, and the rest displayed the look of a man worried and frustrated. Immediately I knew that if Ria woke up today, tomorrow, or whenever, it was not the sight she needed to see!

Reaching behind my ears, I grabbed hold of the elastic cords and jerked off the mask! The first deep breath I took allowed me the courage to smile. Glancing back at my reflection in the window, it was more in line with the face I wanted Ria to see. I loved that woman more than she knew. Whenever she did come back, she needed to see that love for her on my face.

Well, I had put it off all evening long, and the time was overdue for me to turn around and face reality. The reality of Ria in her hospital bed, with oxygen, IV medications, and monitors from head to foot. Okay, here goes! Slowly I turned away from the window and around toward Ria.

Oh My God! I couldn't believe my eyes, she was awake with her head tilted toward me and a little curled-up smile on her lips! I rushed to her side and quickly grabbed hold of her hand she held open and lifted toward me. There was no question in my mind today about my own heart; it was beating strong and alive! The love of my life had come back to me. As tears started to form in my eyes, I leaned forward and kissed her on her lips. They felt softer and tasted sweeter than I ever remembered from before.

"Where have you been, sweetheart?" were the first words I had been able to speak to her face-to-face in over twelve days.

Ria's smile grew bigger, and a tear rolled down her right cheek. I gently wiped it away with my hand and touched the corner of her lips.

"I wondered where that smile had gone to? I am so glad to see you!" I felt she probably was too weak to talk, but I wanted to make certain she knew—so I told her, "I love you."

Without warning, as if someone had unplugged her body, her eyes shut, and her head shifted hard to the side, and she let go of my hand. Noises, lights, and monitors started flashing and beeping all around her! Almost instantaneously, medical staff poured into the room and surrounded Ria in her bed and the intercom announced, "Code 19, Room 525!"

What was happening?!

Someone took hold of my arm and was pulling me out of their way.

"Sir, come with me! You need to leave the room," a woman's voice instructed and moved me out of the way and into the hallway.

"Where is your mask?!" I was now being questioned by someone else just outside her door.

I didn't answer but instead moved side to side, trying to keep my eyes on Ria and what was happening. There were four, maybe five, staff in the room all doing something with Ria. And next thing I knew, they shut the door to her ICU room. I couldn't see what was happening!

"What's happening with my wife?! I need to know what's going on. Tell me what they're doing to her!" I shouted out to whoever was in listening distance. Somebody needed to tell me something, anything, about what was happening to Ria!

"If you'll come with me, Mr. Grayson, I will get you up-to-date on what's happening to your wife, Ria. And you need to put on a mask, please." The words were spoken calmly and tenderly by the woman standing next to me. She held out her hand for mine and then handed me a mask with her other hand.

"You'll need to put this on before we go anywhere," she told me matter-of-factly, but not as if criticizing me for not having one on—just stating a fact.

I did as she told me and put on the mask. Then she took my hand, and we headed away from Ria's room and down the hall. We took the first left and went about thirty more feet before we stopped in front of an elevator marked "Staff Only." I watched as she pressed the Down button, and we waited.

"I need you to tell me what's happening to my wife!"

"Hang in there, Mr. Grayson. We'll be somewhere private we can talk in a minute."

"Hang in there?!"

"Here's the elevator. Let's go."

Once inside, she let go of my hand and stood there silently, looking as the floor numbers flashed one by one as we went down. Finally, when we stopped, it was the first floor.

"Just around the corner now," she said and pointed for me to exit the elevator.

We walked only a short distance, and then she stopped.

"We're in front of the chapel. Why?!" I asked.

"Mr. Grayson, we'll be in the second family room on the right side of the chapel. The minister will be joining us momentarily. We had dietary bring a couple of bottles of water in case you're thirsty while we are waiting for him to arrive."

"Listen to me! I don't know what's happening with Ria! And I don't understand why you brought me to the hospital chapel. I need to know what is going on!"

"This is the family room," she said as she opened up the door and nodded her head for me to go in.

She waited for me to have a seat on what looked like a church pew; it had a red-covered cushion on the seat and a wooden back. Next to it was an end table with two bottles of water and a box of tissues. I was starting to feel very uneasy about being in the room.

The young lady sat down next to me. "Mr. Grayson, my name is Dublin," she started.

I suppose she had seen the look on many a person's face when she told them her name. She must have seen it on mine and felt she needed to explain.

"I know it's different. My mom and dad are both Irish by heritage and went back on vacation one year to locate some family members. They named me after the city in Ireland because they think they were in Dublin when my mom got pregnant. Different, right? I know."

"No, it's not! Ria would love that story. She is only a third-generation Irish American and was named after her great-grandmother who was born in Dublin, Ireland."

"Really? That's too cool."

"Yeah, I know," I answered back but had to know what was happening with Ria. "Please, no more waiting around. What's going on with Ria?!"

"Ever since the COVID pandemic, we have made it standard protocol to bring the primary family member in for us to discuss what could transpire when certain significant markers change or the patient has a respiratory or cardiac code. You probably heard the overhead intercom system announce the call for a Code 19 in Ria's room?"

"I did. Yes, I remember hearing that with all the madness going on. Somehow I do remember hearing that."

"All right then. We're here to let you know in private that they did call a Code 19 on your wife. This code is standard protocol and was called in this case because your wife—I'm sorry, Ria—has COVID-19 and had a cardiac event. This event was signaled and recognized by multiple reliable…" She was reading off all that she was supposed to say from a small card she had in her hand.

"Dublin, I know you're doing your job, and I am sure it must really be hard to do this so many times since the whole coronavirus thing started, but I'll sign whatever you need me to sign saying I understand, but please just tell me what has happened!" I leaned forward toward her and put my hand on her hand holding the card. "What do we know for certain at this point beside the fact that they called a cardiac code on Ria?"

Dublin looked at me dumbfounded on what to say next. "Usually the chaplain is here by now with more news or the primary ICU nurse is here to explain more details and answer your questions."

"All right then." I couldn't be mad at her. She didn't know and was only doing exactly what she was supposed to—following protocol. "No need to let those two waters go to waste. I'll have one. How about you?"

"That would be nice," she agreed. "I guess I can call the floor and see if someone is coming or maybe get more information, if you would like me to."

"Yes! I would. If you don't mind."

Dublin went across the small room and picked up a wall-mounted phone that went direct to the hospital operator. "This is Dublin, and I'm in the chapel, family room 2, with Mr. Grayson. His wife Ria is in room 525. They had called a Code 19. Could you patch me through to his nurse on the floor, please."

I watched and waited. Dublin looked a bit nervous and kept rocking slightly side to side, anxious for some news. Finally, someone on the floor picked up the phone and started to talk with her. I carefully tried to pick up on all her facial and body language changes. The call lingered longer than I anticipated it would, and I wasn't sure what to expect.

"Yes… No, that would be great. Okay, thank you," Dublin concluded the call.

When she hung the handset back in the wall unit, she turned to look at me and came over immediately. She looked as if she might cry before she started to speak.

"Listen, the chaplain is on his way down now."

My heart stopped, and I flopped back against the hard bench. This couldn't be good. Oh God! I took a deep breath and looked at Dublin. "Just tell me what they said!"

"Well, I'm supposed to wait on the chaplain. He will tell you everything."

"I know he will. And I know it's probably against hospital protocol, but for God's sake, Dublin, please tell me." I was ready to hear the worst. I reached over and touched her hand. "Dublin, please tell me!"

Nervously, she exhaled and squirmed on the cushion. "Not supposed to tell you, but Ria did have a cardiac event. It was rated as only mild. She made it through without complications and is stabilized now. They are even going to let you see her again today, even though it's...kind of...against protocol. The chaplain is on his way down now to tell you the news and take you back upstairs."

I began to cry and reached over and hugged Dublin around the neck. "Oh, thank you, Lord!" I hollered out as I cried on Dublin's shoulder.

About that same time, the chaplain came in. He had heard my holler outside the room. "Yes, thank you, Lord, for giving Mr. Grayson the faith to believe you would take care of Ria. Good news, all right! Yes, good news today," the chaplain said, joining in with my celebration as he shook my hand. "They said I could bring you back up to the room now that she is stabilized. Bet you would like that, huh?"

I looked at the chaplain and was grateful for the news and his offer, but I decided to refuse.

"If you don't mind, I would rather Dublin take me back up to the room. I feel I have discovered a kindred spirit for Ria, an Irish woman with as much spunk as her. Dublin, if you would do me the honors..." Taking her by the hand, I helped her up off the bench, and we made our way back to see Ria.

Now I don't consider myself to be a man of great faith. Even as a child, I had a hard time having faith in stressful situations and certain difficult circumstances. Maybe it was losing my dad at a young age that sent me down that road, I am not sure. My mom and grandma used to always tell me to have faith. My answer was that I would try. And then, they always gave me their answer back of "It only takes faith the size of a mustard seed to move a mountain, Connor."

Well, as you guessed, I never moved any mountains as a child, but if they were right (which I passionately believe they were), my faith may have grown to the size of that mustard seed that day when Ria came back from that code! And He had given me hope! Thus, both my prayer requests had been answered that day! I haven't and don't want to ever lose that newfound hope again! I don't want to ever become paralyzed by fear and uncertainty again. And the only way I see to prevent it is to become energized by faith and hope in *the* Lord!

What happened with Ria opened the door for us to be there for a lot of people who were affected by the COVID-19 pandemic of 20/21. It lit a fire for us to utilize all our little town's resources in ways that, well, only a pandemic could do! As I learned with dear Dublin, many infected in our town also discovered that the people who were the greatest blessing to them were oftentimes the people who themselves were unaware of having been a blessing. Just ordinary people doing what they thought they should do, not wanting or needing any recognition for their caring or acts of mercy and love to others. This virus awakened multitudes who now see and have a greater appreciation for the many blessings in their lives that they previously took for granted. What were once little things now take on a magnitude of meaning, not to ever be neglected again!

There were so many changes in all our lives during the pandemic. We each learned new and different ways to enjoy life and developed more genuine appreciation of the little things and blessings that we do have in our lives. There are people in our lives who have always been special, but without direct contact with them, each of us had to develop new means to survive and thrive in the new world of the COVID pandemic.

Ria and I were blessed with two new and incredibly special life-changing habits that our children helped establish for us. The first they called our Blessing Box. Although it originally wasn't a physical box of sorts, after only a short time, the blessings did end up in an actual box. Let me explain a little. When Ria was first admitted to the hospital and none of the children were allowed to visit her, our oldest, Cara, decided she had to do something to let her mom know how she felt. She realized it might be sometime before she could see her, so she created a box, an electronic mailbox.

Cara started writing notes to her mother each day describing one particular way her mother was a blessing to her or one specific way she had blessed her through something she did for her over the years. As the days turned into weeks, Cara kept writing to her mother and presented the idea to her sisters. Meghan and Alana were all about writing notes to their mom, and they dropped them daily in the electronic mailbox Cara had created.

Before long, the mailbox had over fifty notes from the girls. It was at that point that Cara, being the administrator/gatekeeper over the mailbox, decided to actually print all the notes. Each one she printed was hand folded and sealed with a small round red foil seal. They were then placed inside a large gray box with a lid and labeled "Ria's Blessing Box."

They didn't know it until later, but I snuck in a couple of notes I wrote to her in the box too. The first note I wrote said simply, "You are the greatest blessing God has given me." The rest are a little more personal, and I am thankful that when she got well enough to come home and finally read all her notes from the Blessing Box that she didn't share them with us, they were hers to cherish and have for all time.

What an awesome new habit and gift from the pandemic. We each have our own Blessing Boxes, and anyone in the family can send us a note for the box anytime they wish to share how we were a blessing to them in some way or fashion. The notes I have received touched me deeply because they pointed out things I had said or done that I had forgotten about or thought didn't really matter to them, but they did! The Blessing Box was truly a blessing!

The second pandemic habit they created was our Counting Walk. None of us could stand being cooped up in the house for too long, so it was inevitable that we go outside whenever possible. Well, if you are going to be outside, why not make the most of it? Meaning help yourself mentally and physically while you are outside. Not all of us (meaning Ria and I) are capable of running anymore, so the kids suggested we walk. It started out as just an occasional walk to clear our minds and get a bit of exercise to burn off all those calories from sitting around and eating.

What developed was a purpose-driven walk. Walk at whatever pace you can or will and count. At first, I thought the girls meant to count my steps like the app that can track such for you. But they didn't mean count your steps—they meant count your blessings! Reminded me of the song from church years ago, "Count Your Blessing." Name them one by one. And that is exactly what we decided to do.

By walking, we were getting exercise and allowing our body to produce endorphins, our bodies' natural chemical antidepressant. Additionally, by concentrating on our blessing for that day or the day before or whenever, we are pouring good thoughts into our brain and pushing out all the negatives from the news and complaining people. The end result is a physical, mental, and chemical improved you, simply by doing a Counting Walk.

I loved these two new pandemic life-changing habits. And Ria and I plan to continue on with them for as long as we can. Something good did come out of something bad, and it always can if we intentionally look for the good or find new ways of creating the good in all our situations. Guess they call that faith, believing and trusting that God is in charge and will create good out of any situation, if we let Him.

Yes, none of us totally escaped the COVID-19 pandemic. While the vast majority of us were not infected, life did change that year and the old norm may never fully be again. But when all this did subside, we realized, without any doubt, that God had been working in

His world and in our lives! If we open our eyes, we will see that there will always be a need for faith, hope, love, and caring. Through faith, we can experience joy despite our circumstances, and with hope, we can break the chains of fear, no matter what lies ahead of us. Love can help soothe our sorrows, heal our wounds, and caring can give us comfort, restore peace, and provide reasons to shout out for joy, just as I did that day for Ria!

Until now you have not asked for anything in my name. Ask and you will receive, and your joy will be complete.
—John 16:24

CHAPTER 14

Football and the South

I don't know what will happen to me, but
I believe what I'm doing will
make the world a better place.
—excerpt from letter my father, Robert Benter Greer Jr.,
wrote to my mom during WWII

Believe it or not (whenever I say that, it reminds me of the Ripley's television show that aired back in the seventies—aging myself again, huh?), the drugstore has been able to play roles in the lives of those in our community in ways nonrelated to medications or health care. The following story might surprise you?!

I heard it said once in conversation that Southern women know their religions—Baptist, Presbyterian, Methodist, and football! Those of you who are not from the South may not understand the humor of this statement and therefore not hold football in such high reverence as Southerners oftentimes do! Thus, for those of you I ask that you simply bear along and enjoy. Maybe try to pretend it's whatever sport you may love or hold dear—basketball, baseball, soccer, hockey, tennis, etc. Or just put yourself in the shoes of the young people you are about to read of.

Like so many small towns scattered across America, Utopia Springs has only one high school. That said, it only makes sense that Utopia Springs High School pulls in young people from five or six tiny towns in the surrounding area. So when it comes time for football tryouts, fine young men emerge from these proud little map-dot towns and make their way to the practice field of the high school. Each one of these young people come, bringing with them high hopes and big dreams of not only making the team but playing on a winning district championship team. Everyone likes to brag a bit about their local teams so... Utopia Springs High School won the district championship in football (once)... Oh, twenty years or so ago! Doesn't mean our community isn't proud of our team, because we are!

We talked about timing earlier, and I guess you could say the timing was right for our high school football coach to step down and watch from the comforts of the stands. Fifteen years certainly qualifies a coach for a well-needed break. In the void left behind, the search began for a new coach. It was a slow, drawn-out process, but the school administration finally found a replacement willing to come to our small school.

The high school boosters and local parents of wannabe players welcomed the new football coach with open arms. Plans were quickly being made for a summer weight program, spring drills, and the all-important game schedule. Anxiously, everyone waited for the day of contact practices with full pads. Of course, it wouldn't arrive until several weeks before the first game, but the countdown was on! Steady and surely, everything was going just as expected until the economy took a decidedly drastic downturn (despite the president's economic stimulus package). Local school board officials reacted as best they could, but cuts, layoffs, and even elimination of some junior varsity sports followed! No one was happy, but the cold hard fact was that there simply wasn't enough money to go around, so sports got cut.

The situation was sad. And making matters worse, the Utopia Springs High School football team felt the financial crunch long before the academic school year began! Being the small town we are, word filtered down quickly, and the team learned the worst only days before their scheduled departure for football camp. Camp was an out-of-town, extensive get-in-shape program, which had been a tra-

167

dition for the football program for more than twenty years. But just like that, it was no longer on the budget! And of course, no money from the school board meant there would be no camp.

It was a terrible blow to the players! All summer long, they had looked forward to getting away and having time to find themselves, hone their skills and not have Mom, Dad, Uncle Charlie, and the boosters breathing down their necks! To make matters even worse, new equipment orders were placed on hold by the school board for at least a year, and new team jerseys could only be purchased to replace torn and tattered ones. Pants were to be recycled from the last two season's uniforms. Torn, tattered, faded, it didn't matter.

The coaches frantically scrambled to make do with the equipment and supplies while desperately struggling to keep the boys' morale up. Due to the ever-increasing severity of practices needed to compensate for the loss of camp, it was almost a no-win situation for both players and coaches. All those of us in town could hope for was that the boys would funnel their anger and frustration outward on the playing field toward the teams they played and not kill each other during practice.

Lots of ideas were tossed around on possible solutions and morale builders for the boys on the team. Local business owners were the first to come to the rescue, raising money for new cleats and jerseys. Then it was the boosters chipping in for shoulder pads to replace irreparable ones from the last season. The athletic boosters also gave money to the team to replace helmets unable to pass safety inspection. All these were essential items they needed, but despite all this, morale remained at an all-time low.

So next, local restaurant owners started doing Friday night team dinners for the players and promised to continue doing the same all through football season. The boys now had new team jerseys and full stomachs, but morale remained dead on the ground.

One day, at the drugstore, an idea emerged...

"Doc, are you ready for football season?" an old-timer and patient named Henry asked.

"You better believe it!"

"I'm thinking the boys should have a good team this year. What do you think?"

"Well…" I had reservations. "I know they've got talent! They've practiced hard and have a lot of heart, but they seem to be running on empty emotionally. Whenever I can break away early, I go down and watch them practice. Play-running wise, everything looks as it should. But when they start to head off the field, that's when I notice it. Can't put my finger on it exactly… Seems like it's no fun, drudgery to 'em. No fun at all. Just going through the motions, that's all!" Maybe I shouldn't have said it out loud, but that was the way it looked to me.

"Fun? What are you talking 'bout? Boy, playing football isn't supposed to be fun! You get out there and kick some ass. That's the fun! Move that ball down the field and score… Now that's even more fun, right! Hunker down and stop the opposition with your defense, create turnovers—that'll get your motor going!" Henry explained how the sport was to be played.

"You sound like one of their coaches! Sure, everything you said gets your blood going and gives you that adrenaline rush, but it doesn't carry over. It doesn't keep you loving it. I think you have to love it to give it your all, your absolute best!"

"Doc, we aren't talking some girly, warm, and fuzzy feeling game here. We're talking football! Put your shoulder pads on, strap on your helmet, pull up your jockstrap, and go hit 'em where it hurts!"

"Yeah, yeah, yeah… I know! But in order for those guys to give it 110 percent, they need to really love it. Not just the hitting and winning, but love the game! You know, love the smell of the grass field, love those spotlights shining down on Friday night, love the sweaty locker room, love the people in the town who come out—win or lose, love it when they say 'Good game' or 'We're proud of you,' and love it even when nobody wants to talk to you because you blew it on a big play. I don't think they love it that way. Those boys end every practice looking like their butts are dragging, as if they don't love the game. Just going through the motions day in and day out?"

"Huh, I hadn't really noticed. Hadn't looked at 'em or given it much thought."

"I know. It sounds weird! But they don't seem to love it. And they sure as heck don't seem to be having any fun, kicking' butt or not!"

"So what can we do, Doc?" Henry asked, perplexed.

"Something that'll be fun for the boys, that's what we need to do! Not laugh—haha—funny, but rather something more on the line of this-is-cool-type fun. A bring 'em together and have a good time type thing."

"And what the heck is that?"

"Well, since they seem most down at the end of practice, something at the conclusion of practice would likely be best."

"Yeah, like what?"

"Not sure. But I do remember one year, way back in high school, when Coach Pugh at the end one of our god-awful killer practices in full pads told everyone on the team to run to the far end of the field. So we did. When we got there, we all stopped and stared at this mound of something covered with brown army-style tarp. Nobody knew what it was! We didn't know what was under it, but everybody started throwing out guesses. Coach and all the assistants let us go on and on for several minutes before he told us to shut up and take a knee. We did as he said and then, out of nowhere, he went into this serious speech about how we were screwing up and not giving it 100 percent! He even said we were worse than a bunch of girls!"

"You think that would help 'em? That'd make it more fun? Beating 'em down at the end of practice?" Henry looked at me with a scowl on his face.

"No, I don't! Let me finish," I told him, and then I continued. "He was yelling, kicking at the ground. Next thing we know, all the other coaches have moved in and are standing behind him, all stern faced with their arms crossed and nodding their heads as if in full agreement with what he was saying. I thought we must have been crap in practice and hung my head down, like most everyone else. Then he suddenly stopped. Nobody said anything, and nobody dared to move. After a moment or two of silence, everybody looked up and locked their eyes on coach. 'Now that I've got your attention,' he said. As he started again, behind him, the assistant coaches moved over to the edges of the tarp. We all watched them, waiting anxiously for what was next."

"All right, I'm listening. So what'd they do?"

"Coach turned his back to us for a moment. I was thinking to myself, here it comes! He's going to really let us have it. But instead of speaking when he turned around, he moved over next to the other coaches and the tarp."

"Yeah, what happened then?"

"Slowly he reached down, grabbed the tarp firmly with one hand, and then simultaneously he and the other coaches threw back the tarp. And that's when all heck broke loose! It was a free-for-all!"

"What do you mean? What happened? What was under the tarp? What was it?"

"Before we could even get a good look at what the mound was, each of the coaches had reached down, scooped up handfuls, and were bombarding us with *ice*! I grabbed my helmet and pulled it on. But not before I got smacked right in the face with a handful of ice! Then another and then more! It just kept coming!"

"Wow!" Henry was laughing already. "For real? They had hidden ice under the tarp. And they were hurling it at you all. I can't believe it! Never in all my days have I heard of such as that!"

"Man, the coaches were flinging it at us with both hands, as fast as they could! My shoulder pads, helmet, and facemask seemed to be getting zinged right and left, nonstop. Man, they nailed us good!"

"Nobody did anything? You just sat there and took it? What was the matter with y'all?" Henry stood up out of his chair in disbelief that we hadn't done anything.

"Not for long. We didn't let them keep at us! The seniors and captains were the first to retaliate. I'll never forget this one guy on our team—Rocky—a big six-foot-six lineman and senior who wasn't about to let 'em get the better of him! He dove headfirst toward the ice, landing only a foot or so shy of the pile and grabbed as much as he could. Then he nailed Coach Pugh right in the face! It was like the green light went off for us. From that point on, it was a crazy free-for-all, ice and bodies flying everywhere!"

"That's wild," Henry said, laughing and visualizing in his mind what the mayhem must have looked like. "Bet it didn't take long before everybody was into it and the ice was gone. I bet it lasted a while though. Probably a big mess too!"

"It would have lasted a long longer had it not been for what was under the pile of ice! There was another tarp under the ice covering something."

"Under it? There was something more? Under the ice?" Henry questioned.

"Watermelons!"

"What? No way! Are you serious, Doc? Watermelons?!"

"The biggest pile of watermelons I have ever seen! Or at least back then it seemed like it! You know how they have them in the big cardboard boxes at Winn-Dixie every year 'round Fourth of July?"

"Oh yeah... They usually have two or three huge crates of them."

"Well, this was at least as big a pile as two or more of those crates full. And cold... Man, they were ice-cold! And good! They were that long kind of striped-looking ones..."

"Charleston grays... They're called Charleston grays, boy! My grandfather used to grow 'em in his garden every spring. I loved those watermelons. They're the best!"

"I tell you what... They were great! Ice-cold, juicy, and a mess! By the time they doweled them out to everybody, we each started with a quarter of a melon and then could get more if we wanted. There was ice, seeds, and juice all over us! No telling how many seeds I spit out at some of my buddies that day. We were a total mess but happy as pigs in slop! Henry, now that was a practice to remember. When I think about it, those still rate as the best watermelon I've ever had in my life. I think I ate two...maybe three quarters before I felt like I'd be sick. But it was a great kind of sick. We had a blast that day!"

"I bet! Doc, that sound like so much fun! No telling how many watermelons a whole team could go through after a hot full-pads practice. Must have been a bunch, all right, a bunch!"

"I think Coach told us we devoured thirty watermelons that afternoon! By the time it was all said and done, there wasn't a single melon left! Or any ice for that matter!"

"No way!"

"Yes way! We ate every single one of those watermelons!"

"And that whole thing with the ice... Man, that sounds like tons of fun!"

"It was unbelievable! The great thing about it though was that I think it was our team's turning point! Not that we hadn't been practicing hard or that we didn't get along with each other, we were missing something before that day. Nothing you could really put your finger on, but something was lacking. After that day, we knew we could work hard, play hard, and even laugh at each other! Things were never the same. They were way better! We didn't go on to be undefeated and win the state championship or anything like that, but we had one heck of a good season. And such fun. I think everybody on that team that was a senior felt it was the best year we ever had together—both on and off the field!"

"So you're thinking the team this year needs a turning point, huh?" Henry asked, taking his cap off and scratching his head. "They need something to bring 'em all together as a team and something fun, huh?"

"Right! I mean, I love those guys, but they've got a lot of little things gnawing away at them on the edges with this recession and how it's affecting the town and the families. They need to firm up as a team. See that they are one unit—good, bad, ugly...whatever! You know what I mean?"

"I do! What'd you have in mind?"

"No need to recreate the wheel! Why not do the same thing for them. I mean, it worked twenty years ago. Why not do a repeat. I think it would work!"

"Don't see any reason why not. Sure, couldn't hurt. The kids would love it. You know they would!" Henry was all smiles just thinking about it.

With a big smile, I nodded in agreement.

"How 'bout the coaches though? Think they'd buy in on this idea or squash it and tell us to mind our own business?"

"I'm good friends with one of the assistants, Coach Gibson. You know who I'm talking about? He used to be head coach at Orange

High School years ago, and he comes to the drugstore. He's helping with the lineman this year. I think he'll buy in on the idea and will help us sell the idea to the other coaches. They respect him, not only for his age, but also for his years in the game. He played with Joe Paterno—you know, Penn State's legendary coach—back years ago and coached in California before moving over to Florida. Great football mind! He can get them to agree to it if anybody can!"

"Then I say, let's go for it!" Henry was on board with the plan. "Talk to him and set it up. I'll help if you want."

"That'd be great! See if you can talk to some of the local guys that farm outside of town and try to find out if they can get us twenty or thirty watermelons for one day after practice."

"Any idea how quick you can make it happen?" Henry needed to know how quick he had to find all the watermelons and get them donated for our cause.

"I'll call Coach Gibson at home tonight and find out what's a good date. Call me tomorrow, and we'll go from there."

"Sounds like a plan! I really think it's a great idea, and the kids will love it! We should call the boosters, if we can make it happen, and get them to set up the ice and help with cutting the watermelons and serving the players."

"That's a great idea! They'll love being a part of this! How 'bout you call the boosters president?"

"No problem. I'll call him!" Henry agreed.

"Okay. Give me a holler tomorrow."

"Will do! We'll make it happen. You bet we will, Doc! This is going to be better than kicking ass on the field!" Henry was fired up.

It was a Thursday, first day of practice with full pads, August 12. High noon, in the heat of summer, we treated the boys of the Utopia Springs High School football team—all sixty-four players, varsity, and junior varsity—to an ice fight and cold watermelons! To quote one of the players, "It was the coolest practice ever! I loved pilling a mound of ice on top of coach! It was way better than the time I dumped a bucket of Gatorade on his head after a district win!"

Word got around town even more that we were trying to help the kids out and boost morale. Suddenly everybody was wearing the school colors of blue and silver. Cars, storefront windows, even the church glass entrance doors were proudly displaying "Go, Eagle!" decals. Parents, friends, business owners all worked to do something special for the players in the weeks before the season started. There was a cowboy hoedown/barbeque on Friday night, an ice cream (scoop your poison) social after a Sunday morning church service, and a hot dog/hamburger grill-a-thon at the city pool one Saturday. If rumor holds true, the grill-a-thon lasted from ten in the morning until past ten at night! There was a dance-your-socks-off/DJ dance party at the gym and more hometown fun than you can shake a stick at!

No matter what the season record of wins and losses was, the boys, the school, and the town were all winners! The tanked economy had done just the reverse of what most people expected. Instead of bringing our little town down, it brought everybody up—that is, up to a brand-new level of caring and a never seen before sense of community. I loved those months surrounding football that year; they were some of the best ever! People stopped and talked with each other. There were more smiles than I'd seen in years. and the overall atmosphere in the town was one of hope and caring. Even if I wrote ten pages more, nothing I could put into words would explain how we all felt!

For all you diehard football fans, it wouldn't be a good football story if I didn't include a quote by a football legend, right? How about this one:

After all the cheers have died down and the stadium is empty, after the headlines have been written, and after you are back in the quiet of your room and the championship ring has been placed on the dresser and after all the pomp and fanfare have faded, the enduring thing that is left is the dedication to doing with our lives the very best we can to make the world a better place in which to live.

Vince Lombardi

And that is exactly what the good people of Utopia Springs did—made the world a much better place not only for these young men, but for everyone in town as well! They replaced all the negatives beating down on those boys into positives. They turned the fear of the economy and viruses into an opportunity to get behind and help the young men of their town trying to play the game of football… and even threw in a few life lessons along with it. The people in our town made our small piece of the world a much better and brighter place to be!

I don't think anyone will soon forget those fun days of football! I know I will always associate football, watermelons, and ice fights with the true meaning of teamwork, community, and caring. And so it is with football and the South.

Therefore, encourage one another and build each other up, just as in fact you are doing.
—1 Thessalonians 5:11

CHAPTER 15

I Still Feel the Pulse

*Deep within many a forgotten life is a scrap of
hope, a lonely melody trying hard to return.*
—Chuck Swindoll

This is Kuhl Avenue, I just know it is! So the Ronald McDonald House has to be up ahead, I kept telling myself.

"You've got the address, don't you? You do know there's not one, but two Ronald McDonald Houses within a few blocks of the hospital, right? It is the correct one, isn't it?" Ria wanted to be certain.

It was the third time since we parked the car, blocks away in the only public lot we could find with open spaces, that Ria had questioned if we were going to the right one. The one on Kuhl Avenue where her sister-in-law, Kathryn, was staying. And what does that make it now? Let's see, today is Monday June 13…so for over a month now Kathryn has called the Ronald McDonald House home. And her mom had remained across the street, fighting for her life, in the cardiac intensive care unit at Orlando Regional Medical Center (ORMC) during her entire stay.

"All these people… Where did they come from? I've never seen so many people in this part of town! Does Orlando City have a soccer game today or is some other event going on?" Ria was really getting antsy and starting to question me about everything as we continued to walk down the crowded sidewalk and looked for the address.

As much as I hated to use Google Maps, Ria had me anxious enough about if we were going the right way that I gave in. Hurriedly I was putting the address in and waiting for a response as we continued to walk. With my head locked down, looking at my phone, I was momentarily oblivious to our surroundings.

"Connor!" Ria hollered out, as she threw her arm in front of my chest and pushed with her hand back against it to make me stop.

"What?" I immediately questioned her as my head popped up. I froze in my tracks as my eyes went into overdrive trying to convey to my mind what in the world all this craziness was happening around us.

Both Ria and I stood motionless as we attempted to take in and understand the people, the crying, the sirens, and the media. The visual and auditory convolution was totally overwhelming!

"What has happened?" a voice said.

We turned to look and listen as a young distraught woman questioned a man hurrying past.

"I don't know! And who cares?" he flippantly replied back to her.

Out of the corner of my eye, I watched as another woman who had heard his answer stepped directly in front of his path.

"What kind of jerk are you, buddy?" she confronted him angrily and moved in closer to his face. "I'll tell you who cares! The families of everybody who got shot down at the Pulse this morning—they care! And so do all the friends and neighbors of theirs—they care! Probably so do a lot of people who live around here and go to the club, all right—they care!"

"What? I didn't know anybody was killed. I walk this way every morning and just thought it was a...a disturbance of some type... Never dreamed somebody was killed," he replied back, looking a little shocked at the news. He then looked at her and said, "Hey, listen, I'm sorry for sounding a jerk. You're right. They are human beings, just like you and I, and it was wrong that somebody shot and killed them. Again I'm sorry."

She took a deep breath, stepped back slightly, and then sighed as she turned away to leave. "Whatever," she mumbled under her breath, then held her hand up, and walked off.

"Yeah, right, lady!" the man spoke back at her as he walked off.

Ria looked over at me and then at the street corner and spied the sign. "Connor, we're on South Orange Avenue, the block behind Kuhl! I asked you more than once if we were going the right way?" Ria glared at me, frustrated.

"Okay, so I turned down one block too soon when we were walking, sorry! It is too late now. We will just have to cut through at the intersection and go back down a block!"

"Were any of you here when the shootings began?" An Orlando police officer, dressed in his midnight-blue uniform, was walking down the sidewalk asking everyone nearby. "Excuse me!" He raised his voice over the noise and commotion. "Anyone here before or when the shootings began? If so, we need to talk with you!"

We were still standing in the same spot, and it seemed we were the only ones frozen in place amidst the near pandemonium of the moment. Suddenly, the sound of a screaming young woman nearly pierced my eardrum as she pushed her way past me, rushing over to the officer.

"My brother! Where is Emmanuel? I need to find him... Please! Help me, please!" she screamed and began sobbing as she fell against the police officer and to the ground next to his feet.

Tenderly he knelt down on his knees. Then, lifting her head up gently, he brushed her hair back from her face and reassured her, "I'll take you and see what we can find out about him." He then wrapped his arms around her and lifted her up off the ground. As she pushed her face down against his chest, he held her, allowing her a moment to cry.

"Please tell me his name again," he asked, as he continued to hold her.

"Emmanuel. My brother's name is Emmanuel Vasquez," she said, and she started to cry harder as his name lovingly sounded off her lips.

Then the officer, in a comforting voice, tried to reassure her, "Let's go see if we can't find Emmanuel for you, we'll check near the club first and then over at ORMC." He continued to keep one arm around her as they walked back in the direction of the Pulse Club.

Ria grabbed my arm and started pulling me in the direction of the young girl with the police officer. I could tell she was a woman on a mission, and I stood next to her as we reached and touched the officer on his shoulder. He stopped, turned around, and looked at us both.

Before he could even speak, Ria was already starting to ask him a question. "Do you mind if we pray with her for Emmanuel?"

The young girl turned and looked at Ria. "Do you know Emmanuel? Have you seen him today?"

"No, we don't know him. But if it's all right with you, we would just like to take a minute and pray with you for your brother, Emmanuel."

Before answering, she moved her hand up to her neck and reached to grab the chain she was wearing. As she pulled it out from under her shirt, she slid her fingers down the chain and began to clutch the sliver cross it was holding.

"Emmanuel gave me this!" she told us proudly. Then reaching for Ria's hand, she nodded and answered, "Please, let's pray for him."

We made a makeshift circle, held hands, and bowed our heads. But before Ria started to pray, she asked, "I'd like to pray for you too. Tell me your name."

"Alexandria… Emmanuel called me his little Alex." She was barely able to get the words out before she started to cry.

"Let's turn this over to the Lord," Ria told us. As we bowed our heads again, she started to pray. "Heavenly Father, we ask that you take Alex in your loving arms right now and give her comfort and peace in knowing that you will be with her as she begins looking for her brother Emmanuel. Dear Lord," Ria continued on, lifting up Emmanuel, the first responders, the families of those who had lost their lives in the shooting, and the extended circle of friends and loved ones this tragedy had and would touch. After several minutes of fervent prayer, she concluded, "We ask all these things in the name of Jesus Christ. Amen."

Alex immediately went to Ria, and they hugged each other tightly, and both began to cry.

"Thank you! Thank you!" Alex kept repeating over and over to Ria.

The police officer also thanked her. "Really appreciate you doing that." He looked at her and nodded his head at her. Then he gently placed his arm around Alex again, and they started walking away.

As I looked around, there were now small groups joining together as one, on their knees praying. Up and down the street on both sides, we could see strangers, neighbors, friends, all uniting in prayer for a common cry in this uncertain time. I am 100 percent certain the Lord heard all those prayers that day and many, many more in the long days and weeks that would follow this unprecedented tragedy.

When we finally made it to the right Ronald McDonald House, we found Kathryn sitting and crying with others in the television lounge room. They were glued to the horrific news that was being streamed live only blocks away. She didn't see us as we entered the room. Ria walked up behind her, without speaking, and wrapped her arms lovingly around her shoulders. Kathryn turned, and the tears from both of them overflowed as they held each other tight. Finally, Kathryn got up, and we left the room.

At my suggestion, we made our way outside onto a small enclosed patio overlooking a lake. Behind the lake was the emergency entrance to ORMC. Unbeknownst to us at the time, being only two blocks away from Pulse, ORMC had been designated as the main emergency response destination for the victims and numerous survivors still struggling for their life.

The sight at the entrance to the Emergency Room was indescribable! From our safe vantage point, we could see the makeshift police barricades holding back the crowds of friends and family—all fearing the worst and desperately waiting for news. The sound of the crying and whaling sent chills up and down my spine.

"Maybe this wasn't such a good idea," I conceded to Ria and Kathryn. We all agreed and instead decided to go up to Kathryn's small bedroom. Upon reentering the building, we heard the tail end of the Ronald McDonald House caretaker's speech notifying everyone that there was a ten-city block lockdown for the next forty-eight hours. We were smackdab in the middle of the lockdown so we might as well make ourselves comfortable. We were now stuck there with Kathryn and all the others at the house!

As we settled into the cramped bedroom, none of us spoke a word. Maybe it was shock, I'm not certain. But I did know that the fear and uncertainty of it all had engulfed every fiber of my own being. Before sitting down, I reached for my phone in the back pocket of my jeans. I was shocked when I saw the screen blown up with over thirty messages from Alana.

"Oh my god!" I exclaimed as I began reading some of the messages.

"What is it? What's the matter? Is everyone all right? Connor, answer me!" Ria asked, almost hysterical thinking something might have happened to someone we knew.

"Give me a minute," I said as I motioned with my hand.

"No, Connor! You tell me now!"

Kathryn had moved over and was now sitting on the edge of the bed next to Ria. She put her arm around her, in anticipation of the worst.

"It's Alana…" I started to try and explain, but Ria couldn't wait.

"Oh my lord." Ria looked at me as if she was going to totally breakdown. She jumped off the bed and came over and grabbed my phone out of my hand.

"She's all right!" I tried to reassure her.

"Then why didn't you say so!"

"You didn't give me a chance!" I shot back at her.

Handing me back my phone, she questioned, "Then what happened to her?"

"Nothing has happened to her!" I stopped and looked at Ria and Kathryn to make sure they heard me. Then continued on to explain, "It's Louis, you know, the sous-chef from the restaurant she works at? He owns the tiny garage apartment Alana rents near Lake Eola. He..."

"Then why the 'oh my god' earlier?"

"Alana got a text from his boyfriend, Oscar, saying that he was shot and is at ORMC in critical condition! She'll text us later when she hears more, but she's safe and fine!"

"Oh my god!" Ria blurted out.

"Right! That's what I said."

"That's terrible! What can we do? There has to be something we can do?"

The room went strangely silent for minute. I didn't know what Ria was thinking, but I felt a tug at my heart to do something... anything to help.

It was Kathryn who broke the silence.

"Do what you two always do. Stop sitting there looking like knots on a log. What is it you and the drugstore do all the time? Help people!" Kathryn lectured to us and held up both her arms in the air for emphasis to her point. "Right?!"

Yes, she was right!

There, in the small bedroom confines of the Ronald McDonald House in Orlando, for the next twelve hours, Ria, Kathryn, and I made call after call and started to mobilize help. As word began to get out to the general public about the tragedy at Pulse, the number of volunteers from Utopia Springs kept getting bigger and bigger.

My friend Jimmy had a large delivery van they were trying to sell at one of his families used car lots, and it was immediately commandeered and converted into a mobile operation and supply transport vehicle. Our little community loaded it with all sorts of things for the friends and families waiting and mourning at the memorial that had been created around the lake next to ORMC. We were able to deliver almost daily for ten days—water, snacks, blankets, personal hygiene items, over-the-counter items, and much, much more.

The darndest thing. I shouldn't say that because everything happens for a reason. But one day, one of our volunteers placed an old clipboard on a hook beside the back door of the delivery vehicle, next to where we handed out free items to anyone asking for them.

At the top of the page, on the cover sheet of the clipboard, she wrote in big, bold letters—PRAYER LIST. No explanation was given, and there were no nice, neat lines or blanks to fill in. What we had at the end of the first day—and every day thereafter—were page after page of detailed heartfelt prayer requests and concerns. Oftentimes the individual was needing to share and gave in depth details of their friend or loved one and had specific prayers they wanted us to lift up to the Lord.

One day as I was walking back from seeing Kathryn's mom at ORMC, I decided to head over and help out. As I made my way around the lake to the side where we had set-up, I heard a couple go by, and they said they had been to the "prayer van" and gotten a few things they needed. One of them said the volunteers were "some of the nicest people I have ever meet since we left Ohio" and came down. I stopped, looked across the lake at all the flowers on the memorial, and whispered aloud, "Thank you, Lord, for allowing us to be here to help!"

During the weeks and months after the shootings, more information came to light, and details were given to the public. Pulse was the deadliest incident in the history of violence against LGBT people in the United States. It also was the deadliest terrorist attack since 9/11. Sadly, at the time, it was the deadliest mass shooting in history!

At the end of the three-hour standoff, between 2:00 a.m. and 5:00 a.m., at Pulse, there were forty-nine killed and fifty-three wounded—most seriously. More than a third of the victims were shot in the head, and most had multiple bullet wounds. Records show that there were over two hundred gunshot wounds inflicted upon our fellow human beings by one lone shooter!

Alana's friend and teacher Louis Colon was one of the dear individuals that lost his life at the club that night. He was shot three times by bullets fired from a SIG Sauer MCX semi-automatic rifle. One of the shots was to his head.

Thanks to the unending perseverance that day of an Orlando police officer, Alex found her brother, Emmanuel Vasquez, in the recovery room at ORMC following surgery to correct an abdominal gunshot that required removal of a portion of his small intestine. He continued to recover nicely and was released twelve days after the shooting on June 25 in the afternoon. Alex drove him home to their parent's house in Miami.

Kathryn's mother, Lynn, remained in ORMC for almost four months after a life-threatening aortic perforation bleed following an open-heart surgery. She was in an induced coma at the time of the shooting and didn't learn of what had happened until months later. She cried for half the day. When she got her strength back, she visited the hospital and personally thanked all the cardiac intensive care staff for saving her life.

I knew my heart was alive during this terrible time because the pain all the deaths caused made me feel as if it was being torn apart! I had prayed the Lord would open the eyes of my heart to the needs of others—all others—and He did! But it shouldn't have to take a tragedy such as Pulse to open our eyes to those around us hurting and in need of hope. My eyes are now wide open, and I still feel the Pulse!

Keep on loving one another as brothers and sisters. Do not forget to show hospitality to strangers, for by so doing some people have shown hospitality to angels without knowing it.
—Hebrews 13:1–2

CHAPTER 16

Contraband Letters and the Power of One

*To the world you may be just one person, but
to that person you may be the world.*

—Candis Goodwin

As we turn away from one "thing" in our daily busyness, it seems we are always turning smack dab back into another wanting our time and attention. Sometimes we believe that other "thing" vying for our attention isn't worth our taking the time to stop right then and there for it, but other times, it is worth stopping for. Sadly though, too often we pretend we can just ignore this "thing" right in front of us. Forget about the issues beating right at our heals or the ones sitting directly in front of us. So we run from this to that, ignoring the "thing" that is right there. Somehow, we have developed this miraculous ability to deflect these "things" or focus intently toward someone or something else to not see it. Or we simply sidestep them and pray to God someone else will see this "thing" and deal with it, talk to it, or correct it before we have to raise so much as a finger in the process! Thus, if we choose not to stop, chances are we might miss it all together. And oh what we might miss!

But there had been no time for stops or breaks for me so far today. The first of the month when coupled with a Monday always means fast-paced, slammed days at the drugstore. One hundred fifty prescriptions filled so far, eighty-five in the electronic work queue waiting for processing, just under twenty doctor messages needing to be transcribed, faxes sitting in the fax machine...and it isn't even one o'clock! Lunch seems extremely doubtful for any of us as we were down one technician who was home, out sick today. Days like this I really feel my age!

For sanity's sake, I felt it necessary to remove myself from the craziness for just a minute or two. I stopped, took a step back, and moved away from checking the prescription on the counter in front of me. Closing my eyes, I inhaled a slow deep breath, then exhaled, and rubbed the palm of my hand across my forehead. For a brief moment, I just stood still in place and kept my eyes shut.

It felt really nice not to be pressured to take a call, look at the number of prescriptions in the queue, answer a question from a patient, check a waiter prescription, help the drive-through, or any number of other daily workflow tasks that were never-ending...even if it was only temporary. Take it in and enjoy it, I repeated to myself.

With eyes still closed, my ears homed in on the music overhead coming from the piped in station. Rarely did I ever hear it during the busyness of the day; it was there more for the enjoyment of the customers looking around in the store or waiting for their prescription to be filled. I recognized the song playing overhead as "New Day" by Danny Gokey. Listening, I began humming along. And as the rhythm of the song and the thought-provoking lyrics bellowed out, I was beginning to feel a layer of the stress slowly peeling off me. A new day...bursting with hope—absolutely ready for that! Music had always been an escape for me, helping me settle down, putting life more into perspective of priorities and realities, or sometimes just helping me to forget and enjoy the moment. Leaning back against the wall behind me, I listened through the end of the song.

It's generally about this time of day that the technicians working in the back of the drugstore describe us... What was it they called it? Yes, *hangry*, that was it! Explained to me by them as a combo-word encompassing hungry, tired, and angry. Guess lack of nourishment and nonstop busyness can bring it on. They probably were right, and maybe it was time for a real break, not simply a momentary step away from it break.

It was time to grab a pack of Lance nabs, open a cold Pepsi, and take a stroll around the store for a little change of scenery that would hopefully provide me with an attitude reset. Looking around, I wasn't the only one struggling, trying to keep their head above water. Whether they took a break or not, I still felt I needed one, and that's exactly what I intended to do!

Then out of the corner of my eye, I saw her rocking back and forth next to the checkerboard table in the patient waiting area. I turned toward Deena, and it was as if I couldn't help myself, and I went back full steam into work mode again. Impatiently I began to interrogate Deena as to if the lady had been helped. Was she waiting on a prescription, or what?

"Yes and no," Deena replied curtly to my questioning.

"What?"

"Yes, she has been helped, several times, in fact! And no, she is not waiting on a prescription!"

"How about simple plain English this time? What does that mean?" I think we both were getting hangry, and it was starting to show in the way we were talking at each other.

With a little edge of attitude, Deena answered back, "It means, 'in plain English,' that I asked her could I help, and she explained to me that she wanted to look at our cards—the thank-you ones, I think. Which she actually did for a while until she came up to the counter. I went over and asked her again if I could help her or did she want to check out, but she replied no. Then she questioned if we sold postage stamps for the cards. After explaining to her that we didn't, she thanked me, turned around, and went to sit in that rocker." Deena stopped and pointed over at where she was sitting. "She's been right there ever since!"

"Well, all right then... Thanks." Clearly, we both needed a break. It was up to her. She could take one if she wanted but I fully intended to take one—now!

I turned away from Deena and toward the woman in the rocker. Starting toward her, I recognized her face when she turned her head to the side. It was one of our patients, Lois Sullivan. She was a sweet older lady who had been coming to the drugstore for many years. Pushing the swinging door open next to the consultation booth, I started her way. I made an executive decision to take my break talking with Mrs. Sullivan! And that was that!

"Lois," I began as I approached the rockers, "it's so good to see you! Don't see you much these days. I just wanted to come over and say hello and see how you have been."

Sitting in the farther of the two rockers located on either side of the checkerboard table in the waiting area, she looked up and smiled as she saw me coming over toward her.

"Doc," she said. Lois's voice was pleasant sounding, sweet, and calm. "It is so nice to see you too! I don't drive any longer since Robert passed; so not much opportunity to visit these days. But I'm doing very well, thank you for asking. At least as well as a ninety-year-old could expect!"

"Ninety? I can't believe you are already ninety! You look amazing!" And she really did look great. She had beautiful white hair, wavy and stylishly cut in a cute, short bob. Her skin complexion looked soft, and she looked healthy and happy with rosy cheeks. But it was her smile that always made her face seem aglow with joy.

"I celebrated my ninetieth with two of my children, six grandchildren, and two great-grandchildren! The Lord has blessed me so to have them all, and it was a grand time being with them! Another perfect memory to add to the ninety years of wonderful memories I already have."

"That's remarkable!" I felt so happy for her. Then I asked out of curiosity, "What is it you're working on so diligently there?" I motioned to the pen, notepad, and card she had precariously balanced in her lap.

She looked down quickly, then back up at me as she explained, "I was able to get a ride this morning to come in and pick up a thank-you card. You always have such a nice selection with your Sunrise series of cards! Seeing as how my ride hasn't come back yet, I decided to write a short note to put in the card, letting him know how much I appreciate all he did for me and all he does for the community!"

Lois pulled the card out from under the notepad which she had been writing the note on and showed it to me.

"Very nice! Whoever it is you are writing, I know they will be glad to get such a nice card, and the handwritten note will really impress them! I know it sure would me!"

"Billy Fletcher does an amazing job every year with the annual cookout, and I wanted to thank him for all his hard work and, of course, all the delicious food!" Lois so graciously explained to me who the card was for and why.

"Absolutely! He does an amazing job year-after-year. Sometimes I wonder how he does it all. And you know, people don't send thank-you notes much nowadays, and even less bother with writing personalized notes."

"Thank-you cards will always be my go-to, and they hold a special place with me," Lois said with a loving sigh.

My curiosity was instantly aroused by the way she explained herself and I had to ask, "Why so special, the thank-you notes, if you don't mind my asking?"

"Oh, a long story, Doc, and one almost as old as me," Lois answered me with a young-girl-sounding giggle to her voice. She looked captured in memories as she sat there in the rocker.

"Okay, Lois, you've got to tell me this story! It must be a good one based on the way you sound talking about it. I sat down in the rocker across the checkerboard from her and leaned forward hoping for an answer."

"But it was so many years ago... It happened so long ago, and it would bore you, I'm certain of it."

"Try me," I encouraged her to share the story with me. Then I added, "Please!"

"Well, all right then." Lois nodded her head and slid to the front of the rocker. Then she put the notepad and pen in her pocketbook, next to her on the floor. "Where should I start?"

"The beginning! Always at the beginning!" I told her as I took a quick gulp of my Pepsi.

"You remember Robert—Bob, my husband—right?" Lois started her tale with a question.

"You should know I remember Bob! We used to talk all the time when he came in. I loved all his stories about growing up around here and then going off to war."

"Yes, yes… He so enjoyed his chats with you, Doc! Well, back when Bob and I got married, Saturday, September 6, 1941, to be exact, he only had the weekend before he was to report in and head off to fight against Hitler and the Germans. It was the Second World War, and Bob was proud to be able to do his part and serve his country. He had finished at Georgia Tech and went in as a commissioned office—a pilot in the Navy." Lois stopped for a second and shut her eyes. A big smile came on her face, and she started right back in with the story.

"I remember Bob looked so handsome in his uniform. He sent me a picture one of his buddies took of him standing in front of his plane. I framed that picture and put it on the nightstand by the bed. It probably sounds silly, but I still have that same picture, in that same frame on the nightstand by my bed to this very day." She paused and looked over at me.

"I don't think that sounds silly at all," I reassured her, with a smile.

"I knew it would likely be a long haul for Bob as the war seemed to be dragging on and on. I would sit down and write him letters, getting him up-to-date on all that was going on with me and all the happenings stateside. I used to buy the postage stamps at this little drugstore around the corner from our one-bedroom apartment in Norfolk, Virginia. Each week they posted specials on a chalkboard displayed outside in front of the store. Almost invariably, they had weekly specials on their greeting cards. I suspect they knew all us wives wrote to our beaus, and they wanted to capitalize on the opportunity for a sale. Money was tight for everyone, and a penny saved here or there meant a lot back then!

"Most of the cards were a nickel, some six cents, and you had to put postage on the card in the amount due based on the location it was to be delivered to. Overseas postage was always more than my cards to Mom and Dad back home. After a month or so, I got pretty familiar with the cards at the drugstore. For some reason, I took a keen liking to the artwork on the thank-you cards, and the messages inside expressed a lot of how much I appreciated Bob, his dedicated service to the country, and the love he always showed to me." Lois laughed after she told me about the reasons she liked the thank-you notes, and her cheeks blushed bright red in a way like I had never seen before.

"It seemed Bob was always changing duty stations, carriers, bases, and the likes. He blamed it on the war and was probably right. It was frustrating trying to keep up with him! First it was the European theatre and then the North African theatre. Yet where he was didn't matter so much. I loved him and continued writing him. Thank-you cards became my go-to favorite! In each one I sent to Bob, I enclosed little notes of appreciation and never forgot to tell him how much I loved him, missed him, how proud I was to be his wife, and how I couldn't wait until he came back home and we could be together again! At one point, I missed him so dearly, I started sending cards with notes every week! My mother said it was too much and frivolous with our little bit of pay, but that didn't stop me for a minute!"

"Little Mrs. Independent back then, weren't you, and hard-headed too! I have a couple of married daughters like that! Yes, I know your type well," I told Lois, and we laughed together.

"That time seems so hard to imagine," I told her. "These days people text, e-mail, or call someone anywhere anytime—no matter how far away."

"But cards were a special treat back then!" Lois immediately spoke up. "And Bob always said they meant so much to him, so I kept on writing! I remember well he had just been notified of his deployment to the North African Campaign in '42. Because of the dire need for skilled pilots, he had been transferred around three times in one year. My letters were hit-or-miss reaching him because of never-ending duty station reassigns. Yes, keeping up with him and where he was seemed almost impossible because of the censorship of his letters. Sometimes half the words in his letter were blacked out by those darn censors!"

"Must have been hard," I said, sympathizing with Lois. "But I know you understood what he did was important, and you were proud of him!"

"Most definitely! I was enormously proud of Bob! Anyway, there was this strong push being made by New Zealand, along with support from Britain and the US. It was the second hard push by the allies against the tenacious Nazi General Erwin Rommel. They called it the Second Battle of El Alamein. Bob was assigned as a squadron leader of a large air group set to go up against the Germans. After being briefed on the intended air strike patterns and going over expected ground support from the allied armies, Bob and his men had about one hour before operations commenced.

"Bob was in the briefing room having coffee, smoking a cigarette, and sharing a laugh or two with the guys when a mail carrier came into the room asking for Lieutenant Sullivan. Bob was known as Sully to his men and no one paid any attention to the inquiry... except Bob!

"He said he stood up and told the young carrier that he was Lieutenant Sullivan. The reply from him was, 'Well, you must be one important person, sir.' 'And why is that?' Bob said he asked curiously. From a backpack, the carrier pulled out a box and handed the whole thing to Bob. The young man explained that every letter in the entire box of letters was addressed to him. 'Looks like it's a compilation of letters from your previous stations that finally caught up with you,' the young carrier said. He told Bob he hoped he enjoyed reading them all and to go show those Nazis a thing or two!

"Bob said he looked down at his black-faced, Mido wristwatch and knew time was short. Immediately he opened the box and poured all the letters onto the briefing table. All the fellows started giving him grief, but Bob said he paid them no mind. When the alarm sounded for ready to stations, he still had over half unread!"

"So what did Mr. Sullivan do?"

"Quick thinking! He took off his leather flight jacket, pulled out his Barlow pocketknife, and began cutting the lining along the seam between his left shoulder and the waistband. Hurriedly he shoved as many of the unopened letters as he could in between the lining and the jacket. They weren't allowed to take contraband of any type in the plane with them, except Bob said they always pretended not to notice the pictures of everybody's honey on the control panel."

"What about the already opened letters?" I questioned.

"Bob said he left them on the table and never saw them again!"

"But when he got back, he was able to read them all again along with the others. That's terrific!" I commented.

"Not exactly," Lois interjected. She looked at me, tilted her head to one side, pressed her lips tightly together, squinted her eyes, and continued. "It was a terrible battle—this Second Battle of El Alamein! The Allies and the Germans were losing men by the thousands, huge losses! Bob's air group was fighting against Rommel's best pilots—most of which were flying Focke-Wulf 190s, or some name like that. Bob flew a new fighter the P51 Mustang that had been developed less than a year before the battle. In the air, Nazi fighter planes outnumbered the Allies by 3 to 1!

"The Nazis took over four thousand prisoners that day, and sadly, Bob was one of them! He was shot down on a low flyover giving air support to advancing ground troops. One of Rommel's notorious tanks shot off Bob's left wing, and his plane hit and tumbled over to a stop in the sand of the North African desert. He was quickly taken prisoner and locked in a cell with three other American soldiers for nearly four months until, finally, they were liberated by New Zealand soldiers. Bob said of the soldiers from New Zealand that they were the nicest of guys to be friends with, but the fiercest of fighters he had ever seen!

"Bob felt lucky when he was taken prisoner because they only searched him for a weapon, never bothering with checking the lining of his flight jacket! He brought that old brown leather jacket home with him and wore it until it was threadbare!"

"I can't believe he never told me this story!"

"Bob never liked to talk much about that day. I did hear him say to someone in his sleep one night that he was sorry he had let everyone down. I think that's how he must have felt. But one thing he did talk to me about was the cards! He explained to me how every day he would open one of the thank-you cards and read the note inside. At first, he read them to himself, but after much harassing by his cellmates, he started to read them aloud every morning to them. Bob swore he knew some of them word for word by memory by the time he was liberated. So many times after the war, he reminded me that he never could have made it through his imprisonment had it not been for my thank-you cards and notes! You see, Doc, that's why thank-you cards hold a special place in my heart!"

"Wow… What a story!" I exclaimed to Lois in amazement. "No wonder you like thank-you cards. They're definitely special!"

"Bob was the love of my life and the most amazing man I ever met! What he saw in me, I don't know? But I do know that I got one heck of a catch in Robert Sullivan!" Lois was beaming at the conclusion of her story.

"Great, great story, Lois! I really appreciate you sharing it with me," I told her as the girls were motioning for me to come back to work.

Lois looked over at the technicians and saw they were getting a bit antsy in the back and then gave me an out, "Looks like you need to get back to work, Doc!" And with that, she reached into her pocketbook and pulled back out the pen and notepad.

"And I thank you so much, Doc, for listening to the memories of a ninety-year-old lady," I heard Lois say to me as I went through the swinging door and back to my work area.

Before picking up and checking the prescription on the counter, I couldn't help but let her know how much what she had shared with me meant. I moved to the front checkout counter, leaned across toward the side closest to her, and let her know, "Lois, if you hadn't told me that story, I would have never felt it was worth the effort to send a thank-you card or write a thank-you note! Through your eyes, I was able to see how a simple action and words on a card brought a ray of hope to Bob's dark situation. I feel certain the love in those letters gave him reason to stay alive and come back home to you! Clearly a thank-you card or note can mean the world to someone— just as it did for Bob! Honestly, I never knew a card could mean so much until now!"

I was so thankful that today I had chosen to take the time to stop from one of the "things" in my life that demands attention (in my case, work and the prescriptions waiting for me) and opened my eyes to see another "thing" sitting right there in front of me. Obviously, there was a choice—a momentary mental decision I had to make between pressing on with the enormous workload of pre-scriptions or stepping away and seeing that other "thing" as equally, if not more, important, Mrs. Lois Sullivan! And what a marvelous gift this stop and look at "thing" choice had given me! Yet I wonder how many times in the past had I missed such a gift?

As you have seen throughout these pages and stories, my life certainly isn't perfect—no, lightyears from it! And my decisions have often been far from the best they can be. But when I think about others who have stopped from some "thing" they were doing and saw another "thing" in front of them—me—and choose to show me kindness and hope... Well, I want to be more like them! I want to be able to stop more! I want to make more right choice, to stop and give back to others!

None of us can fully know exactly what others are going through. What their circumstances, difficulties, demons, and obsta-cles truly are all about. But we all have that choice to make. That decision to stop that "thing" we are doing and to open our hearts and ears to them and their "thing" they are dealing with. They might need to share or simply want to know they exist, that they are visible to the world. There is no way we can share kindness, hope, caring, listening, understanding, love, or respect to our neighbors if we don't know them. And the only way to know them is to stop that "thing" of ours that seems so important and engage them. It only takes one person to create a spark of hope where there was none, and that hope can totally transform someone's life forever!

I wasn't sure that day how to engage Lois or what might happen when I did. But when I chose to walk over and say hello, I just did it! Usually that's the beginning of it—just doing it! Put one foot in front of the other, then repeat, and smile. Once you are there, it's amazing how the walls start breaking down, the words start coming, and before long, you have engaged someone new and possibly even unpacked a little hope for them!

That someone you engage might be totally different than you, look entirely different than you do, be from a different city, state, or country than you, or may actually be more afraid than you are! None of us are immune; troubles besets us all at some time or another, but when we engage another with love in our hearts, we find that hope and friendship become a common tread binding us together as fellow human beings. Engaging and showing love to someone isn't merely something we do. It's something we become—a giver of hope, so to speak!

There are people out there among us who have no hope. The tragedies of their life have them living in fear. I used to not see them because my eyes didn't want to focus on them, but I see them now. I can't say how I will react each and every time. And yes, I know I alone am the one who has to live with those decisions. We all have to decide how we are going to handle each day. So then why not make each day count. Why not take and put that one foot in front of the other, smile, repeat, and approach someone you know needs hope? It may seem like only a small thing, yet small beginnings often grow into mountains of impact. Live your life to the fullest. Have no regrets for taking that step to help another. Just look what those small cards did for Lieutenant Robert Sullivan during the Second World War!

And look at what happened with my friend Billy Fletcher to whom Lois was writing the thank-you note. He is just an everyday local kind of guy who made the decision to stop the "thing" he was doing and follow through on a small idea to help one or two people in need.

While sitting around his old tire store, shooting the breeze, and telling stories of the ones that got away to a couple of his fishing and hunting buddies, he came up with this so-called *crazy idea*. He suggested a way that they could clear out their freezers from last year's hunting good fortunes and make room for this coming season's bounty. Up front he made it clear that he wasn't asking or suggesting any of them dip into their wallets or run down to the Winn Dixie in town and bring back bags of groceries for these folks he had a mind to help! Instead, he proposed a straightforward and simple solution to benefit them all. (I love it when life's great ideas are so simple!)

Billy suggested to them that they pull out of their freezer expected overflow to make room for what they would likely bring back this year. If they thought it wouldn't be a good year for them—only take a little out. If the year looked really promising, clear out and make plenty of room for the new! Once they knew what amount of game (fish, venison, quail, pork, etc.) they were dealing with, they could decide on the number of smokers, cookers, and grills needed to cook up a mess of food.

"If we each come up with one or two people we know or have heard about around town needing some help, we'll just invite them over for a cookout. We can tell them to bring their family and hangout with us while we're cooking everything." Billy told Doug to bring his cornhole boards, Lyle to bring horseshoes, and he would "volunteer" his grandson to drive over his pickup and play some tunes out of that expensive system he helped foot the bill for last Christmas. "Nothing fancy, mind you, and nothing pretentious and no strings attached." These were his only stipulations!

Billy went on to suggest to his buddies that they get their wives involved in whatever way they would like to help. Cooking, baking, or whatever they felt led to do would surely be appreciated by the families they were trying to help. It was also mentioned, to avoid spending any money, that they take a look in their pantries, at their hunt camps, or wherever else and snag whatever paper supplies they had to be used in serving the meals. Billy pointed to a box over in the corner of his shop and donated the five-hundred-count cardboard box containing red Solo drinking cups. He emphasized several times the need to have paper plates, napkins, plastic knives, forks, and spoons. Billy reminded them to let their wives know that they came up with this crazy idea and would clean up afterward. He didn't want to deal with upset wives at the conclusion of the cookout!

Doug remembered he had a fifty-pound bag of cornmeal and said it could be used to batter the fish and make hush puppies. Lyle said his wife usually made coleslaw for the youth cookouts at the

Baptist church and volunteered her to make several large batches for the event. Things were falling in place without Billy even asking if everyone was in on the idea. Finally, he slapped his hand on the counter and hollered out, "How 'bout it, guys? Everybody in for it?!"

Based on what I understand from Doug (who just happened to be there and is one of my best friends), there wasn't a word of discussion, disagreement, or hesitation. They were all in! It was a done deal! And since July 4 was just a weekend away, they decided to make it an Independence Day cookout behind the old tire store. The cookout was set in motion and several families were identified by the guys and asked to drop by and hangout between 11:00 and 2:00.

One of men in a family they invited had some issues with his pride and wanted no part of "charity." It was amazing to see a good old boy like Billy immediately come up with a solution. Billy suggested that they go fishing the morning before the cookout and bring their fresh catch to add to the rest of the food for grilling. That was it—problem solved! Sometimes obstacles are simply opportunities waiting to be embraced! Billy didn't have an agenda for this whole thing. His motives were pure and straightforward. It was an idea with three ingredients: compassion for neighbors in need, faith in believing it could be done, and a willingness to serve others, thereby showing them love!

That first cookout was a success! Not for the number of people feed or any fancy fixings, but by the way it showed true caring for neighbors in need. Billy is a man of few words; there was no speech, announcements, or mention of why they did the cookout that day. All there was that day was laughter, fellowship, a few hunting and fishing stories, and lots of delicious food! Of course, I feel certain Doug blessed the food and included in his prayer a few thank-you words for the bounty the Lord had provided, the country we live in, and the neighbors and family we share our lives with. What more could anyone ask for?!

You might be questioning to yourself what, if anything, has grown from this so-called *crazy idea* of one man to help his neighbors? I don't blame you for wondering, and it's doubtful any of us could have ever imagined how his idea would grow. Billy would never brag about it or even bring it up for that matter, but how about I share it with you?

After eleven years, Billy's small, simple idea has grown and is still growing! Though now it has been given an "official" name by the city and townsfolks—Riley Park Cookout—it still is on the Fourth of July, and it still is free to anyone wanting to hangout, have fun, and enjoy a delicious meal with their neighbors. First and foremost, helping and caring are at the heart of all the day's activities!

And this grand day begins bright and early at 8:30 a.m. That's when it is kicked off with two casting tournaments—one for youth and the other adults. Then next there is the fishing tournament on the Harris Chain of Lakes, generally with over thirty boats and teams of fishermen snagging crappie and bass for the cookout. Wonder where the idea arose for the fishing tournament? (Remember Billy and the man going fishing that morning before the first cookout?)

Hunters, fishermen, and businesses throughout town and the surrounding area contribute with food from their freezers and supplies for the meals. The food for the cookout itself is no longer prepared on only a couple of grills behind Billy's tire store; now there are large elaborate grills and smokers starting to prepare the meats twenty-four to forty-eight hours before the event. The location—Riley Part—is on land donated to the city over seventy-five years ago by (you guessed it) Billy's grandfather. And the large pole barn in the center of the park was built by money donated by attendees over the past six years!

It now takes upward of fifty-plus volunteers to help get things set up and prepare the food, side dishes, and desserts. At last year's cookout, the small "crazy idea" Billy thought up had grown to mammoth proportion and gave out *free* meals to over 1,500 neighbors in our small town and surrounding communities! Not only are meals served to those at the park, but there were twenty-eight volunteers that personally drove to and delivered free meals to better than four hundred shut-ins! Wow, what that must have meant to them?! A hot home-cooked meal brought to them in their home by a caring neighbor!

I shared with Billy once the story of an older widowed woman who had moved to our community from another state years ago. When first arriving, she was able to get around and care for herself but in later years became homebound. Even though she had family in town that cared for her, she missed coming to the cookout. For years, we delivered her prescriptions to her home and always around time for the cookout each year she expressed to us how much she thought it meant to homebound individuals to have meals from the annual event brought to them.

"What a blessing," she would always say. Though she had never personally met Billy, she asked me if I would let him know how much it meant to her when they started delivering a meal to her each year and how delicious it was! I promised I would tell him, but with helping each year and the cookout getting bigger and bigger, I forgot.

Then one year, I made a point to mark it on the calendar to go see her the day of the cookout. I was there talking with her when an elderly husband and wife stopped in to deliver her a meal from the cookout. It was in a Styrofoam container and included a chicken breast, fried fish, coleslaw, two hush puppies, and a side salad. She thanked them both and bragged over how wonderful the meal looked and how she could eat on it for several days!

As she was readying to eat the meal, I followed the couple out to their car and personally thanked them. Not meaning to be nosey, I wanted to know how they knew to deliver to her and how they got her name. They both looked at me rather puzzled and told me to wait a minute. He opened the back door to the car and picked up a clipboard with a list of deliveries on it. Not hesitating for a minute, he handed it to me.

It was simply addresses (maybe one or two had a first name handwritten next to them) without names of who the delivery was actually going to. Still I wondered why no names were on the delivery list? The older gentleman explained that Billy asked people with the various local churches and community service organizations to submit only addresses—no names—of those shut-in or in financial need who can't make it to the cookout. He goes through the lists and then passes them on to volunteers to group by area, neighborhood, apartment complexes, and the like. The lists are then divided up between the volunteer delivery drivers, and it goes from there—made sense!

"Where is her address on the list?" I questioned, wanting to make certain it was on the list.

Quickly moving his hand down the list, he stopped at hers. "It's right here." He pointed firmly at it.

My eyes locked in to where he was pointing: simply an address with no name.

"Thank you," I told him and patted him on his back. Now I knew without any doubt that Billy didn't even know the names of the individuals he was helping, and I felt certain that was exactly how he wanted it to be!

As the older couple drove away, I suddenly realized how Billy's blessing to the community was so nondiscriminatory, so open and so genuine! The original pretense of simply helping those in need hadn't been lost one bit. The blessing the woman was receiving was genuine, and Billy didn't know, and still doesn't know to this very day, who she was! But I knew who she was, and I knew what a blessing it was to her every year to be visited and receive that meal .... For, you see, the women at that address was my mom!

Was Billy's idea a good one? Well, I certainly think so...and so did my mom! Though she passed a few years back, she loved his *crazy idea!* And I passionately believe that if you decide to do something to help others and don't convolute it with personal agendas, then that idea can succeed and deliver hope (as well as food) in more ways than we can number. Hope placed in Christ never fails. And not only can it succeed, but oh, how it may impact another's life.

What dreams are stirring in your soul right now? Like the stories of Lois Sullivan and Billy Fletcher, it only took one small idea to greatly impact the world of another. So it is that we are introduced to an idea out of nowhere in our head or we are given the opportunity to think outside the box when a need arises. That little idea or need can lead to action—if we are only willing. Willing to unpack that secret thought, that small idea, that person we know who needs us, that something or someone just waiting for that moment in their life to see faith, hope, and love in action.

You may say that we can't change much if we aren't willing to risk much, and I would agree. I would also follow-up and say that change and risk aren't always going to be easy. Of course not, but do it anyway without retreat! Don't you remember that there was a risk to getting on a bike for the first time? Wasn't there a risk to crossing a busy street by yourself for the first time? Wasn't there a risk to telling someone you loved them for the first time? There were no safety nets for any of those, and there is no safety net for unpacking hope to someone—so do it!

Live deliberately! Make a purposeful choice and decision to take a risk to bring hope and love closer to those around you! Once you have done it a few times, it will start to be a habit—and a good one at that! Although there is only one of you, your words, actions, and thoughtfulness will change the world for someone! And trust me on this, it will not only make you feel good to help someone, it will make them feel great!

Got any thoughts or ideas about something to do or someone to help? Have you written a thank-you note to anyone lately? Have you given someone an encouraging call, text, or e-mail? Have you ever brought someone a home-cooked or baked item—cookies, cupcakes, dinner? Have you ever volunteered to babysit for a couple so they can have a "date night"? If you have never done any of these or thought about any of these, what are you waiting for? Your one small action may change the world for one small part of it or one small person! It's a big world out there… Think small!

Commit to The Lord whatever you do, and
He will establish your plans.

—Proverbs 16:3

CHAPTER 17

I Admit It, I Am Vulnerable

Clouds are all around, rays of sunshine are needed.
—Mike Deegan

It was a beautiful autumn day for early September, but for the funeral of a father, is there ever a beautiful day?!

I remember sitting there at the graveside rites, tightly squeezed between my mother on the left and my grandmother on the right. We were in rickety foldup, wooden chairs provided by the funeral home, and there was some type of artificial green grass rug covering the ground around the gravesite.

Mom lovingly patted my leg and whispered she loved me only seconds before a rather large and rotund minister walked by, touched Mom on the shoulder, then turned to face the family and friends grieving with us that day. He looked over at someone and nodded his head, cleared his throat with an awful sounding upheaval, wiped his mouth with his handkerchief, and belted out the words, "Dearly beloved, we are gathered here today…"

If you have ever wondered when you see funerals in movies and here the preacher say those words and question if that truly is how they started funerals back in the day, well, the answer is yes. As he continued on with the eulogy, I fixed my eyes on the dress-attired Navy servicemen behind him standing at attention. Without even knowing it, my hand had reached over to hold my mother's hand.

She was clutching a dainty white eyelet handkerchief, and when I turned to look more closely at it, a tear from her eye fell against my thumb.

I turned my head up, only to see her face covered with tears, her lips quivering, and the red lipstick she was wearing smeared at the corners of her mouth. Her eyes were puffy, and her nose was starting to run. Looking back over to my right, my grandmother's black hat had shifted, and her snowy white hair looked unkept around the edges of the hat. She had her face almost completely covered with her handkerchief and was shaking her head side-to-side.

Uncle Roy sat next to Grandma, and as I stared at him, I knew it was the first time I had ever witnessed him crying. He was a wounded war veteran…a Marine. Crying was not something I expected to see! And my Aunt Elizabeth next to him was even a bigger mess than Momma and Grandma!

So what was the matter with me? I asked myself. *Why wasn't I crying?*

I shifted back in my chair and turned to look at everyone behind us. They were all crying too! Just as I got ready to whisper in my mother's ear… *Bang! Bang! Bang!* I covered my ears and put my head down until they had stopped firing the rifles. When I looked up, Mom was taking a folded flag from the Naval officer and a letter written to her by the President of the United States of America. Momma placed the flag in my lap and told me, "This is yours, son. Your dad was a hero."

At only six years of age, my idea of a hero was Superman in my comic books or The Phantom in the Sunday newspaper. Dad, Mom and Grandma had all read me those. But how could Dad be a hero like them if he was dead? Maybe when I got home, the *World Book Encyclopedia* or my *Websters Student Dictionary* could help me understand more. If not, I would just ask Mom.

Lots of people came over to hug me and mess up my hair. Thank goodness Mom had let me use some of Dad's Brylcreem to push back my crewcut, or my hair would have been an even bigger mess by the time we got home. Everybody kept using that word *hero* when they talked about Dad. And if they all had been crying over a hero dying, why wasn't I?

Three Navy officers, with wings like my dad's on their chest, all saluted me at the same time and reminded me to be proud of my dad. Each had served and flown with him, one over Germany and the other two in North Africa.

"Your dad saved my butt one time," one began, only to be cut off by another reminding him I was just a kid and didn't need to hear any stories.

"Really?" I wanted to know everything about my dad.

"All you need to know, son, is that your dad was a hero, and he saved a lot of people's lives with the courage he displayed in the air and on the ground."

"Can you tell me something about what he did? What was he like?"

Mom heard me ask and interrupted, "Thanks so much for coming, guys. Connor is just a little too young to hear any stories about his dad... Maybe when he's older, huh?"

"Yes, ma'am," all three answered immediately.

Then with another salute to me they turned and left. Although at the time I thought they were saluting me, but looking back now, I realize they were saluting my dad—honoring him one last time through an act of love and respect to his only son.

What I remember most from that day were the words *hero* and *courage*. What's confusing though is when I got home and looked up the word hero in my dictionary, the definition said it "was someone who shows great courage." And if that's true, then *hero* and *courage* go hand in hand, and yes, my dad was a hero! And if that's true, then I knew I was not a hero!

A hero would have the courage to mourn the loss of his father. A hero wouldn't put up a make-believe shield of anger for thirty-five years against someone who never intended to leave him and exhibited nothing but pure courage when he went to fight for my freedom as his son and as an American!

A hero would have the courage to talk proudly of a man who was a second generation solider, a Navy pilot, an escaped prisoner of war, a Purple Heart Medal holder, and his father! Yes, that would take courage! A courage far greater than any within me for too many years. Why couldn't I cry that day and why couldn't I talk about him, not even with my mother?

I didn't know the word then, but if you asked me now, I would say the answer was *vulnerability*. I refused to let myself be vulnerable that day! I just couldn't take the risk of being physically or emotionally wounded one more time. So a shield of impenetrability became my only protection that day.

Trace back in time with me some of the events that possibly made me the way I was:

First, it made me sad when my grandpa (on my dad's side) died, and my dad was away fighting in a war against countries and ideals I didn't understand.

Next, it made me sadder still when my Uncle LC came home that same year with his feet nearly frozen off after fighting in General George Patton's infamous Second Armored Division of tanks, Hell on Wheels, during the Battle of the Bulge in the winter of 1944. I would have rather he died by a shot from the Germans in the head than to have seen him dead that night on the floor from shots of whiskey!

Then to have my other grandfather (on my mom's side), a fourth-generation bright leaf tobacco farmer from Southside Virginia, die less than one month after Uncle LC... Too much! And of all places for Grandpa to die, it was in the living room of the house we were staying in with my grandparents when my father was still away at war! The snowball of deaths was nothing short of pure devastation to me! Of all things, Grandpa—a tobacco farmer—died of lung cancer!

Last was where we started this story, with the death of my father in a plane crash. When the officer came to the house that night to notify Mom, I was between her legs holding onto her housecoat. When she started to cry, I ran and hid under the end table in the living room. I felt there were demons swirling around me, and I curled up in a ball, frozen with fear. His death was more than I could take at the time!

The family loss count for me, in less than three years, amounted to—two grandfathers, one father, and one uncle! My world would never be the same. And suddenly I became a "little man" and was referred to in conversation as the "man of the house." What? How could a six-year-old boy possible be equated to a man?

Because he couldn't, it caused me lots of problems over the years, truck loads full of mistakes, unimaginable insecurities, anger, and lots of walls! Until finally, I quit trying to justify and admitted all my mistakes and all my faults. By admitting and exposing my flaws, it allowed grace a chance to heal me. And that grace cleansed me and allowed me to get out from behind my walls. Admitting vulnerability and exposing all my insecurities and emotions opened an amazing door that slammed right into and through my so-called shield of impenetrability! At last I was free!

But vulnerability felt scary and really uncomfortable, especially after years of trying to protect my feelings and emotions. However, it was only through this vulnerability that my life was opened up to take risks. I had no choice but to take risks, for no longer was I locked in behind my walls. My life was now out there for all to see! These risks exposed the transparency I have talked about throughout this journey of hope. With all I have been through concerning the losses in my family and the physical state of my heart, I have learned that transparency and vulnerability were not only necessary but were actually the only means by which I could survive!

To keep my heart beating and pumping, there had to be faith, hope, and love in my life—three things that were nowhere to be found behind my walls. And it couldn't be that those three only be given to me by others, it had to also be that those three were given *by me* to others needing the same. I had to now risk my heart beating not only for myself, but for others around me who were hurting and in need.

The walls were broken down, and a change started in my messy life that day when I left my cardiologist's office. I have had so many fears and doubts along the way, but those gifts of faith, hope, love, joy, vision, and purpose, that I have shared with you from the stories of others' lives, have appeared around every corner and at every roadblock laid out before me. A questioning or doubting mind might call my still being alive, still being blessed, and still having hope a coincidence or luck, but really, do you think that?

Open the eyes of your heart and see the world around you. Allow the flames of love within it to burn and shine a light on all that is around you. An open heart on fire can never deny the existence of love. And where there is love, there is hope for a brighter tomorrow. Now that we know there is love and hope, the existence of faith can no longer be questioned. For it is alive and living in the two! With faith, hope, and love, my heart can beat stronger. I know this for a fact, and so can yours!

One of my sons-in-law is a firefighter, and he once told me that a hero was someone who, without hesitation, would run into a blazing fire to save someone they didn't even know. I won't be running into any fires, but as long as my heart is beating, I will be running with all my might and with all the resources available at my disposal to help save anyone who comes to me or the drugstore needing hope. I intend to take my father's example and live courageously for others, claiming victories as they come every minute, hour, day, week, month, and year…for as long as my heart is beating!

I pray that the eyes of your heart may be enlightened in order that you may know the hope to which He has called you.
—Ephesians 1:18

CHAPTER 18

Hope: Our Foundation of Happiness

Being hopeful helps you to press on instead of giving up.
—Joyce Meyer

Worrywarts is probably not a real word, but it was an expression my Grandma Lovelace used to describe Miles and I when we were children and had lost all hope in a situation or circumstance and we feared what the consequences might be.

Whether it is a real word or not doesn't much matter to me because she was right in her analysis! For, you see, far too frequent were the times when Miles and I had forgotten to wipe our feet and turned around halfway down the hall only to discover a trail of red clay behind us on the floor! It was at moments such as this when we were truly worrywarts!

In our minds, there was no hope! No hope whatsoever for avoiding a spanking with that darned weeping willow branch that would inflict tingling pain as it wrapped around my leg with just the slightest flick from Grandma's wrist! That slightest flick happened within an instant, but the sting was hard enough to forever remain engraved in my mind. That memory has continually served as a reminder to me never to track dirt into the house. Feel free to validate that with my wife Ria, if you like. Even to this day, I stop at the door, rub my shoes back and forth across the mat several times, and usually even turn them to the side to see the bottom and make sure I'm not going to track the outside inside. For me, lessons learned the hard way are never forgotten!

Nowadays it is far too easy to be what Grandma called a worrywart. To cave in to all the negative news and negative attitudes of people around us and…to worry! If we don't intentionally and consistently work at it, I honestly believe we could all be sucked into the spiraling vortex of dread, pessimism, worry, and fear. I mean it! Ria calls me a Negative Nellie when I worry! But truthfully, if we don't try to keep our mind on the positives, we do succumb to the negatives. And what a terrible place that is to be!

Fortunately, there is always hope! Even if it is only the faintest glimmer at the end of a long dark tunnel, it is the distant light that is always there! Hope never leaves us. Instead, we allow ourselves to leave it behind. To lose sight of it, to take our focus away from the good, and be distracted by the bad! You have heard me say before that every day is a new beginning. A beginning where we must deliberately choose each day to be positive, to be hopeful, and to make a difference. And I know for a fact that it certainly made a difference to all of us at the drugstore when one day we had a surprise delivery at the drive-through window!

Although Gabby may not have been the first to come up with this unique idea, she was the first to bestow it upon the drugstore. What am I talking about? She may kill me for divulging her age with this little story (so, Gabby, please forgive me in advance), but as the occasion of her fortieth birthday approached, she began to do a little soul-searching and retrospective thinking about her previous thirty-nine years. We all do that on "big" birthdays—*18, 21, 30, 40, 50,* and even *100*, a milestone that was recently celebrated by one of our drugstore customers!

On these big birthdays, we look back, then look forward, and stop on the here and now to ponder a few things. Really we have no choice in the matter because we can't go back and change what has already happened in the past, and we can't accurately predict all that is going to happen in the future. We all would agree we found that out with the recent COVID-19 pandemic. We can't get so hung-up on what we would rather be doing or where we would rather be that we forget to make the most of where we are! So that leaves us with the reality of now—the present.

We all must decide for ourselves what we will do with each day we are given. What is it that we will do with the here and now? I think we all have heard it said dozens of times before that each day is a gift, a chance to open the present and make it worth remembering. What is inside that gift is what is inside us, the business of our heart. It is what we choose to do on that one day that matters.

Gabby choose to bring the staff at the drugstore homemade redneck caviar (salsa), a couple bags of chips, and a made-from-scratch pound cake. Absolutely yummy! When I stuck my heard around to see her at the drive-through window, I asked, "What's the occasion?"

Sheepishly, she looked at me without answering. I knew good and well that she had heard me and was about to repeat my question when she hollered out for us to enjoy and pulled away in her car.

That was strange, I thought to myself.

Usually she's all chatty and in no rush to leave. Nonetheless, I followed Meghan who was carrying the goodies back to our break area. The reason for her generosity moved to the back of my mind as I maneuvered to get my hands on some of that pound cake.

As I began to remove the clear wrap covering the cake, my hand reached under the plate and pulled off, with the wrap, a small round piece of paper. At first glance, I paid it no mind and proceeded to slice myself a piece of cake. Grabbing a fork out from the drawer, I took the wrap, paper, and slice of cake with me as I sat down at the table. Flipping the paper over, I could see it was colorful and probably printed off the computer.

It was round with blue scalloped edging and trimmed with red polka dots. A tiny flag banner streamed across from one side to the other of the paper. On each flag was a letter of the alphabet, the compilation of which spelled out the word *kindness.* Below the banner I read:

kindness INSPIRES kindness

Then in a semicircle outlining the lower portion of the circle, it read simply, "Given to you with joy on my fortieth birthday!"

The salsa and cake were delicious. The card was genuinely nice! But what did it mean exactly? I decided to call Gabby on her cell phone and ask. After talking with her and listening, her explanation made the note the most special part of the gift. Not to get too far ahead of myself, but the note was so special to me that I placed it in my desk, center drawer, in plain view so that every time I open it, I am reminded of what kindness and deliberateness of purpose can accomplish.

Gabby's explanation to me was easy to understand yet most likely not as easy to accomplish (or think of, for that matter). What she had chosen to do, how she had decided to spend her fortieth birthday was a 180-degree shift of the paradigm of life. There would be no party, no cake, no cheering her on to blow out the forest of candles. (Sorry again, Gabby, but forty candles do take up a lot of room on a cake.) Instead, she had opted to take a part of every day of her life for the next forty days and perform forty acts of random kindness! Not forty selfish things for Gabby, but rather forty kind-hearted things for forty other people! Her car must be loaded down and her mind bubbling over with joy as she sets out on such a worthwhile mission!

I felt that the impact of forty random acts of kindness on forty people would be phenomenal! Only wish I could have been a fly on the wall and seen the joy that such kindness produced in the lives of those forty people. Her kindness inspired me to push on with this book at a time when I was ready to push it in the trash. Thank you, Gabby! And as your little card said, and I do believe, *Kindness inspires kindness.* Yes, truly it does!

Oftentimes in our lives we are able to plant seeds, so to speak, in the lives of others. Though we may not be the ones to water or prune as those seeds germinate, grow, and spread their branches, we have done our part! Gabby planted a lot of seeds, seeds of love and kindness. She did it with a pure heart—having no expectations of return of any type. I couldn't help but ask Gabby to share with me the details for some of the forty acts of kindness. As expected, she wanted no part of telling me anything. I don't blame her. That wasn't her intention or reasoning behind the random acts!

What is interesting though is how I have found out secondhand what she did with a few of those acts. Actually I would have to call it firsthand, sort of, because I learned of what a few people did because I questioned them as to why they wanted to help with this or that, why they wished to give someone this or that gift. Each explained to me that their desire to help was first sparked by a random act of kindness that happened to them once upon a time.

One nice lady who had received one of those random acts of kindness turned around and bestowed an act of kindness upon our little town. She gave the city a small vacant parcel of land she owned that was smack dab in the middle of three intersecting streets loaded with small, little homes with zero lot lines and nice families. Her only stipulations were that it be made into a safe, family-friendly park with slides, swings, picnic tables, basketball court, and a covered gazebo surrounded by a butterfly garden. That was certainly one small seed that blossomed and bore fruit for everyone in town to enjoy. But remember, you didn't hear that from me!

When my three daughters were young (how oftentimes I wish they still were, but I am thankful to still have them—young or old), I would sometimes find myself alone early in the morning, drinking coffee and feeling sorry for myself. If you are blatantly honest with yourself, you know you have been there before too. We don't just wake up every day happy as a lark, singing joyous for the world to hear, now, do we? You know what I am talking about on certain mornings. It's when we have one of those private, poor-pitiful-me parties with our coffee.

It was on those type mornings, when the whole house was dark and still, that I would let my mind drag me into thoughts of worry—finances, children, work, etc. And if I wasn't careful, those thoughts would grow and bring pessimism along with it for the ride. When that did happen, it ended up being a bad morning, an unbelievably bad morning for me and for the girls. When they woke up and came downstairs, not only was I short and snappy, but also negative and nitpicky about everything! Maybe none of you have snapped, "Go do something with your hair. It looks awful" or "What kind of outfit do you have on? Go change, now."

Well, one morning, I walked outside on the back porch when I started to feel those emotions overtaking me (and I didn't want a repeat performance from the day before). That's when I saw it. Something utterly amazing—the sunrise! It was nothing new; it was there every morning. The thing was… I hadn't been noticing it. Sure, I always told Ria every new day was a new beginning and a chance to start over and put the past behind, but I wasn't paying any attention to these amazing new beginnings. All I was giving her was lip service. Sort of my way of getting out of a mistake I had made and being allowed a redo the next day.

Somehow, I had overlooked the sunrise. With all my worrying and busyness, I had missed it. I had actually missed the fact that day in and day out, the sun still rose in the same place it always had behind the house. And like it or not, mornings always came around, and nothing that happened in my world would ever be bad enough to stop it. Though sometimes battles with the loss of friends and family and fights with my heart disease made me wish I could stop it, I couldn't!

I am not saying that I didn't realize there was a change from darkness to light every morning, rather that I didn't look closely enough to see that the sun was so beautiful every day as it slowly crept up over the eastern horizon and blazed a reflection across the lake toward our house. There it was this morning, streaming straight at me standing there on the back porch! How could I have not seen it each and every day? How could I have missed that every day of my life started anew with something so marvelous and beautiful?

Another of Grandma's expressions *"If it had been a snake, it would have bit you!"* was absolutely right! If it had been a snake, it certainly would have bitten me every day, and I would have noticed it was there, but it wasn't a snake, and I hadn't noticed. I was too busy being self-absorbed with my personal worries to even look up and see it. I felt a little ashamed and wondered how many days I must have looked down or straight ahead and never bothered to look up.

It was that very morning when I saw the sunrise like never before that I decided it was time to stop and look at things with a more realistic perspective, to intentionally hunt out and find that thing everyone called hope. Even if it was the smallest of small, I intended to capture it! Whether it was in a moment, a sight, a word, a sound, or a deed, I intended to purposefully look and discover it every day. I knew it wouldn't be easy, but I knew that where there was hope there was also happiness. The two, I remembered from years gone by, were hand-in-hand, inseparable. My life and my family needed to know I had hope, and they needed to see there was a lot of happiness in every day!

Yes, I believe we do have to hunt it out sometimes, pursue it, and find it in whatever place, person, or thing we can. One of our Founding Fathers, Thomas Jefferson, challenged us to do just that when he gave this country the immortal words "life, liberty, and the pursuit of happiness." Mr. Jefferson realized, as I have also, that we need to make it a daily task. Put it on our electronic to-do list: *pursue happiness today*!

Not only pursue it, but when we find it, *drink it up*! Fill ourselves with it to overflowing! Then as we allow it to overflow from us, we pour it out and onto those around us who may desperately need hope and happiness. I used to love playing in the lake with our girls when they were young. It never failed that after a short while, one of us would sneak back over to shore and grab a bucket. Next, they would purposefully fill the bucket with water, intentionally seek out one of our family members and pour it onto whoever it was they had chosen. Just a game, but it was all about being intentional and utilizing the element of surprise. We wanted to deliberately cover them with the water without their knowing it was coming. Of course, Ria liked to sunbath and was frequently the recipient of this intentional gift. Sorry about that, honey!

I have come to look at hope and happiness much in the same manner as this simple summertime family event. When people aren't noticing me, I am intentionally looking for that bucket and the water of hope and happiness to fill it with. Sometimes I struggle to find even a drip-drop, but I don't give up! I know it's there; I just need to keep positive and never stop looking. Oftentimes in the midst of my searching, when I am about to give up, it shows up without me even going to look for it!

Take the examples of the drugstore. How many times did I actually have to go looking for people to help? Not many. Usually they came to me! Or more accurately, they were there just needing me to notice them, kind of like the sunrise I discovered that was there every day. It wasn't anything new, just something in the day-to-day of life that had gone unnoticed by me!

Think about the number of times we walk into a convenience store and don't notice those around us. I've thought about that very situation numerous times and have tried to change it. Surprisingly (although it shouldn't be), I have been rewarded with some unexpected drops of hope, usually followed by happiness! Enough over time to fill my bucket more than once, once empty, twice full, and even more!

Last week, I was in a hurry to get in and out of the convenience store and had forgotten all about trying to look around and make a positive change. As I parked and got out of my truck, without my even realizing it, there was a young man who had stopped and watched me as I hurriedly made my way toward the door of the store. Patiently he waited for me and even held the door until I made it safely inside. He didn't have to, but he did! As I walked past, he stopped me in my tracks when he said in a kind tone, "Hope you have a great day, Doc!"

Suddenly, my need to rush was put on hold. I hit the brakes, and whatever it was that had made me in such hurry was moved to the back burner. I thanked him and told him to have a great day too. Then, turning around to head toward the aisle and get what I needed, unexpectedly I ran into a lady rushing to leave the store. She was just like I had been only moments earlier, too consumed with herself and her own needs to even look up or around.

Instead of pushing on past me without a word, as I feel sure she would normally have done, she stopped instead. "My, oh my, that sure is a nice-looking smile! You need to share that with the girl at the checkout counter! I think she got up on the wrong side of the bed this morning."

We both laughed and exchanged a pleasant word or two before parting ways. But the suggestion she had made stuck in my mind. I had gotten not one, but two unexpected, unsolicited buckets of happiness since I stopped at the convenience store this morning. It was time I let some of that same happiness flow over to the girl at the checkout counter. It was time for me to give and not simply receive—to share it with someone else needing a morning dose of happiness.

I waited off to the side and sort of out of sight until there was only one other customer in the line. I then went over and shared with her how good of a job she was doing keeping up with the never-ending volume of customers. Admittedly, I exaggerated a little when I complimented her on how well she handled all the customers' attitudes and demands and that I was sure she must get tired of dealing with so many difficult situations. But truly, I did admire how she was able to put up with all the junk that probably got thrown at her every day. I knew for a fact that I couldn't do what she was doing day in and day out!

My words must have caught her off guard. She moved away from the cash register and leaned on the counter in front of me. I watched as a smile took over her face. It looked nice on her.

"Just last night, I told my husband that I didn't know if I could take another day of this place. People are always complaining, talking on the cell phone while I'm trying to help them, and downright rude half the time! I bet him there wasn't a single nice person left in the world!"

I answered her, "You can't imagine how many times I have felt that exact same way when I go into stores. People have lost all sense of manners and respect and treat each other like dirt more often than not! So yes, I know exactly how you feel!" I agreed with her and smiled.

"But my husband told me to hang in there. Besides, we need the money, he reminded me. He's out of work right now, and we need the money I make to cover the bills and buy groceries. There's not much left after that."

"Looks to me like you're doing a great job of supporting your family! Anyone who's been there knows how tough it is to be the primary breadwinner. To be the only one bringing in money, the one everybody depends on. Hey, at least you've got a job that pays the bills, right?!"

"Right. And I'm so thankful for that," she acknowledged and then went on, "You won't believe what my husband told me last night."

"Try me," I suggested.

"I'd been complaining all night long about my job and how horrible everybody had treated me the last couple of days. He listened but didn't say a lot. Guess he's heard my complaining a thousand times before and has gotten immune to it. But finally, he looked over at me and said, with this sarcastic attitude, that if nobody was nice to me today, we'd talk about me looking for another job. He said we'd leave it at that and see what happens. If somebody was nice today, then it was a sign to stay. But if nobody was nice today, then it was a sign to leave. Know what, mister?" she asked me, with an even bigger smile than before.

"What's that?"

"You're that sign! The one we were looking for."

I shrugged and answered, "I doubt that."

"No, really... I mean it. You're the first person in the last three days to acknowledge I even existed. Everybody else comes in here and doesn't say hi, bye, or kiss my butt. Well, they do sometimes say that—or worse. But you know what I mean? They throw their money on the counter, have their cell phone glued to their ear, talk to the person with them, ignore me all together, or just fuss and complain about the way things are—politics, viruses, you name it. It makes me so mad sometimes!"

"You're looking at it all wrong," I interjected with my thoughts on the matter, "They're so down on themselves and the world, they can't open their eyes wide enough to see any of the good things around them. People walk around everywhere, every day too down in the dumps to see up! It's really not that hard to find the good... You just sometimes have to look harder for it than others and want to find it. I think some people enjoy moping around, complaining, and feeling sorry for themselves and the world with all its messes. What is worse, they want to bring others down to their level. Join their pity party. You know, misery loves company."

"I never thought about it that way. Do you come in here regularly?" she asked with a puzzled look on her face.

"Almost every day on the way to the drugstore. Why?"

"So have I ever seen you before? I don't remember ever talking to you, have I?"

"No, you haven't. But we have both seen each other before, just never spoken. It's not your fault. It's both of our faults."

"Yeah, guess you're right. You're right...about both."

"Both? Both what?"

"We've never spoken, and you do have to look. You have to look for the good hidden under all this bad."

"Yes, you do have to look to find the good!"

"That's it! I mean, just look at us. We've never spoken, but we've seen each other...maybe a lot."

"Right."

"You could have been like all those other rude people, but you weren't. I can't remember seeing you, and I'm pretty certain I've never spoken to you before. So you see? It's like you said... If I'd have taken the time to look, I'd have seen you, and we'd have probably spoken before now. Right? Man, do I wish I'd have seen you before now! Some days I think I'm going to strangle the next customer who says something ugly or mean to me. On those days, I could really use someone like you." She laughed and then jokingly said, "Maybe I can just call you next time I'm having a crappy day?!"

"It's my fault about the past, but it's behind us. I can't tell you how sorry I am for not speaking to you before now, but you can sure bet it won't happen again. Every time I come in, I'll make it a point to speak to you, and if somebody's really giving you grief... Well, you can turn around and say, 'Got a problem with me? That's my dad over there.' That'll shut 'em up for sure!"

We both laughed at the thought of telling some irate customer I was her dad. It was no telling how embarrassed they would be to think they had treated her that way in front of her father (even if I wasn't really her dad). Some would say it might serve them right?!

From that day on, I had a new friend! We talked every time I came in, and before long, she was talking with lots of other customers besides me. Her words and expressions were positive and uplifting. And I am incredibly happy to report she has now been promoted to assistant store manager, and her husband got a part-time job in Oviedo. Things are looking up! Can't say for sure, but I'm thinking all the positives started happening for her because she chose to look up. She intentionally sought out happiness, and sure enough, she found it.

I like that story, and I am proud to have Nan as a new friend. Seems to me each of us has a role in our time and in our season of life. How we live during those times and seasons of our life and the attitudes and choices we make are ours.

With one minute, one hour, one day, what could happen if we were more deliberate and purposeful in our life? What small act of caring or compassion could we do that could literally rock and change someone's world? The hope and happiness we could show to someone could bring them back, turn them around from fear and dread, and point them in a new direction. What if you put yourself wholly at God's disposal? The end result of your service wouldn't be up to you but rather would be in the hands of the Master who leads and guides you. Why can't we just bring a willing heart and ready hands and allow God to supply the guidance and strength?! No magic wand needs to be waved over any of you. Simply meekness and an open heart for others is all required—one minute, one hour, one day, and one person at a time.

Remember this though, life cannot be phoned in, texted to, or the likes of such. It is face-to-face, day-to-day, real-time, the next person you meet, then the next after that, and on and on. I know it takes risk and effort to deliver hope and happiness to someone, but *please make the effort!*

I like to think I made the effort and made the right choice at the right time with Nan. And I hope I will do the same the next time the opportunity presents itself. My challenge to me and you is that we both should try to make the right choice at the right time with someone we meet today. We both know that if we do, it will be worth the effort to that individual.

As for my kids and the story of how I used to get a poor attitude before I discovered the morning sunrise on my back porch... These days they remind me on a regular basis of what I used to tell them. They've now shared it with their children (my grandchildren) who also remind me, and so now I share the rest of the story.

The morning after I first realized how gorgeous the sunrise was each day, I decided I needed to say something to let the girls know I had discovered happiness to replace that dark cloud that sometimes came around and engulfed me. At the time, they were too young to understand any complicated explanation of how adults let the pressures and stresses of day-to-day life drag them into the doldrums, so I decided no heavy-duty, detailed explanation was necessary. Just a few simple statements should suffice.

The adage "actions speak louder than words" was an expression I often threw up at them when they began to pout or give me attitude about something Ria and I had decided they needed to do or not do. Put in other words, I knew they would most notice if I wasn't in a bad mood and didn't bite their heads off first thing in the morning. Thus, the actions part was an easy demonstration and was a good starting point. I would show them each morning with how I greeted them and how I talked with them around the breakfast table.

But I still needed something more, maybe words that could explain it. I mulled around all kinds of catchy clichés and easy-to-remember kid expressions, but none really said what I wanted to say. None I thought of got across the whole thing, but it would come to me.

Unexpectedly, it did! One morning, when we opened the back door and were making our way across the porch, toward the van, to load up and head off to school, I saw that amazing sunrise again. It was just as, if not more, stunning than the one I had seen only mornings earlier! Inside me, I suddenly felt as if I knew for certain that God's creation of a sunrise was one of His overflows of beautiful and intense loving feelings for us. A daily painted masterpiece given to us as a reminder of His love for us. Without even thinking, the words came out my mouth—"*Thank you, God, for the pretty day!*" I had meant it as an open expression of how I felt about seeing the sunrise, but my three daughters took it more as a parental directive of some sort.

All three were on the back porch only a few steps ahead of me. I was a little slower than them due to the fact I was carrying all three of their backpacks. Without any warning, they stopped. I nearly tumbled over them before I could halt my momentum. All three were looking over at the sunrise I had commented on. I watched curiously as they moved their heads and surveyed the yard. Almost simultaneously, they said, *"Thank you, God, for the pretty day!"*

My mouth hung wide open in disbelief. Then the reality of what had just transpired hit me, and I almost started to cry. The genuineness with which they had said the words made me realize they had actually stopped, looked around at the sunrise, and been thankful for something good—something wonderful that God had created for them. Finally, they had found that morning dose of happiness I had so desperately wanted to give them every day. Right there, in their own backyard, they had looked and discovered something they had missed every day, something to be thankful for—a reason to have hope and be happy! Every day, when they saw that sunrise, it would remind them of all the blessings God had given them and all the blessings He still had in store for them! And that would change everything!

After looking at each of them, I dropped the backpacks and got down on both knees. With my arms outstretched, they moved over next to me, and we group hugged each other. This time, I couldn't hold back the tears. They began to stream down my face, and I hugged them even more tightly than before. Meghan, my middle daughter, wiped the tears from my cheek. Alana, the youngest of the girls, gave me a kiss and said, "It's all right Daddy! You don't have to worry. We're right here!"

And then my oldest, Cara, pointed at the sunrise and exclaimed, "Look, Dad, God's made a path of sunlight just for us! It's shinning straight at us! Isn't it beautiful? Do you see it?"

"I sure do! I see it, sweetheart," I told her as I gave her a kiss on her cheek.

The question is, Do you see it? Do you see that ray of happiness and hope shinning straight at you? Oh, it's there every day… Look again! Once you find it, capture it in your heart, and pour it onto someone else!

The joy of the Lord is your strength!
—Nehemiah 8:10

The End

EVERLASTING HOPE

For all have sinned and fall short of the glory of God.
—Romans 3:23

God demonstrated His own love for us in this way:
While we were still sinners, Christ died for us.
—Romans 5:8

The wages of sin is death: but the gift of God
is eternal life thru Christ Jesus our Lord.
—Romans 6:23

If you confess with your mouth, Jesus is Lord, and
believe in your heart that God raised him from the
dead, you will be saved. For it is with your heart
you believe and are justified; and with your
mouth that you confess and are saved.
—Romans 10:9–10

Everyone who calls on the name of the Lord will be saved.
—Romans 10:13

For it is by grace you have been saved, through
faith—and this is not from yourself, it is a gift
of God—not by works, so that none can boast.
—Ephesians 2:8–9

AUTHOR'S NOTE

I can't speak for you, but as for me, I intend to use today, tomorrow, and every day given me to live! I plan to live every God-gifted second, minute, hour of every day to the utmost fullest! I intend to shine that bright and amazing, hope for all to see as I walk this path we call life!

As this effort of remembering and recording hope moved to publication, it became ever apparent that the Lord isn't quite done with me yet! And…news flash: He isn't done with you either! Thus it is my humble and simple suggestion that you use all your time, moments, and paths along the way wisely and completely! Leave nothing undone—no wish-I-had, no put off, and certainly no regret! Truly never let it be said of you that you took for granted one sunrise in the morning or any of the precious minutes that followed until the sunset that night! Tomorrow may never be… Live out hope today!

ABOUT THE AUTHOR

Rich Greer is a pharmacist who centers his works around the lives of patients—stories of their hurts, victories, blessings, and hopes. His experience during the last forty years has spanned over hospital, managed care, home infusion, and independent retail pharmacy. Currently, he enjoys practicing in a small one-pharmacy town in Central Florida.

His characterizations and settings reflect the rural Southern influences of growing up on a farm in Virginia, attending pharmacy school in Georgia, marrying a beautiful lady from Charleston, South Carolina, and living in Central Florida's farm and agricultural belt.

He and his wife are blessed with three wonderful daughters, three amazing sons-in-law, and five very active grandchildren.